THE BEAST OF LOCH NESS

A GASLAMP GOTHIC VICTORIAN PARANORMAL MYSTERY

KAT ROSS

The Beast of Loch Ness

First Edition

Copyright © 2022 by Kat Ross

All rights reserved.

This story is a work of fiction. References to real people, events, establishments, organizations, or locales are intended only to provide a sense of authenticity and are used fictitiously. All other characters, and all incidents and dialogue are drawn from the author's imagination and are not to be construed as real.

ISBN: 978-1-957358-10-9

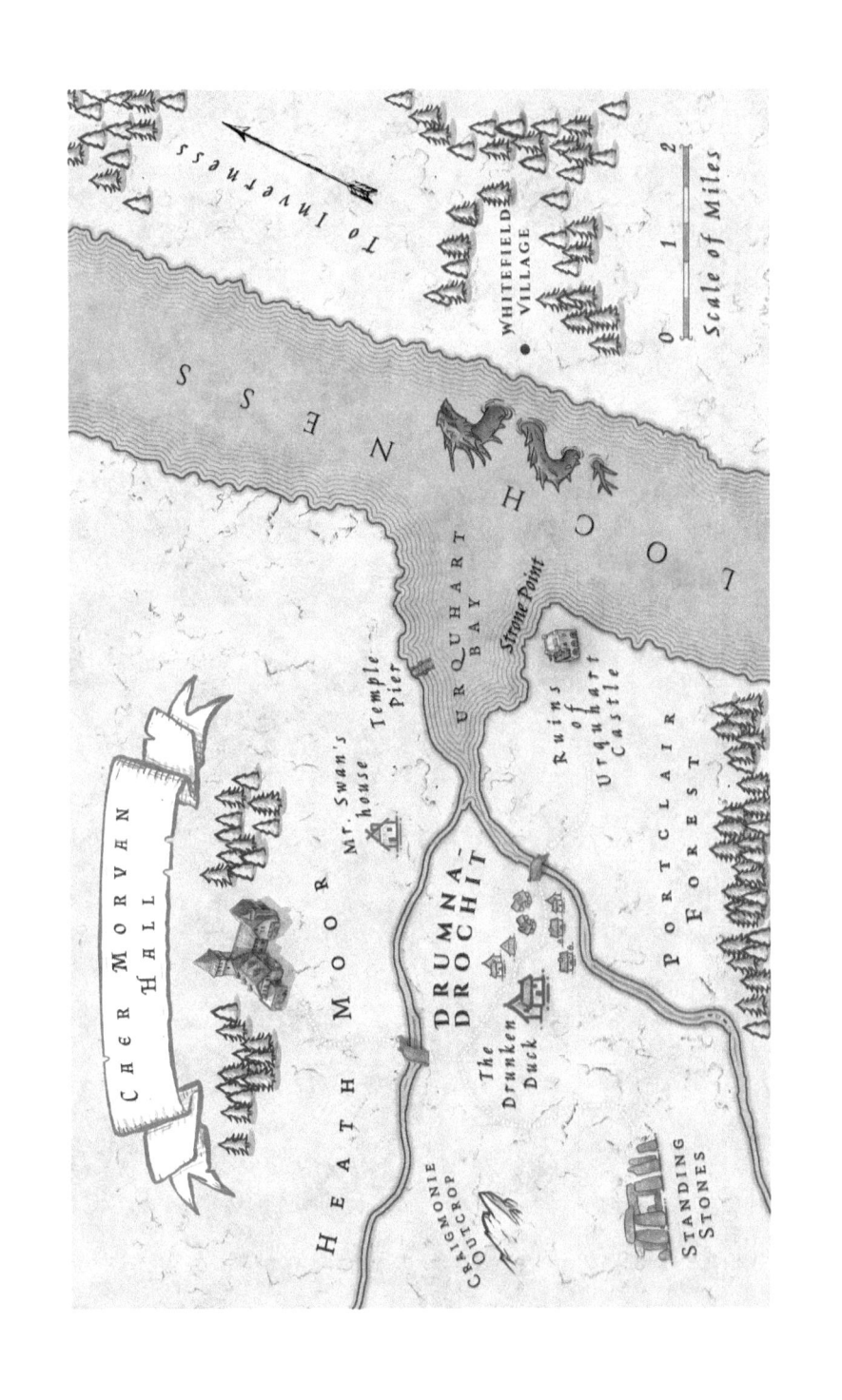

CHAPTER 1

"*H*oneymoon?*" Mrs. Davies looked appalled. "In *Drumnadrochit?*"

John Weston, my husband of sixteen days and closest friend since childhood, flashed his dimples. "Is it truly so hard to believe, madam?"

Mrs. Davies arched a plucked brow. She wore a dress of plain black bombazine. A widow, though not above vanity. Dyed chestnut curls framed a round face with powdered cheeks and rose-tinted lips. The effect reminded me of a cursed doll I'd glimpsed in a glass cabinet back in New York, though there was nothing blank about Mrs. Davies's stare. It drilled into us like the vanguard of a Roman legion.

One hand rested on a silver-tipped cane. I put her somewhere in her mid-seventies. She occasionally gave a discreet cough into a lace-trimmed handkerchief, but her voice was booming and she looked hearty enough to me.

"Well," she said with good-natured malice, "if it is solitude you seek, I wish you both luck. The hotels are all booked. I hope you secured advance reservations."

I accidentally made eye contact with the small, squishy-looking dog in her lap, eliciting a sharp bark. Mrs. Davies made no attempt to soothe the wretched creature.

"Full?" John echoed.

"Because of ze monster," muttered Miss Neiderberger, Mrs. Davies's companion.

The dog, whose name was Caesar, let out another high-pitched bark.

It required little imagination to deduce that Miss Neiderberger was German or Swiss. She had the ruddy complexion and athletic build of someone who skipped up icy alpine peaks without breaking a sweat. Thick blonde braids coiled around her ears. Her blue eyes were as inscrutable as a glacial lake.

John feigned innocence, though I could tell he was enjoying himself immensely.

"Dear God!" he exclaimed. "What monster?"

"Ze loch monster," Miss Neiderberger replied helpfully.

Mrs. Davies waved a gloved hand. "It's a leviathan, Dr. Weston. A sea serpent. My late husband Algie, God preserve his soul, told me about it when we communed at a séance in London three weeks ago." Her gaze grew misty. "In life, we were united by a passion for exotic fauna. The obscure and recherché."

The last word was spoken in an exaggerated French accent. "After some debate, we agreed that I must travel to Scotland and bear witness to the aquatic abomination."

Miss Neiderberger took this statement in stride, but John was struggling. His face was too smooth, his chin trembling ever so slightly. The dog's beady eyes fixed on him with malevolence.

"Oh, look!" I said, before disaster struck. "The loch!"

The four of us, plus Caesar, were sharing the mail coach from Inverness to Drumnadrochit, a journey of about sixteen miles. We all leaned towards the window on the right-hand side as the expanse of misty gray water came into view.

Loch Ness was long and narrow, with steep forested hillsides rising up from either shore. The monster that reputedly dwelt in its depths was the reason we had come all the way from New York City to the Scottish Highlands, although it was also true that we were on our honeymoon.

After a whirlwind courtship, Weston had proposed the previous Christmas. Over the following spring, he'd completed his degree at Columbia's Medical College and secured a position at Bellevue Hospital, where he meant to train as a surgeon. As for myself, I was now a full-time investigator for the Society for Psychical Research, handling cases that ranged from simple hauntings to graveyard ghouls, doppelgängers, golems, and even a vampire or two.

You would be forgiven for assuming that I was the one who had suggested Loch Ness as the locale of our honeymoon. In fact, it was John's idea. Though medicine was his primary calling, he dabbled in monster lore and had assisted me on several major cases. It was no exaggeration to say that I would not be alive without Weston's timely intervention.

But where I tended toward skepticism, John believed in everything under the sun. When one of his acquaintances in Edinburgh reported that a serpentine creature had been sighted near the sleepy village of Drumnadrochit, it was like dangling the Hope Diamond in front of Mrs. Astor.

My husband gazed out at the loch with excitement. It was late October, the leaves turning umber and gold, a crisp bite to the air. I expected we'd be doing a good deal of drifting about in the cold and wet, but I didn't mind. I was in love, unencumbered by children or responsibilities beyond those I owed to my employer, Mr. Harland Kaylock—who, though disapproving of holidays, had commanded me to enjoy myself—and the northern region of Scotland boasted a rugged beauty unlike anything I'd ever seen.

It seemed as far from the grimy streets and raucous crowds

of Manhattan as one could get and I was relishing every moment.

"There's a reward for the first photographic evidence of the monster," Mrs. Davies said with a sniff. "It's drawn all the lunatics out of the woodwork. Isn't that right, Caesar?"

She chucked the dog under the chin. He gazed up at his mistress adoringly.

"Er, that *does* put a damper on things," John said, turning to me with an amused look. "But we'll manage, won't we, darling?"

"You did make reservations, I hope?" I said.

"Of course I did. We're staying at the finest inn in town. The Drunken Duck!"

I laughed. "Sounds perfect."

"That iz where we are staying, as well," Miss Neiderberger said.

The coach slowed to climb a hill. The Royal Mail guard who had been standing on the back hopped down to give the horses a rest.

After eleven days confined to a steamer, followed by the Caledonian Railway from London to Perth, and then the Highland Railway from Perth to Inverness, I was itching to stretch my legs.

"Let's walk," I said to John. "Just for a bit. I could use some fresh air."

He nodded and leaned out the window, asking the driver to stop. Mrs. Davies appeared scandalized, but in short order, we were strolling along beside the slow-moving coach. It was a handsome conveyance, with big red wheels and a Royal Mail crest on the side, drawn by four black steeds. A box at the rear carried the mail, safeguarded by a fellow with a white beard and whiskers wearing a black top hat, a red coat with gold double buttons, and black collar and cuffs.

"Is the village really full?" John asked him.

"Och, it was," the guard responded. "Never seen so much

traffic on the road, though it's tapered off. I ken most of 'em are starting to give up. All the hired coaches are headed back toward Inverness. Naught's been seen in the loch for months."

"Do you think there's really *something* in there?" I wondered.

He cast me a wry look. "I canna say, Missus. But the lochs have many legends."

It was easier to doubt before I'd seen it myself. But looking out at that opaque water, cloaked in streamers of fog, it seemed more than possible that ancient mysteries lurked beneath the surface. We crested the hill and the view spread out around us, a patchwork of green valleys and stark crags.

"What's that?" John pointed across the moor to a large stone manor house about two miles distant. It had a central square with wings extending to either side and a broad emerald lawn sloping down toward the loch.

The guard's face hardened. "Caer Morvan Hall."

"Who lives there?" I wondered.

"T'was the seat of the Montagues for nigh on four hundred years."

"Is it empty?" John asked.

His lips pursed. "Just heed my advice and keep away," he muttered. "The Hall is a haunted place."

John caught my eye. "Really?" he said in a casual tone. "How so?"

The Royal Mail guard didn't answer. He shared a meaningful look with the driver, who tugged the reins and drew the coach to a halt.

The guard climbed back to his perch at the rear. "Ye'd best get inside, sir. We aim to arrive at Drumnadrochit before sunset. Things roam these hills in the night."

John shot me his own delighted look and we rattled forward again.

"Have you heard of Caer Morvan Hall?" he asked Mrs. Davies.

"No. The local laird, I suppose. Algie would know. His third cousin was an earl."

We passed the rest of the trip listening to stories about her late husband and the origins of the Pekingese breed, which turned out to be rather bloody. Thirty years before, during the Second Opium War with China, British troops sacked and burned the Imperial Palace. In the apartment of the emperor's aunt, who had committed suicide as the foreign invaders closed in, five pups were discovered.

One was bestowed upon Queen Victoria, who named it Looty. The rest went to various members of the English nobility. Caesar, we were informed, descended from the stock bred by the Duchess of Richmond in her famous Goodwood kennels.

"My little boy comes from noble blood that stretches back for millennia," Mrs. Davies declared, stroking the long white ears. "Caesar's ancestors dined on shark fin and the milk of the antelopes that frolicked in the imperial park. You can see it in his eyes, can you not, Mrs. Weston?

I reluctantly lowered my gaze to her lap, earning a low, savage growl. Mrs. Davies made a tsking noise. "He dislikes strangers, but I'm certain he will warm to you once we're settled at the inn. How lovely that we'll be neighbors!"

I smiled. "It is, indeed, Mrs. Davies."

The road meandered along the shore of the loch, turning west at a bay from which the ruins of Urquhart Castle were visible across the water. The driver spurred the horses to a brisk trot. Minutes later, we saw clusters of cottages and he announced that we had arrived in Drumnadrochit.

It backed up against a hillside, occupying a flat bowl amid the rolling highlands surrounding the loch. Smoke trailed from chimneys of the slate-roofed dwellings. I'd expected a carnival atmosphere, but few people seemed to be about.

The coach drew up before a large two-story inn of ivy-draped stone. A young man emerged, broad-shouldered and black of hair. He greeted the driver in a friendly fashion and started to unload the baggage, which was hauled inside by a boy in knickerbockers and brightly striped socks.

John offered his arm to Mrs. Davies, who released Caesar to do his business in the bushes. Miss Neiderberger took her employer's cane and after much huffing and rearranging of skirts, Mrs. Davies emerged from the carriage to study the inn with narrow eyes.

"I suppose it will do," she said. "I hope they'll have a hot supper waiting for us."

"Ye can be certain of it," the young man said, striding over. "Welcome to the Drunken Duck. I'm Finn Brody. The hen's my ma, Ursilla."

A wan, delicate blonde woman in a green dress and spotless white apron hurried up. "You must be Mrs. Davies," she said with a smile.

Introductions were made all around. John stuck his hand out and gave Finn's a warm shake. Dusk was falling fast now, and with it an icy drizzle that worked its way behind the collar of my red wool coat.

Mrs. Davies had a mountain of baggage. Finn ordered the boy to hop to and get her trunks inside before they soaked through, though not unkindly.

There was a delay as Caesar led us a merry chase through the dirt yard—during which my suspicions were confirmed that Mrs. Davies was far more nimble than she admitted—but at last the fugitive was captured and I bent my ear toward the coach.

"I feared ye wouldn't make it afore dark," Finn was saying to the driver and guard, whom I gathered were planning to spend the night. They all spoke rapidly, with thick burrs, but I managed to decipher the conversation.

"We had a broken axle in Inverness," the driver replied, crossing himself. "But the Good Lord brought us through safe."

Finn nodded. "Ye can take the usual rooms."

Again, I sensed an anxious undercurrent in the looks the three men exchanged. They didn't realize I was listening so it wasn't just to have a bit of fun with the tourists.

No, something genuinely frightened them.

I had a premonition that our honeymoon might not be as restful as I'd anticipated, but this faded as we entered the common room, where a toasty fire crackled in the hearth.

CHAPTER 2

T he inn was just as I'd pictured, with low beams blackened by age, cozy chairs and tables, and the low murmur of conversation.

A plump orange cat dozed at the end of the bar, tail wrapped over its nose like a muffler. The sweet scents of pipe tobacco and woodsmoke mingled with delicious aromas wafting from the kitchen.

The only off-putting note was the array of heads stuffed and mounted on the walls. Mainly deer and foxes—though at least they didn't bark when I looked into their glassy eyes.

A few people were drinking, but I scarcely saw them before Finn led us up a crooked flight of stairs.

"Yer rooms," he said with a wink at John. "The largest suite in the Duck."

I felt a rush of fondness for my husband's foresight as we entered a charming sitting chamber with diamond-paned windows that provided a spectacular view of the town and glimmers of the loch half a mile beyond. Sprigs of fresh fir gave off a minty aroma.

A large landscape painting showed almost the exact same

view in winter, though the angle was broadened to include Caer Morvan Hall in the corner, a dark smudge against the snowy fields.

As Finn carried my luggage into the adjoining bedroom, I noticed a webbing of extra skin between the thumb and forefinger of his right hand. It must be a congenital condition, though it didn't seem to hinder him. I looked away before he saw me staring and thanked him for carrying my bag.

John's trunk was already waiting, along with his leather doctor's valise. I'd teased him about that when he insisted on bringing it along, but I'd secretly felt pleased. It had been my Christmas gift to him the night he'd proposed. And, as Weston pointed out, one never knew when his skills might be needed.

"Supper's ready downstairs once you're settled," Finn said. "Unless you'd rather have it sent up?"

We looked at each other. "The common room is fine," I said. "Thank you, Mr. Brody."

He nodded and withdrew, shutting the door behind him. The instant we were alone, John wrapped his arms around me and gave me a kiss that lifted me to my toes.

"I've been waiting all day for that," he murmured.

"As have I," I replied a touch breathlessly.

More kissing ensued and it became clear that two choices awaited. I was sorry when he sighed and stepped back, but my stomach *was* rumbling.

"Food, then bed?" he suggested, reading my mind.

"I'd choose the other way 'round if I weren't starving," I replied with a grin, "but I suppose I could use a bath anyway. Do I smell frightful?"

His gaze lowered and my cheeks warmed pleasantly. "You never smell frightful."

John reached for me and I danced back with a laugh, walking to a basin and splashing water on my face and hands. I stuck a hand out and John handed me a towel.

"What do you make of all that about 'things roam these hills'?" I asked, my words muffled through the towel.

"And Caer Morvan Hall. We must get a closer look."

"Oh we must, must we?"

"Merely for the exercise, Harry. Daily walks are an essential ingredient of good health."

I patted myself dry and twined my arm in his. He was tall and I was short, but we fit like two puzzle pieces. I regarded my handsome young husband in the mirror. His brown hair curled winsomely in the damp.

"Right," I said. "Let's see about supper."

Only two people remained in the common room besides Ursilla and Finn Brody. The first was an elderly man in a tweed cap who hunched over a pint in the corner, chatting quietly with the inn's mistress.

The second was a woman in her forties with piercing dark eyes and a clever face. She wore an elegant walking dress of dark blue, but her boots were muddy. She sat near the fire, nursing a glass of something and jotting in a notebook. We nodded to Finn, who stood behind the bar, and took a table.

The meal was simple but excellent, steak pie and minced potatoes, along with a smoked haddock soup and hunks of warm brown bread. It was served by a pretty girl named Cassie who kept casting furtive glances at Finn when he wasn't looking.

Mrs. Davies and Miss Neiderberger did not appear and I gathered they'd chosen to dine in their rooms, which made me uncharitably relieved. When the repast was cleared, we carried our mugs of ale over to the fire and joined the woman there, who had been watching us with unabashed curiosity. She rose to her feet as we approached.

"Fellow Americans!" she declared with a smile of delight. "I heard you talking. I won't ask what brings you so far from home." She waved her glass at the empty common room. "But

I'm afraid you've missed the party. There's only a few of us monster hunters left."

"Mrs. Harrison Weston," I said, smiling back. It still felt strange not to be Miss Fearing Pell anymore, but I minded it less than I'd expected to. "This is my husband, Dr. John Weston."

He bowed at the waist. "A pleasure. Mrs—?"

"Gryffin," she replied. "Henrietta. But you may call me H.N."

"Not *the* H.N. Gryffin?" John asked.

She looked surprised and pleased. "You're familiar with my work?"

"I've read every one! *The Horror of Vordek Castle. The Fortune-Teller's Confession. Raven Red. The Secret Chamber at Mont Morrone Abbey—*"

I suppressed a laugh. "It seems you have an admirer, Mrs. Gryffin."

"Just H.N., please. I'm divorced. It's a pen name, anyway. My maiden name is Grunt and my last husband's surname was Nipple, if you can believe it." She eyed me seriously. "Would you want to be Hetty Nipple? Or Hetty Grunt, for that matter?"

"Er, no."

"Nor did I." H.N. sank back into her armchair by the fire. "Everyone except my publisher thinks I'm a man, so please don't reveal my deep, dark secret." She laughed a bit loudly and I got the impression she'd been drinking for a while. "Won't you join me? It's been terribly quiet these last days."

One glance at John and I knew I couldn't deprive him of the opportunity to rub elbows with a literary star. Besides which, I liked H.N. Gryffin. I knew what it was like to navigate the shoals of a man's world and she had my admiration for finding a way to hoodwink the small-minded public.

"So I take it the Drunken Duck is no longer bursting at the seams," John said dryly as we settled ourselves before the hearth.

"Fabulous name, isn't it? I might steal it for one of my

stories." She leaned forward, black eyes twinkling. "Did you know there were actual intoxicated waterfowl involved?"

I laughed. "Not really?"

"Oh, yes. A leaky beer barrel was discovered by the ducks in the yard. When the innkeeper at the time—this was a good century ago—when she woke up the next day, she thought they'd gone to their Maker and prepared to pluck them for the cookpot."

"No!"

"Don't worry. The ducks revived just in time to avoid becoming supper, though I imagine their poor heads ached like the dickens." She signaled to Finn for another brandy. "But I digress. You were wondering where everyone went. Well, they got bored when no one saw anything in the loch, I suppose."

"But not you?" John ventured.

"I have interests beyond the supposed monster. The folklore of this region is a rich seam, Dr. Weston, and I came to mine it. Kelpies, selkies, Muckle Black Tyke. I could go on for hours." She patted the leather-bound journal at her elbow. "The villagers are a taciturn bunch, but I've managed to collect a few tales."

I could practically hear the gears whizzing in Weston's brain. So much for early to bed.

"Kelpies and selkies I'm familiar with, of course," John said with a professional air. "But what's Muckle Black Tyke?"

"A variation on the black dog myth."

He nodded. "Yes, of course. Unnaturally large with glowing red or yellow eyes, associated with the Devil or Witches' Sabbath. Sometimes an omen of death. Also connected with electrical storms. Said to haunt crossroads, gallows, and ancient byways."

She cocked a brow. "You do know a few things. More than those other gawkers."

I almost explained that we were here for our honeymoon,

not to hunt monsters, but it seemed futile at this point. H.N. smiled and patted Finn's hand as he delivered her brandy. It was his left, which appeared normal. He must have been self-conscious about the webbed fingers for he kept the deformed hand out of view.

"Still on about Black Shuck?" he asked with a grin.

"That's another name for it," H.N. explained to John. "Also Yeth Hound, Wisht Hound, Padfoot, or Uktena—"

"In the Cherokee tongue," he finished.

Finn shook his head in amusement and went back to wiping the bar. To my surprise, H.N. turned to me with an expression of genuine interest. "And what do you do, Mrs. Weston?"

It was a question rarely asked by strangers. Most people assumed I stayed at home tending to domestic duties.

"I'm an investigator for the Society for Psychical Research," I replied. "In New York, of course. Not London."

Her brow furrowed. "Wait a moment . . . Harrison. Not *the* Harrison Fearing Pell?"

John beamed. A blossom of warmth unfolded in my chest.

"Oh, well," I fumbled. "So you've . . . heard of me?"

"Heard of you? I'm a great admirer! Mr. Hyde! The golem case. Oh, many others." She shook her head. "Well, it all makes sense now. How wonderful to meet you in person!"

I felt awkward and elated at the same time, my estimation for H.N. Gryffin rising steeply.

"I'm here in an unofficial capacity," I said. "Just a holiday."

She winked. "Of course. I understand perfectly. We'll have to share notes, won't we?"

We chatted for a while. It turned out that she'd met my boss, Mr. Harland Kaylock, and was familiar with the Night Squad, the obscure detectives' division that dealt with the occult in New York City. The icing on the cake was that she didn't mention my sister Myrtle, whose fame, in all honesty, far surpassed my own.

"How did you hear about the golem?" I asked.

"Because the Night Squad hushed it up, you mean?" H.N. laughed. "I have my sources. Well, I must say, things were looking dreary, but they've improved in the last hour. How long are you staying in Drumnadrochit?"

I was about to reply when the door banged open. A tall, stooped man entered the common room in a swirl of rain, furling a black umbrella and jamming it into the stand with ill humor. Thinning brown hair lay plastered against his skull. He wore rubber boots and a woolen greatcoat. A net of the sort used to catch butterflies dangled from one hand.

"Filthy weather," he muttered to no one in particular.

"And here we are in Scotland," H.N. remarked. "Who'd have guessed it?"

The man cast his gaze around the room, neck bent like a wading bird in search of frogs, then stomped up the stairs. A door slammed somewhere in the depths of the inn.

"Professor Carlton," H.N. said in a stage whisper. "He's a biologist. One of the hardy souls who refused to leave. Now he's obsessed with finding an emperor moth for his collection, but the skies aren't cooperating." She took a gulp of brandy. "He's always creeping about, not exactly the social type. I think he likes insects better than people."

"And the elderly gentleman with Mrs. Brody?" I prompted.

She glanced at the pair sitting together near the window. "That's Mr. Swan. He was the groundskeeper for Caer Morvan Hall. Retired now."

It was the perfect entrée. "Speaking of the Hall," John said, "I heard it was haunted."

"Not exactly. Cursed is more like." Her eyes narrowed as she regarded the caretaker. "I've tried to coax him into talking about Duncan Montague—he was the last of the line, died nine months ago—but the fellow's about as chatty as the Standing Stones at Portclair."

Sensing the attention, Mr. Swan glanced our way with a guarded expression, then returned to his ale.

"Died how?" John asked.

"Heart failure. He was only thirty-nine, but the Montagues have a habit of dying young. None make it past the age of fifty."

"The coach driver was afraid of arriving after dark," I said. "He claimed strange things walk the night."

H.N. Gryffin gave a slow nod. "The locals pretend ignorance, but I pried loose a few scraps. It seems Duncan was terrified of something in his final months. He barely left the Hall. Rumor has it that Montague sold his soul to the devil."

The author raised her glass in an ironic toast. "And the devil came to claim his due!"

CHAPTER 3

H.N. Gryffin's voice rose on the last bit, loud enough for Finn Brody to cast her a sharp look. But she wouldn't be deterred.

"Isn't that right, Mr. Swan?" she called over merrily. I realized to my dismay that she was more than a little drunk. "Did Auld Nick pay Duncan Montague a visit?"

The elderly caretaker flushed red. Ursilla Brody laid a hand on his coat sleeve.

"It's all right," she said. "She's just making a jest."

"An ugly one," Mr. Swan grumbled.

John shot me a look that said he agreed with this assessment. "We ought to head up to our room," he said, rising. "It was a long journey."

I set my ale down. A tense silence settled over the common room.

The author frowned. I think she realized she'd gone too far. "Of course." She stared into her glass with bleary eyes. "I ought to do the same."

Mr. Swan was donning a hat and overcoat. He looked a bit unsteady and Finn offered to see him home in a cart.

"I've walked from the Duck for forty years," Mr. Swan declared. "Think I can manage it once more." He jammed the hat down on his curly white hair, then turned to stare at H.N. "Ye'd best watch yer step, hen. Tisn't wise to mock Auld Nick on a night such as this, nor any night."

The words were spoken solemnly, without the anger he'd displayed before. A chill prickled my spine. Auld Nick was what the Scots called the devil.

H.N. started scribbling in her notebook. I leaned over her shoulder. She'd copied Mr. Swan's words down verbatim.

"What?" she muttered when I lifted a brow. "It's a good line."

Mr. Swan stumped to the door. He nodded at the Brodys and set off into the blustery darkness. Finn stared through the window for a minute, then set about clearing the old man's glass and wiping the table down.

"I suppose I shouldn't have said that," H.N. conceded. "Swan's a touchy sort. Stiff as a clergyman's collar." She tipped her gaze to the stuffed heads on the wall with a crooked smile. "Wouldn't you agree?"

I wasn't sure whether the question was directed at me or the heads, so I made a noncommittal noise. John and I bade the innkeepers goodnight and went upstairs. Cassie had left us a tub of steaming water and a stack of fluffy towels with little ducks embroidered along the hem.

John helped with the little pearl buttons down the back of my dress and unhooked the corset stays. I shed my chemise and petticoat and stockings and knickers, dropping them all in a heap.

"What shall we do tomorrow?" I asked John, sinking into the bath with a happy sigh.

Once I'd gotten over feeling shy, watching my husband undress became one of my favorite amusements. He did it in a precise order: cufflinks, watch and suspenders, then the starched white shirt and tie and undershirt and trousers. Weston had magnificent legs.

"I'm more interested in how we might amuse ourselves tonight," he replied.

Water sloshed over the edge as he sank down opposite me.

I smiled.

An hour or so later, we snuggled under the quilt as the rain dashed against the window.

"I want to go out on the loch," John murmured sleepily. "In answer to your question."

"Even if it's still raining?"

"Yes. Don't you want to look for the aquatic abomination?"

I chuckled. "As long as there's another hot bath at the end of it."

He pulled me close. "Oh, there will be."

That cheered me and I drifted into a peaceful sleep.

The last, as it would turn out, for many nights to come.

———

MRS. DAVIES AND MISS NEIDERBERGER APPEARED AT BREAKFAST with Caesar, who was brushed to a gleam and bouncing off the walls in his eagerness to go out, unlike H.N. Gryffin, who barely uttered a word to us.

The author sat alone at the farthest table, clearly hungover, sipping from a mug of black coffee and scribbling in her notebook.

Professor Carlton thumped downstairs and snatched a piece of dry toast from the sideboard. In the daylight, he resembled one of my husband's autopsy cadavers returned to life, with sunken cheeks and deep-set eyes under wispy brows.

"Who are you?" he demanded, brushing crumbs from his greatcoat.

John gave our names.

"More of the usual lot, I suppose," Carlton muttered, eyeing Mrs. Davies. "I imagine you're one of them, too?"

"I beg your pardon, sir," she said icily. "One of *what?*"

"Monster chasers." He bit off the words with disdain. "It never bloody ends, does it?"

The professor propped his butterfly net over one shoulder like a soldier with a bayonet. He strode to the inn's front door, slamming it on the way out. H.N. didn't look up from her notebook, but Mrs. Davies stared after him with an affronted expression.

"What a perfectly awful man!" she exclaimed. "Don't you agree, Miss Neiderberger?"

"Very rude," the companion said with a sunny smile.

She wore a blue silk dress that matched her eyes. I watched her carve up an apple with surgical precision and offer a sliver to Caesar. The dog sniffed it, then dragged it under the table. Crunching sounds ensued.

"Oh, Carlton's always like that," H.N. Gryffin said, still not looking up from her notebook. "It's probably why his college sent him on sabbatical. Get rid of him for a while."

"And which college is that?" Mrs. Davies asked. "I might write a letter of complaint to the dean!"

"Haven't a clue. He's not much of a conversationalist, as you might have noticed."

"Well, if he speaks to me again, I shall pretend I'm deaf," Mrs. Davies said.

H.N. laughed. "You really should." She finally roused herself from the notebook, gaze settling on Miss Neiderberger. "I've been meaning to ask, are you Swiss or German?"

"Swiss," the companion replied. "From a small valley in the Graubünden region."

"How charming! You must tell me all about the folklore from your childhood. I'm familiar with most of the German legends, but less so the alpine regions."

Miss Neiderberger opened her mouth to reply and was cut off by her employer. "When her duties permit," Mrs. Davies said curtly. She turned our way. "Will you be going to the loch today?" she boomed.

"Yes," John replied, enunciating his words as though she really were deaf. "And what are *your* plans today?"

"The same, of course." She brandished a pair of binoculars. "I do hope Caesar doesn't get seasick."

"You're bringing the dog?" I asked.

He'd leapt into her lap and was boldly licking the egg yolk from her plate.

"Where I go, he goes, Mrs. Weston. We are inseparable." She cast a fond glance at Caesar. "Now, you must promise to behave yourself."

He gave a loud bark. The orange tabby, which was slinking down the stairs, puffed its tail and streaked into the kitchen.

Finn brought a dog-cart around for Mrs. Davies and Miss Neiderberger, but as the day was fine, John and I chose to walk. I donned my new high-crowned Tyrolean hat, made of brown felt with a wide grosgrain ribbon. John wore the battered Homburg that had seen him through many an adventure.

Cattle and sheep grazed in stone pens on the village green. A few dozen men stood around haggling over prices. John tipped his hat and bid them good day. The greeting was politely returned, though I felt their gazes on our backs. After that came a weaver and smithy with smoke pouring from the forge chimney and the sounds of hammering within.

H.N. Gryffin must have hopped onto the dog-cart when I wasn't looking because she was already down at the shore when we arrived. She stood with a ruggedly attractive man, no more than twenty-five or so, with curly brown hair and a cleft chin. He'd just set up a camera on a tripod and was peering through a magnifying loupe to check the focus.

The writer seemed in better spirits. She beckoned us over and made introductions.

"This is Mr. Cormac Ferguson," she said. "He's renting Kinlach Cottage."

"Oh, where's that?" John asked.

"Over at the north edge of town," Mr. Ferguson replied. "I suppose you're staying at the Duck."

"That's right. You're aiming to capture the beast on film?"

"Nae, landscapes are my specialty. I come down to photograph the loch at different times of day, that's all." A dry chuckle. "But perhaps I'll get lucky eventually."

"You've never seen it yourself?" John persisted.

Ferguson shook his head. "I doubt the creature exists, but I know that won't sway ye. I've seen dozens come and go in the last few months, every one bent on finding the monster. To be honest, I'm glad things are finally settling down. I left Glasgow for quiet and solitude, not a bloody circus."

"Don't pay him any mind," H.N. said with a mock scowl. "He's always grumpy in the mornings."

Ferguson looked abashed. "Aye, she's right about that. I meant no offense. T'was a pleasure to meet you both. Enjoy your row."

The photographer busied himself adjusting the angle of the tripod and John and I walked down to the water, where enterprising townsfolk were renting boats. Two strong men levered Mrs. Davies onto the stern bench of a dinghy. A frantically barking Caesar was pressed into her arms by Miss Neiderberger. Once they were settled, the Swiss woman took the oars and began to vigorously row toward the center of the loch.

John handed over a few shillings to one of the villagers. The sun came out. We climbed into our own white-trimmed boat. I sat back, enjoying the breeze on my face and smell of fresh water. It was turning into a pleasant morning—except for one thing.

"I don't suppose there's any chance of seeing the creature with that dog about," John muttered, yanking hard on the oars.

Caesar's high-pitched cries echoed off the hillsides like a yodeler. They could probably hear him up in Inverness.

"Unless the monster gets hungry for a morsel," I said. "Do you think Mrs. Davies could be persuaded to let him have a swim?"

"Now, Harry." He frowned at me in mock severity. "It could be an herbivore for all we know."

I looked around at the breathtaking scenery. "Tell me about Loch Ness. I suppose you know everything about it."

"Not everything, but I did do some research. Are you sure it won't bore you?"

"You never bore me, Weston," I replied honestly.

He grinned. "For starters, it contains more fresh water than all the lakes in England and Wales combined. The deepest part is estimated to be at least seven hundred feet. That's twice as deep as the North Sea."

We were a fair way out at this point. A sensation of vertigo made the soles of my feet tingle.

"Loch Ness is twenty-three miles long and runs through the Great Glen," John continued. "This is Urquhart Bay. You can see the castle just across the way."

"Is it open for visitors?"

"Yes. I thought we could have a picnic there."

"Is there some blood-drenched ghost?" I asked. "A shrieking banshee, perhaps?"

"That's Irish," he corrected. "It would be a Ban Sith. And no, I only wanted to enjoy an outing with my new bride."

"Huh." I kept my face neutral. "That would be a first."

John's brow creased. "I've been awful, haven't I? Preoccupied with curses and black dogs. Fawning over that drunk author—"

I leaned forward and flicked his knee. "I was teasing. You've chosen the perfect place and the perfect inn. And you weren't *fawning*. If you had been, I would have told you so. Now what about the monster?"

"The last sighting was nearly two years ago," he admitted. "But it wasn't the only one. The first on record is in a biography of St. Columba from 565 A.D. And stone carvings by the Picts depict a mysterious beast with flippers."

"That would make it more than thirteen hundred years old," I pointed out.

"If there were two, maybe they can breed." He waggled an eyebrow.

"I hope that's the case. It saddens me to think it was the last of its kind."

He looked over my shoulder. "Is that the professor?"

A spidery figure was leaping across the moor, slashing the air with his butterfly net. Some ways up the loch, I heard Mrs. Davies exhorting Caesar to *hold still, for God's sake, before we all go overboard.*

"They should have called it the Odd Duck," I said. "We seem to be the most normal people staying there—which is alarming."

Caesar's yapping protests faded into the distance as John rowed us south down the loch. His brown eyes scanned the surface, searching for ripples, but I was content to relax and listen to the gentle lap of water against the prow and soft splashes of the oars. Autumn gilded the hillsides, turning the alders a glorious yellow.

Then a cloud passed across the sun. A wind sprung up, tugging at my hat. I clamped a hand down just in time to save it from sailing across the loch. My gaze lit on a crag above Drumnadrochit.

A dark silhouette crouched there. Despite the distance, I had the powerful impression that it saw me looking. The shape spun and loped off.

"John!" I exclaimed.

He looked around wildly. "What is it?"

"Up there!" I pointed.

He twisted around, but the shape was gone. "What did you see?"

I shaded my eyes with a hand. "An animal. Something fairly large."

"A wolf?"

"Perhaps. Let's ask the Brodys."

Dark clouds had swallowed the sun. It was starting to drizzle again. John rowed us back to Temple Pier where the photographer was packing up his equipment. H.N. Gryffin hung around talking to him—flirting, actually. She was quite a bit older, but he didn't seem to mind.

I asked if they'd seen the animal, but both had been focused on the loch not the hills behind them.

The boat carrying Mrs. Davies and Miss Neiderberger scraped onto the pebbled beach a minute later. Miss Neiderberger lifted her skirts and hopped out, tossing the oars to one of the villagers as if they were toothpicks. Caesar looked damp and chastened. His long ears drooped as she attached his leash and deposited him on solid ground.

"Like Odysseus, he pines for home," Mrs. Davies declared with a smile. "After a long and rather wet journey."

"I vill try to finish knitting his new sweater," Miss Neiderberger said. "I fear he has taken a chill."

The inn's errand boy returned with the dog-cart. By the time we reached the common room, it was lunchtime. John and I took a table. I asked the serving girl if there were wolves in these parts.

"Not since my great-grandfather's time," Cassie replied with a laugh.

"What other animals are native to the area?"

"Pine martin. Deer and badger."

"Well, it wasn't a badger," I muttered when she left.

"What wasn't?"

I turned to find H.N. Gryffin standing behind us.

"Oh, probably nothing," I said. "I thought I saw something from the loch. Up on one of the crags."

Interest sparked in her eyes. "What did it look like?"

"To be honest, a large black dog. Someone's pet, I suppose."

"Do you remember exactly where it was?"

I nodded. "In the direction of Caer Morvan Hall."

"What do you say we walk up there?" John asked. "Maybe it left paw prints."

"Excellent idea!" H.N. said, waving her notebook. "I hope I wouldn't be a third wheel?"

I suppressed a sigh. "Of course not. We'll fetch umbrellas."

In short order, we were crossing the footbridge over the River Enrick. Cultivated fields surrounded the village, but across the river the land rose and became more rugged. Caer Morvan Hall perched atop a hill in the distance.

"Does anyone live there?" I asked.

"Some rich American bought it," H.N. replied, tucking a lock of dark hair behind her ear. She wore a fashionable straw hat adorned with feathers. They flopped in the wet breeze. "He's living there with his family."

"An American?" I echoed in surprise.

"Name of Goodnight. From California, I hear."

"Why would someone move from California to Scotland?" John wondered.

"Not a clue. But he's very wealthy. A hotelier, I believe. They've been there for a few months now, but they never come down to the village."

"How peculiar," I said as we crested a rise that overlooked the loch.

It was just a barren hilltop, but the angle looked right. I'd taken my bearings from the rowboat, marking the distance to the Hall on the right and the village below.

"I'm certain this is the spot where I saw the animal," I said, studying the sodden ground.

We spent a few minutes poking around, but the turf was rocky and held no traces.

"A trick of the light?" H.N. suggested. She looked disappointed.

I nodded, even though I felt sure of what I'd seen.

"We could ask whoever lives there," John said, gaze turning to a primitive stone cottage not far away. It had a single door and two windows facing south toward the loch.

"That's Mr. Swan's croft," H.N. said. A pink flush crested her cheeks. "I suppose I owe the man an apology. My tongue ran away with me last night."

I studied the dwelling with a prickle of apprehension. "Why is the door standing open?"

No smoke drifted from the chimneys. No welcoming light shone in the windows. If the elderly caretaker was home, I saw no sign of it.

The rain grew heavier, blowing sideways now.

"We'd better look in on him," John said.

I picked my way down the hill, struggling to close the flapping umbrella. John went first, calling ahead so we wouldn't startle him.

"Mr. Swan? It's Mr. Weston from the Drunken Duck!"

There was no reply. H.N. shared a worried look with me as we crossed the yard. A bedraggled vegetable garden sat next to the house. It was late in the season and most of the plants had withered.

"That looks like a footprint," I said, pointing to a circular indentation in the earth. "Leading away."

"Could be," John agreed. "Maybe it's Mr. Swan's."

The cottage had a turf roof and gabled chimney at each end. We climbed two rough-hewn steps and entered a flagstone kitchen. A three-legged iron pot hung from a chain inside the cold hearth. The pungent, mossy aroma of peat smoke lingered in the air.

Against one wall sat a dresser with white china plates and other crockery on the shelves. The center of the room had a bench and trestle table marked with overlapping rings.

Nothing looked amiss, yet my nerves were taut. The wind banged the door against the thick stone frame and John hurried to close it properly.

I peered through a stone arch to the living quarters. A much larger hearth occupied the far end. A barrel chair was positioned by the fireside, with a fiddle resting against it.

Only a little daylight came through the curtains, leaving most of the chamber in gloom. The house was quiet save for the throaty murmur of a pigeon up in the rafters. Then a match scraped. H.N. stood at my side holding a paraffin lamp. She drew a sharp breath.

A table lay overturned on the rag rug in front of the fireplace. Next to it, Mr. Swan sprawled in a pool of blood. John ran forward and crouched down, pressing his fingers to the old man's neck. The face was pale, the eyes open and staring.

After a few seconds, John let his hand fall. "He's dead!"

CHAPTER 4

"Stay back," I said to H.N. Gryffin, who had gone very pale. "We must preserve the scene for the police."

She nodded and retreated to the kitchen door, still holding the paraffin lamp. I stood for a moment, studying the room. The pool of blood around Mr. Swan looked dry at the edges but tacky in the center where it was deepest.

"I'd say this happened shortly after he got home from the Duck. John?"

Weston looked over. "It takes roughly twelve hours for a body to cool, though that depends on the ambient temperature. If the fire was going it would delay things." He touched a stiff hand. "Rigor mortis is complete. So yes, I'd estimate time of death as late last night."

"Do you think it was an accident?" H.N. whispered. "Or murder?"

"That's what I'd like to find out," I said.

John gently turned the head. "The back of his skull is cracked. There's a severe hematoma. It could have been a bad fall." He glanced at the overturned table. "If he tripped over that and hit his head against the fireplace."

The table was high and narrow. It must have held a daguerrotype photograph in a silver and glass frame, which lay next to the body.

But something looked odd.

"If the picture fell from the table to the flagstone floor, why didn't the glass crack?" I said.

It showed a young man with dark hair posed in a formal seated portrait with a woman and child on his knee. The man was thirty years younger, but I felt sure it was Mr. Swan.

"You think the scene was staged?" John asked.

Other than that single off-note, I saw no sign of another person. No bloody footprints. No murder weapon. Except . . . .

"There's two hooks on the hearth," I said. "One has a bellows. But the other is empty. I'd guess it held a poker. So where is it?"

John beckoned H.N. Gryffin to come closer with the lamp. He examined Mr. Swan again. "The wound was inflicted by blunt trauma. I suppose a blow from a poker is possible, though it's hard to say for certain."

"But there's a smear of blood, see?" H.N. pointed to the hearth.

One of the stones above the fireplace had a red splash.

"It could have been put there by the killer," I said. "To make it look like he tripped."

She regarded me seriously. "Of course it could. I was merely pointing it out. Either way, we must notify the authorities. And Caer Morvan Hall is much closer than the village."

I nodded. "We'll go there first. John, will you stay with him? If it wasn't an accident, better you keep an eye on the house."

"Of course." He took the lamp from H.N. and moved to the window. "I'm glad you're together, but be careful. I'll watch from here."

The two of us set out, shoulders hunched against the rain. I paused for a moment to examine the impression I'd seen when we arrived. It seemed to be the edge of a man's heel, but it was impossible to judge the shoe size.

"If it *was* murder, who would want Mr. Swan dead?" H.N. wondered.

"You've been here longer than we have. Any ideas?"

As the cottage dwindled behind, it occurred to me that H.N. Gryffin was the person who'd had an altercation with Mr. Swan last night. And accompanying us when we discovered the body would be a clever way of disguising her own guilt.

"Well," she said slowly, "I've hardly spoken to him, but he's close to Ursilla Brody. He comes in most nights for a drink—or three. The man seemed harmless." She shot me a look. "But you never know in remote villages like these. Bad blood can go back centuries."

"And his new employer?"

"Jack Goodnight?" H.N. shrugged. "I already told you what I've heard, which isn't much. Never met the man."

We walked up the drive to Caer Morvan Hall. The manor was even grander up close with pointy turrets and two wings extending out on either side, though only the left half showed glimmers of light. The other side was pitch dark.

Carved heraldic sigils flanked the heavy oaken doors. H.N. banged on a knocker until a servant appeared. Like Mr. Swan, she was in her late sixties, with lank gray hair pulled tight into a bun and a pinched, weary face.

"We must speak to your master about an urgent matter," I said. "My name is Mrs. Weston. This is Miss Gryffin."

"What is it?" The servant peered at us warily. "The family doesn't like to be disturbed."

"It involves Mr. Swan. There's been . . . an accident."

Her demeanor changed from suspicion to concern. "Oh! Is he all right?"

"We'd better speak with Mr. Goodnight first," I said.

She stepped back and allowed us to enter the gloomy, chill

entrance hall. Every single window was covered by heavy drapes. Dark oil portraits lined the walls.

"They're out in the gardens," the servant said.

"In this weather?" H.N. asked with surprise.

The woman didn't reply. She led us past doorways that gave glimpses of a drawing room and formal dining room, across a wide central passage, and into a salon with French doors opening to a stone patio. Stairs led down to a manicured lawn on which a white pavilion had been erected.

It had the look of a luncheon party with tiered platters of cakes and fruit and sandwiches, though only five people sat at the table erected beneath—three women, a man, and a child wearing an enormous sun bonnet. They looked over as we approached.

"Sorry to disturb you, sir," the servant said, wringing her hands. "But there's been an accident with Mr. Swan."

The man leapt to his feet and hurried up to us. He had thick dark hair, worn swept back, and strong features. He wore a tweed coat, flannel trousers and well-polished boots.

"I'm Jack Goodnight," he said, searching our faces. "What's happened?"

"We're staying down at the village," I said. "We passed Mr. Swan's cottage and saw the door open so we went to investigate. I'm afraid he's dead."

"Dead?" he stared at us. "What on earth happened?"

Mr. Goodnight might be the picture of an English country squire, but he had the broad accent of the American West.

I quickly related the scene, omitting my suspicions. His wife had joined us. She appeared shocked.

"How terrible," she murmured. "I just saw him yesterday."

Mrs. Goodnight had an upturned nose and bright green eyes. Her slender frame was draped in a fashionable rose-hued tea dress with long flowing sleeves. She didn't seem more than thirty-five, yet her mouth was bracketed with lines of bitterness and disappointment.

It was only a first impression, but I thought she had the look of a woman who was unhappy long before she heard the news about Mr. Swan.

"My husband stayed with the body," I said. "He's a medical doctor. I don't suppose you have a telephone?"

"No, but I'll order the carriage," Mr. Goodnight said. He turned to his wife. "You'd best get Louisa back inside. Don't tell her what happened."

Mrs. Goodnight frowned. "Of course not. Mr. Swan was always so kind to her." She shook her head. "Oh, how sad. That poor man."

She returned to the pavilion, leaning down to speak to her daughter. The girl wore a long-sleeved, high-necked dress with gloves and I could scarcely make out her face beneath the bonnet, though she looked uncommonly pale.

The two other women studied us curiously. One was quite young—a governess, perhaps. The other was older, early forties, and wore the cap of a nurse. She had a handsome, intelligent face.

Mr. Goodnight turned to the servant who had escorted us outside. "Miss McKenzie, tell Mr. McKenzie I need the coach brought around."

She bobbed a curtsey and ran off. The three of us started walking back to the house.

"Was he the worse for drink?" Mr. Goodnight asked in a low voice.

"I can't say," I replied. "That will be a matter for the authorities to determine."

Goodnight grunted. "I suppose the townsfolk will claim it's the curse."

"Curse?" H.N. said innocently.

He cast us a weary glance. "Surely you've heard the talk. It's one of the reasons we keep away from the village. They're a superstitious bunch. Would you mind waiting while I fetch my coat and hat?"

We stood dripping in the entryway as he dashed up a curving fight of stairs.

"Caer Morvan Hall," H.N. said softly, her gaze devouring the portraits. "It looks like he bought the contents, too. Those must be Montagues."

The resemblance through the generations was uncanny. Coal-black hair, board-straight backs, and haughty expressions. The main difference was in the style of whiskers. The more ancient scions were bearded and clad in dark velvet, while their descendants were clean-shaven and wore frock coats. All had a cruel aspect and I wondered what sort of landlords they'd been.

Also why on earth no one had taken them down.

Mr. Goodnight returned and we got into the waiting carriage.

"Take us down to the village," he told the driver, Mr. McKenzie.

I settled against the leather seat, tucking the umbrella between my boots.

"I kept on the old servants," Mr. Goodnight explained as we sped down the drive. "Those who wished to stay at least. It seemed the right thing to do. Mr. and Miss McKenzie have lived here all their lives. Mr. Swan, too."

"It's a terribly big house," I ventured. "You must have other staff."

"A cook, of course. Three chambermaids and a scullery. The governess, Miss Parker, is a local girl. But we don't entertain. One of the wings is sealed completely. I saw no reason to have an army of servants underfoot." He forced a smile. "Where are you staying?"

"At the Drunken Duck."

"Hunting the loch beast, I imagine," he said without much interest.

"My husband and I are newlyweds," I said. "We came on holiday."

"And I collect legends," H.N. said vaguely.

Mr. Goodnight gazed out the window. "I suppose you think it strange that we were picknicking in the rain, but my daughter has a rare condition. She's allergic to sunlight. It causes terrible burns. That's why we relocated to Scotland."

"I'm sorry," I said. "Is she doing well here?"

He gave a mirthless laugh. "Better than California."

An awkward silence descended.

"How did you choose Caer Morvan Hall?" H.N. asked.

"It was cheap," he said bluntly. "No one else would touch the place. Like I said, superstitious."

"But you haven't encountered anything . . . unusual?" I asked.

"Nothing except for spiders and mice, Mrs. Weston. The Hall was an excellent investment opportunity. I'm a builder, you see. Own a chain of hotels out west. Have you ever heard of the Coronado?"

I blinked. "Why, yes. It's in San Diego, isn't it?"

He nodded, perking up. "The largest beach resort in the world. We brought in water, built a railroad and ferry service. Even an electrical plant! The hotel has more than two thousand incandescent lamps," he added proudly. "Just opened the doors last year."

"You must miss overseeing things," I said.

His smile died.

"I'm sorry, I shouldn't have said—"

"No, it's all right." Mr. Goodnight sighed. "Yes, I do miss California. But Louisa's health comes first. I wanted to be sure my family was settled before I traveled back again. We're very close."

"Well, I'm sure they're grateful," I said. "I imagine it could be lonely out here."

"Yes." He fell silent.

"We'll have to inform Mr. Swan's next of kin," I prompted. "There was a photograph in his cottage. A wife and child?"

Mr. Goodnight gave me a sharp look. "They died a long time ago," he said. "A fire at the Hall."

"How tragic," H.N. murmured.

"The estate agent told me the story. It happened on Christmas Eve some thirty years ago. Preston Montague—he's the father of the late Sir Duncan—died, as well."

The popular belief in a curse was starting to make sense. "So Mr. Swan had no surviving family?"

"Not that I know of. It's one of the reasons we kept him on, though I paid lads from the village to do the heavy work. I don't think he had anywhere else to go."

We crossed the bridge and slowed to enter the narrow village lanes, where poultry and children ran about freely. The driver stopped in front of the Drunken Duck.

"I'll inform Constable Robb," Mr. Goodnight said, handing us down from the coach. "I'm sorry you had to see poor Swan, but I thank God it wasn't my wife and Louisa. They go to visit him sometimes."

I was eager to speak with the constable myself, but it would have to wait. H.N. and I went into the Duck, where we had the sad task of telling the Brodys. Ursilla covered her mouth with a hand and burst into tears. Finn wrapped an arm around her shoulders and led her upstairs.

H.N. went behind the bar and poured two glasses of whiskey.

"I don't usually partake this early," she said, handing me one, "but I think I'll make an exception."

I took the glass but didn't drink. "I really should go back for John."

"The constable will head to Swan's cottage straight away. I'm sure he'll give your husband a ride back to the village." She downed her whiskey in one swallow and made a face. "But I promise you he won't want any *women* underfoot. Even though we're both more clever by half."

Besides the two of us, the common room was empty.

"Are we?" I asked, taking a swig of whiskey.

H.N. laughed. "Without a doubt." She shook her head. "Poor thing."

"The constable?"

"No, *you*, Mrs. Weston. First day in the village and you've got a murder on your hands."

"Oh no," I said. "We're on our honeymoon. Let the constable have this one." I squinted at her. "And I thought you said it was an accident."

"I said nothing of the sort. You were right about that picture. The glass should have broken if Swan bumped the table. His killer was sloppy." H.N.'s eyes glittered. "If it was a person at all."

I frowned. "Of course it was."

"Tell me something, Mrs. Weston. Did you really see a black dog up on that ridge?"

I thought back, trying to convince myself that it was just a trick of the light, but the image of the crouching shadow was too vivid.

"I'm certain," I said, taking another bracing sip.

"Because your husband was right. They're omens of death." H.N. gripped her glass and leaned forward. "I have a confession to make."

I raised a brow, though I didn't really expect her to admit to being a murderess.

"I wasn't entirely honest last night. I have heard a few things about Duncan Montague. He thought he was being stalked." She leaned forward. "By a great black hound!"

CHAPTER 5

I took H.N. Gryffin's words with a large grain of salt. The
woman penned gothic mysteries for a living.

"Where did you hear that?" I asked.

She smiled. "My source is confidential. But it's common
knowledge in the village. Duncan Montague used to frequent
the Duck, but he stopped coming not long before he died."

"Maybe he saw the same animal I did and it made him
paranoid."

She splashed another measure of whiskey into her glass. "It's
not paranoia if the monster really is out to get you."

"Are black dogs part of the Montague curse?"

"Not that I've heard," she admitted. "But it seems quite a
coincidence that you saw it up near Swan's house and then we
found him dead."

"True. Except I saw it *after* he died, so it wouldn't really be an
omen, would it?"

Finn came back downstairs and people started drifting into
the inn as the news spread. John returned with Constable Robb,
a bluff-faced man with bushy white side whiskers. H.N. and I
gave our statements in a private dining room. The constable

nodded when I mentioned the missing poker and glass portrait that failed to crack when it supposedly tumbled from the table, but I could see he was doubtful.

When I came back out, John was talking with the local doctor, a fellow named Martin Gibson. He had short-cropped red hair and rather buggy light-colored eyes with deep creases at the corners.

"I'll have to rule it death by misadventure," Gibson said. "There's no evidence of foul play. And plenty of witnesses who admit he was drinking the night before."

"What about the heel print outside the cottage?" I asked.

"The rain had washed it away by the time they arrived," John said. "Though I did tell the constable about it."

"If there were any conceivable motive, I'd recommend an inquest," Dr. Gibson added with a note of apology. "But Jacob Swan had no enemies. He was well regarded by everyone in the village." The doctor cast a glance at Ursilla Brody, who sat next to the window, a handkerchief balled in her hand. "She was like a daughter to him."

There was more in the doctor's eyes than mere sympathy. They held a fondness that spoke of long admiration. It wasn't hard to understand. Ursilla Brody was a beautiful woman with a prosperous business. I wondered where Finn's father was.

"I saw something," I said. "Up on the moor."

Dr. Gibson frowned. "A person?"

"No. Some kind of hound."

The conversation around us dwindled.

"I don't doubt that you saw *something*," Dr. Gibson said in a patronizing tone. "But it was probably a stray sheepdog. There are plenty of flocks around here."

"It was huge," I persisted.

Two men drinking at the bar exchanged a look.

"I've seen the hound," said one. "Black as a tar pit with flames for eyes!"

The pair might have been brothers. They both had square jaws and curly ginger hair. The one who spoke sounded a pint or two on the wrong side of sober. I wondered if he was H.N's "confidential source."

There were murmurs, some villagers nodding, others shaking their heads. Ursilla Brody glared at the men.

"Hush, Lachlan," she said fiercely. "Don't act the fool!"

He stuck his nose back in his mug. "It's true," he grumbled.

Dr. Gibson looked a bit disturbed—and thoughtful. "Well, if you see it again, let me know." He produced a pipe and pouch of tobacco, filling the bowl and tamping it down, then lighting it with a match.

"You served abroad, didn't you?" I said. "India? Decommissioned five years ago, unless I miss my guess."

He looked startled. "I was in the Black Watch. Royal Highland Regiment."

"Which accounts for the initials engraved on your pipe," I replied with a smile. "And the date."

He looked at it with a rueful grin. "Your husband mentioned your skills of deduction. But how did you know I was in India?"

"You bear the signs of prolonged exposure to a tropical sun."

"Aye, it aged me," he admitted.

I looked around. The villagers had returned to their own conversations.

"Have you been called to Caer Morvan Hall?" I asked quietly. "Mr. Goodnight told me about his daughter, Louisa."

"Poor wee lass," Dr. Gibson said, puffing on his pipe. "She has xeroderma pigmentosum. I stop in every now and again, but there's not much to be done except keep her out of direct sunlight."

"I read about that, though I've never seen an actual case," John said. "A peculiar affliction. It often runs in families."

"The parents deny any history of it. The nurse they brought from America seems competent." Gibson picked up his doctor's bag. "Well, I must be off. I hope the rest of your stay is more pleasant."

He departed in a cloud of blue pipe smoke.

"Are you game for a row on the loch?" I asked John.

He smiled. "Hoping to see your beast again?"

"As a matter of fact, yes."

"Then your wish is my command."

Dusk was falling as we walked down the road. "If this were one of H.N. Gryffin's horror tales," I said, "who would the culprit be?"

He took the question seriously, as I knew he would. "Let's start with motive. Mr. Swan had no fortune, nor living heirs. It's doubtful he was having a torrid love affair with a married woman. That rules out both money and jealousy, the two perennial favorites. Which leaves one thing. He saw something he oughtn't have."

"Eliminate a witness." I nodded slowly. "But to what? If he went straight home, what could he possibly have seen? It was dark and rainy last night."

John stuffed his hands in his pockets. "Maybe we'll find another body."

"Lord, I hope not. But that constable didn't even look into people's alibis."

"Och, they'd all claim they were home abed, wouldn't they?" John said in a terrible Scottish accent.

The loch was a slate gray expanse roiled by little whitecaps. I turned to gaze up at the hillside, hoping to spot my beast, and instead saw two tiny sparks moving across the moor. They would have been invisible from the village and I felt a small thrill. John saw it, too.

"Fairy lights!" he said.

"Or lanterns. But who's meeting up there at this time of night?"

We looked at each other and ran back up the road. Night

was falling swiftly. I wrapped my red scarf tighter against the chill.

"Do you see anything?" I whispered when we reached the edge of the moor.

"No . . . ." He pointed. "Wait, over there!"

It was on the other side of the river from Caer Morvan Hall, south of the village. The light bobbed along for a minute, then vanished. We hurried to the spot where it had been as the last daylight drained from the sky. A fog was rising, obscuring the moor. Out of the mist, I saw a jagged circle of weathered stone pillars in the distance.

"The Portclair Standing Stones," John said.

They looked unearthly rising up out of the fog. I saw no sign of the lantern, but I did have the sensation of being watched. It lifted the hair on my neck.

"It'll be pitch dark soon," I said. "We'd better get back."

I startled at movement in the corner of my eye, but it was just a tawny owl gliding past, wings silent in the white. The bird soared above the Standing Stones and vanished.

But a moment later something stirred the fog low to the ground. I touched John's arm.

Whatever it was, the mist cloaked it. Yet I could see billows as it moved among the stones, like ripples on a still lake. I told myself that it was a fox or some other moorland creature, yet my heart beat swiftly as I took John's hand and tugged him away from the stones.

A figure loomed out of the fog. I bit back a shriek when I saw it was Professor Carlton. He wore his greatcoat and carried the butterfly net.

"Well, hullo," he said. "What are you two doing out here?"

"We saw lights," John replied. "I don't suppose you brought a torch?"

The professor shook his head. "I have very keen eyesight."

"Any luck?" I asked.

He stared at me.

"With the emperor moth?" I prompted.

"Ah, yes. I managed to obtain several male specimens, but the female *Saturnia pavonia* is nocturnal. They're gray and white. About three inches across. I don't suppose you've spotted any?"

We shook our heads. "Listen, Professor," I said. "I think there's an animal roaming the heath. A large one. Perhaps you should come back to the inn with us."

Carlton frowned. "An animal? There's nothing dangerous to man in Scotland anymore."

"Nevertheless," I replied, "I would strongly suggest—"

"Nonsense," Carlton said, his scowl deepening. "I heard what happened to old Swan, but that was an accident. He drank to excess and took a tumble. I can assure you that these moors are perfectly safe. Now good evening to you both."

We watched him vanish into the fog.

"He could have been one of the lights," John said thoughtfully. "He might have hidden the lantern when he heard us coming."

"Are you suggesting we follow him?"

The fog had already closed in, muffling all sound.

"I doubt we could. But it's hard to believe he thinks he can find a moth in this weather."

"And it's the perfect excuse to skulk about," I agreed, chafing my frozen hands. "But I vote for the Duck."

John nodded. We made our way back to the village without incident and my spirits lifted to see warm light spilling from the windows of the inn.

"Hot tea and a hot bath," I said as we entered the common room. "Then it's straight to . . . ."

I trailed off at the sight of two men sitting before the fire. One was fair and clean-shaven, the other big and burly with dark hair and a walrus mustache. They turned and the second man's expression of perfect astonishment mirrored my own. I rushed forward with a laugh.

"Uncle Arthur! What on earth are *you* doing here?"

"Harrison!" He leapt to his feet. "And John Weston! I hear congratulations are in order."

"Dr. Doyle," John said warmly.

They'd met before—Arthur Conan Doyle was a friend of my father's. The men shook hands and Arthur introduced us to his companion, a Welshman named Frank Thomas.

"I had no idea you were coming here for your honeymoon," Arthur said, looking abashed. "I didn't mean to barge in on you. We won't impose on your privacy—"

"Don't be silly," I said, as we joined them in two armchairs near the hearth. "I'm awfully pleased to see you."

Arthur was one of my sister's many admirers, so I caught him up on Myrtle's latest escapades hunting a priceless relic that had been stolen from the Maharaja of Bhurtpore.

He informed us that Frank Thomas was a friend from the University of Edinburgh, where they'd both studied medicine. They had come because of the loch beast, though in a roundabout way. Mr. Thomas hoped to raise money for charity by swimming from Drumnadrochit to Fort Augustus. The recent publicity helped to gain attention for the stunt, and Arthur had used his contacts at the Ghost Club to secure backers. He was an avid sportsman himself, cricket and rugby among other things.

"And your writing?" I prompted. "Will we be getting more tales of Sherlock Holmes and John Watson?"

I'd heard from my parents that his medical practice in Southsea wasn't going very well, though readers had devoured *A Study in Scarlet* and *The Sign of the Four*. Arthur had written loads of other adventure stories, but Holmes was the character that seemed to capture the public imagination.

Now he made a face. "My publisher Ward Lock took advantage of me," he grumbled sourly. "But I've moved on. I'm working on a fresh batch of short stories now. In fact, I had supper at the Langham Hotel in London this summer with the editor of Lippincott's Magazine and who do you guess was there?"

I leaned forward. "Tell me."

"Oscar Wilde! He'd read one of my stories and liked it very much. I must say, Harry, Wilde's conversation left an indelible impression upon my mind. He towered above us all, and yet had the art of seeming to be interested in all that we said."

Arthur smiled. "But as much as I enjoy my scribblings, I doubt it will ever pay the bills. I'm considering going to Vienna and studying to be an eye surgeon next year."

"John just earned his medical license," I said proudly. "He'll be interning at Bellevue when we return to New York."

"That's wonderful news," Arthur replied. "I wish you both every success." He frowned. "But what's this about a death in the village?"

"We discovered the body," John said.

"Did you really?" Mr. Thomas ventured. He spoke with a rapid Welsh brogue.

"And that's not all," I said. "Not by a long shot."

We took turns filling them in on Caer Morvan Hall and the black dog sightings. I could see Arthur was intrigued. "Black dog, you say?"

"It's called Muckle Black Tyke in these parts," John said. "Harry swears she saw it just before we found Mr. Swan."

Arthur's brown eyes narrowed. "The hellhound legend. I—"

"Is that A.C. Doyle?" a voice rang out.

We all turned as Mrs. Davies hobbled over with Miss Neiderberger in tow, holding a wriggling Caesar firmly in her arms. The men shot to their feet.

"I'm afraid you have the better of me, madam," Arthur said, bowing in a courtly fashion over her extended hand.

"Mrs. Algernon Davies," she said. "Surely you recall my late husband? He was an esteemed member of the Ghost Club."

"Oh yes, of course," Arthur said in a sympathetic tone. "Mr. Davies is greatly missed. You have my sincere condolences on his passing."

Women, I knew, were not admitted to the Club.

Mrs. Davies brushed this off. "Algie has merely moved to a higher plane," she replied. "We still commune on a regular basis. Are you here to hunt the leviathan?"

"Not exactly. Mr. Thomas means to swim the loch tomorrow morning."

Caesar barked. Mrs. Davies pressed a hand to her breast. "Do you think that's wise?"

Mr. Thomas asked something unintelligible. She squinted at him. "Pardon?"

"He's wondering if you've seen the creature," Arthur said.

"Alas, no. But what about the chill temperature? Surely he'll drown!"

"Mr. Thomas has several long-distance swims under his belt. He nearly made it across the Channel last summer but was turned back by a storm. In any event, I'll be accompanying him in a rowboat. You're welcome to come down and watch."

Her steely gaze regarded us. "I shall do so. Miss Neiderberger will arrange it."

Frank Thomas smiled. Miss Neiderberger blushed to the roots of her tightly braided blond hair. "I am certain you vill do vell," she said.

Mrs. Davies turned to John and me. "I hear you discovered old Swan. How dreadful. Drink is a sure path to the Devil."

"I'm not sure he was drunk, Mrs. Davies," I said.

"Murder, then?" She didn't seem entirely displeased at this prospect. "How exciting. Well, I must be to bed." Her attention settled on Mr. Thomas. "At what hour do you propose to swim the loch, young man?"

"Crack o' dawn," the Welshman replied cheerfully.

She nodded. "Then I shall pray for you, Mr. Thomas. Goodnight."

Mrs. Davies sailed off, her cane rapping against the floorboards. Caesar cast us a condescending look and permitted Miss Neiderberger to attach a leash and drag him outside.

"We shared a coach from Inverness," I whispered. "But Uncle Arthur, they're all like that! The other guests, I mean. Miss Gryffin is . . . ." I trailed off, remembering my promise to keep her secret. "A bit peculiar, too. And Professor Carlton claims to be hunting moths, but I've never seen him with a single one!"

He chortled. "Perhaps I'll find some material for my Holmes stories." The smile faded. "I'm on deadline to deliver six by next year so I mean to get some writing done on this trip."

"We won't disturb you," I promised, reaching up to give him a peck on the cheek. "But I hope you'll help unravel the multitude of mysteries?"

Arthur winked. "I wouldn't miss it for the world, Harrison."

CHAPTER 6

We ate breakfast in darkness the next morning and hurried down to Temple Pier. Besides the other guests at the Duck—excepting Professor Carlton, who slunk off in his rubber boots with barely a nod—most of the village had turned out to watch. It was a festive gathering, though the sun barely penetrated the ominous dark clouds to the east.

The ruin of Urquhart Castle hunched across the bay. Most of the keep had been shattered in the wars for Scottish independence. Only a corner tower stood intact, a dark silhouette against the hills beyond.

John and I joined Arthur in a rowboat. Mr. Thomas stripped down to his swimming costume, which had weights sewn into the hem so it wouldn't rise in the water. Cormac Ferguson, the photographer staying at Kinlach Cottage, took a picture of him with the castle in the background.

Mr. Thomas performed a few squats and stretches. The time was noted. Then he waded in and began to confidently breaststroke down the loch.

John and Arthur planned to take turns at the oars, though a second boat was waiting at the halfway point in Alltsigh some miles south. I had to admire Frank Thomas's hardiness. The water was about fifty degrees, which, while not freezing, was cold by any measure. Yet he plodded on, striking a steady pace of about a mile an hour.

Several other boats were following, including that rowed by the indefatigable Miss Neiderberger, who could probably have given the loch a go herself.

It started to drizzle. The fog thickened. At times, we lost sight of Frank entirely and Arthur would shout his name, steering for the answering call. I could see the other boats well enough. The mist sat above the surface, perhaps a foot thick, making it seem as though we drifted on a sea of clouds.

"It wasn't even this bad on the English Channel," Arthur muttered. "Frank?"

No answer.

"Halloo! Frank!"

Something bumped the boat. A gentle nudge, but I gripped the gunwale, heart hammering.

"What was that?" I squeaked.

"Floating log?" Arthur ventured, though his knuckles were white around the oars. "Frank!"

The wind picked up, though it barely rippled the fog. Then: a muffled shout from off to the left. Arthur began to row toward the sound.

"Mr. Thomas!" John called. "We're coming your way!"

"I don't want to run him over," Arthur said anxiously. "Frank!"

Another cry came, this one with an edge of panic. "Somethin' brushed m' leg!"

If I hadn't felt that nudge, I might have thought they'd arranged it all ahead of time. Some sort of prank—though that wasn't Arthur's style. Like John, he had a deep fascination with the supernatural, and, I believed, a healthy respect for it.

The boat began to rock from side to side, riding a sudden tumult of wavelets. Fog blanketed the craft on all sides now.

I wondered how far we were from shore.

And whether my skirts and petticoats would drag me to the bottom when I plunged into that icy abyss.

"Mr. Thomas!" I called out, reminding myself how much worse it was to actually be *swimming in the loch.* "Where are you?"

It seemed pointless, but I tore my coat off and began to wave it about in a bid to clear space at the bow. To my surprise, this worked. The mists parted enough to reveal a figure flailing in the water about ten yards ahead.

Arthur made for him, John calling out encouragement. Frank's eyes were wide, his face bloodless. He was treading water in circles and glancing over one shoulder.

"Nearly there!" John shouted as we closed the distance.

That's when I spotted the line of ripples. It was moving swiftly in Frank's direction.

"Row," I urged Arthur, who had his back to the bow and thus couldn't see what was coming for his friend. "For God's sake, row!"

My face must have conveyed the urgency of the situation because he didn't waste time turning around to look. At thirty-one, A.C. Doyle was a powerfully built, vigorous man. The oars dug deep into the black water.

I counted the seconds in my head, trying to calculate the two trajectories and determine which would arrive first.

It would be a very close thing.

Then the line of ripples vanished.

"Oh God," I muttered. "It's gone under."

Frank Thomas flicked wet hair back from his eyes. I met his gaze for a brief moment. Somewhere in the fog bank, Caesar began to howl.

A whispered prayer left my lips. Arthur gave a tremendous heave on the oars. The boat skimmed the last few feet.

The instant we came aside, John leaned over and seized Frank Thomas around the chest. Arthur dropped the oars and they dragged him, dripping and swearing in Gaelic, into the boat.

Only I glimpsed the thing that passed a moment later.

A hint of something even darker than the loch, long and sleek. Two greenish glows like emeralds held to a flame. Eyes, I thought numbly.

Then it was gone.

The surface stilled. The mists closed in again.

Frank was shivering from head to toe. John offered his coat.

"Are you injured?" he asked, running a professional eye over Frank's shivering body.

"Nae. It just bumped me." He gave a strangled laugh. "Did ye see it?"

"No, did you?"

Frank shook his head. "Made it worse, didn't it?" He managed a grin through chattering teeth. Then he tugged a crucifix from beneath his tunic and pressed it to blue lips. "How far'd I get?"

"Er, about two miles," Arthur replied, relief on his face.

Frank glanced over the edge of the boat. "Tha's good enough for me."

Him and John wordlessly shared the stern bench as Arthur rowed us back to Temple Pier, where we found Mrs. Davies bobbing about with Miss Neiderberger.

"I heard shouting," she called. "Is Mr. Thomas quite all right?"

"He's fine!" I shouted back. I turned to my companions. "Should we tell her?"

"You bet your boots," Frank managed.

We all reassembled back at the Duck, Mr. Thomas bundled

up in blankets and nursing a large whiskey as he told the story of his encounter of the loch beast.

Mrs. Davies glowed with excitement, tempered by disappointment that she'd missed the spectacle of his near demise. "I *told* you to keep up," she chastised Miss Neiderberger.

"You said you were cold," Miss Neiderberger objected.

"Because you forgot to pack the blanket for my feet!" Her frown faded. "But Algie was right. He'll be so pleased to hear it. Still, one must wonder why the beast did not simply overturn the boat and devour you all?"

I was a question I'd considered myself. "Maybe it's not evil," I said. "Just misunderstood."

"But you said it was swimming straight for him!" Mrs. Davies protested.

"And we don't know what it would have done." I glanced at Frank, who watched us with amusement. "Although I'm grateful we reached him first."

"A new species," Professor Carlton put in, rubbing his spidery hands together in glee. "If it appears again, perhaps I can have the honor of naming it."

I'd been surprised when he joined us—and more surprised that H.N. Gryffin was nowhere to be found. I'd seen her briefly down at the shore when we first set out, flirting with the Scottish photographer, but she seemed to have disappeared.

"Are you sure you didn't get a good look?" Professor Carlton pressed.

"It was too foggy," John said ruefully. "And the creature never surfaced. We only saw the ripples."

"So it could have been anything," he sniffed. "A giant carp, perhaps."

Mrs. Davies rolled her eyes.

"It wasn't a carp," I said. "I saw the eyes. They were like . . . ."

Everyone leaned forward.

"Like burning copper. Bright green."

Professor Carlton cast me a skeptical look. "Well, I hope you keep it under your hats. The inn was intolerably full just a week ago. If word gets out, they'll all come back."

"Perhaps ye riled the beast up." It was same villager who claimed to have seen the *other* beast—Black Tyke. He scowled at us from the bar. "Never had trouble from it before."

Finn stared at him for a long moment. "Lachlan is right. Not that we minded the extra custom, but some folk weren't so keen on all the outsiders in Drumnadrochit. Mr. Swan's funeral is tomorrow and we'd like to mourn him in peace. Better if you let it lie for now."

"I wasn't planning to wire the papers," Frank Thomas said good-naturedly.

Finn nodded. "Good. But 'tis better if all of ye stay off the loch from now on."

No one objected to this. He caught the eye of the serving maid, Cassie. "Could ye help me with the milk delivery?" She smiled and they disappeared into the kitchen. My stomach rumbled and I realized I hadn't eaten a thing since my painfully early breakfast.

"I'll ask Cook when lunch is served," I said to John.

She was rolling dough on a floured table when I entered. The tabby watched with a heavy-lidded gaze from the windowsill.

"Sorry to trouble you," I said. "But—"

"Yer famished?" she said with a wink. "Supper'll be ready shortly. I hope you fancy a mince pie."

"Very much," I said, returning the smile. "It smells wonderful in here."

"Teddy agrees with you," she laughed, regarding the cat with fondness. "He's a shameless beggar, aren't you?"

Teddy closed his eyes in evident disdain.

"We used to have a terrible mouse problem," she confided. "The little devils chewed through four sacks of oats in a single week." Cook glanced at a small wooden box in the corner. "Mistress gave me these traps. Supposed to catch the wee buggers without killin' em. Has a soft spot for animals, she does."

I frowned. "But all the stuffed heads . . . ."

"Och, those are ancient. Came with the inn. Mrs. Brody only bought it fifteen years back." She made it sound like a brief interlude. "The traps never worked anyway. The bait always disappeared, but nary a mouse to be found. Clever, they are. So I brought in Teddy and never saw another!"

"Might I examine one?" I asked.

She looked surprised. "Go ahead, missus."

I crouched down, thinking it was the sort of device my sister might invent—if she cared a fig for the life of a poor mouse. The mechanism proved to be quite simple. The box had a seesaw mechanism so that when the weight shifted to the back—presumably where one placed the bait—a door would drop shut, trapping the interloper inside the box.

"Ingenious," I said. "I wonder why it didn't work."

Cook shrugged. "Clever, they are," she repeated.

On my way back to the common room, I nearly collided with H.N. Gryffin, who was slipping through the front door. She stifled a gasp as I loomed in front of her, then covered it with a shaky smile. "Oh, hello, Harrison. I hear I missed some excitement."

Her hair was in disarray, her cheeks flushed. I detected an oddly guilty look in her eye and wondered what she'd been up to all morning.

"You can ask Mr. Thomas yourself," I said, pointing to the group at the hearth. "He'll give you a firsthand account."

"Wonderful, I'll do that," she replied brightly, turning to beeline for the stairs up to her room.

I watched the author go with a frown, then rejoined my companions. It rained until nightfall, at which point Professor Carlton suited up for his nocturnal pursuit of the elusive emperor moth. Arthur retired to his room to get some writing done. After a vicious round of Old Maid with Mrs. Davies and Miss Neiderberger, John and I did the same.

"So your loch beast is real," I said, uncoiling my auburn hair from its pins.

"And I'd wager your black hound is, too," he replied. "Plus a possible murder."

"What else could I ask for in a honeymoon?" I said lightly, feeling instant remorse. "Oh, that's awful. We shouldn't joke about Mr. Swan."

"I knew what you meant," John said, pausing for a moment of respect. Then he flung himself to the bed. "Damn, I wish I'd gotten a better look. Do you think Finn Brody would find out if—"

"I'm not going back out there," I said flatly. "Not even in a battleship."

"Right." He folded his hands across his chest. "But didn't you say it was a kind, peaceable creature?"

"Pure speculation. I was scared spitless. Weren't you?"

"Well, yes, but more for Frank Thomas."

I shook my head and perched on the edge of the bed. "You're a piece of work, Weston."

He grinned. "Isn't that why you love me?"

"One of the many reasons," I said, blowing out the candle.

CHAPTER 7

I t was still raining the next morning, so we decided to stay in bed until our stomachs finally drove us down to the common room.

Cassie served us eggs and toast with a saucy smirk. Ursilla and Finn Brody had already departed for Mr. Swan's funeral. We hadn't been invited since we barely knew him, though I did wonder if his killer was among the mourners.

"Or they could be sitting right here among us," John said cheerfully when I voiced this thought aloud.

I glanced around. It was the usual motley assortment. Mrs. Davies carried on about spirit photography to Cormac Ferguson, who'd stopped by for lunch and been corralled into her orbit. He nodded with a polite expression but kept glancing at the door.

Miss Neiderberger had been given the task of taking Caesar for a nice long walk so it was relatively quiet. Once Ferguson managed to extricate himself, Mrs. Davies coaxed H.N., John and me into another round of Old Maid. It was only after the horrid old woman stuck me with the queen of spades for the third time that I realized one of our party was missing.

"Has anyone seen Professor Carlton?" I asked.

"Not since last night," H.N. said. "But he keeps odd hours."

"The professor *always* comes down for breakfast," Mrs. Davies said with a frown. "He's an early riser." Her gaze lingered on me and John with faint accusation. "But I didn't see him this morning."

"I'll ask Cassie," John said, walking over to the bar where the serving maid was wiping glasses.

"You don't think something's happened to him, do you?" Mrs. Davies asked, pursing her rouged lips.

"Let's not jump to conclusions," I said quickly. "Though with all that's happened, we ought to keep an eye on one another."

The statement was intended to be reassuring, but we ended up staring across the card table with mutual suspicion.

"He never turned up for breakfast," John reported a moment later. "Sometimes he asks Cook to pack a hamper, but neither woman spoke to him today."

"Let's check his room," H.N. suggested. "It's across from mine."

The four of us squeezed up the narrow stairs, Mrs. Davies jabbing a sharp elbow in my ribs to gain the lead. Repeated knocks on Professor Carlton's door brought no response.

"Shall I see if it's unlocked?" John said. "Or would that be an invasion of privacy—"

"Oh, I'll do it," H.N. snapped, gripping the knob and throwing it wide.

There was a collective intake of breath, followed by sighs of relief. The room was cluttered with books and specimen jars, though most looked empty. The bed was neatly made, a pair of socks hanging to dry on the footboard.

"No corpse," H.N. said. "But his bed hasn't been slept in." She rounded on us. "Who saw him last?"

"Well, we all did," I replied. "When he went out last night."

"We'd better organize search parties," John said. "He might have fallen into a crevasse or something."

The look he gave me indicated that *or something* was a more likely scenario, but John had the grace not to say it aloud. Mrs. Davies had no such compunctions.

"What if the leviathan got him?" she said, eyes gleaming.

"Or Muckle Black Tyke," H.N. added.

"Oh dear!" A hand flew to her mouth. "My darling Caesar is out there!"

Mrs. Davies plodded heavily down the stairs, shouting for an umbrella.

"Poor Miss Neiderberger," I said. "Though I suspect she can fend for herself."

After some hesitation, I decided to fetch Arthur. He would be upset if I neglected to include him in the search, deadline or no. I found him bent over his writing desk. He seemed grateful for a break and roused Frank Thomas from the room next door.

In short order, we all headed back downstairs, where frantic barks signaled that the Pekingese was alive and well. Miss Neiderberger stood in the doorway shaking rain from her hat. Mrs. Davies showered Caesar with kisses.

"None of that," she said, poking Miss Neiderberger with her cane when the companion started to peel her coat off. "We're going back out. Professor Carlton has vanished!"

"Ze professor?" Miss Neiderberger echoed in alarm, tucking an errant strand of wet hair behind her ear.

"We ought to find Constable Robb," I said.

"He's at Mr. Swan's funeral," a youthful voice replied.

I looked down. The scullery boy waited expectantly.

"They're in the churchyard," he said. "I'll show ye."

We all bundled outside into the raw October afternoon. The church wasn't far. A small crowd was gathered in the cemetery listening to the white-haired minister give a eulogy. Ursilla Brody wept in silence, Finn at her side. Dr. Gibson stood on her left, his flame-red hair marking him out in the sea of black-clad mourners.

Jack Goodnight and the two elderly servants from Caer Morvan Hall were there as well. Mr. Goodnight caught my eye with a slight frown, then turned back to the service. I saw no sign of his wife and child.

"Duncan Montague is buried over there," H.N. whispered, pointing to the far corner of the cemetery.

The headstones in that section were far grander than the rest, with marble plinths and statues of mournful angels.

"It's all Montagues going back three centuries." The author pulled out her notebook. "I already examined the graves. Not one of them lived to see fifty."

H.N. showed me the page where she'd recorded a list of birth and death dates in neat, precise script.

"The women, too?" I asked.

She shook her head. "Just the male heirs. Don't you find that peculiar?"

"Very," I agreed.

"And here's another thing. They never die *terribly* young. For a Montague, one's twenties are safe enough. Thirties are the last hurrah. Somewhere between forty and forty-five seems to be the magic number. Then—" She gave a little hop.

"You go . . . dancing?" John hazarded.

"I was kicking a bucket," H.N. said.

"That's rather morbid," Arthur said disapprovingly.

She cast him an enigmatic smile. "My point is, the curse likes to play with them. Let each one think that *he'll* be the one to get away."

"Or prolong the dread," Frank Thomas said.

"Clever man," H.N. said. "Like Duncan Montague. I've tried to learn more about him, but the townsfolk have a funny attitude towards the family. I don't get the impression the Montagues were well-liked, but they ruled over these parts since the 1500s. I'm not sure if it's fear or stubborn loyalty, but most people refuse to speak about them."

"Perhaps it's a bit of both," John said.

"Well, I haven't given up." She pitched her voice for John and my ears only. "Cross my palm with silver, Lord Burgundy, and I shall reveal the shocking truths you seek."

"That's a line from . . . er, don't tell me . . . *The Fortune-Teller's Confession*," John exclaimed.

"So you mean to bribe the villagers for information," I said dryly.

"Whatever works, Mrs. Weston," she replied. "Someone knows *something*. And I mean to ferret it out."

"I don't mean to interrupt," Arthur said, "but a man is missing." He turned to the scullery boy from the Duck, whose name was Arran, and sent him to fetch the constable.

"Carlton will probably turn up," H.N. said, turning her collar up against the drizzle. "Perhaps he found his moth."

No one bothered to refute this, though standing beneath the skeletal trees as Mr. Swan's coffin was lowered into a muddy hole, I experienced a host of misgivings about not only my fellow guests but the village of Drumnadrochit as a whole.

There comes a point when disparate tragedies begin to form a larger picture. I could barely discern the outline, but it struck me as sinister.

Ursilla Brody stepped forward to toss a handful of earth on the coffin. The two servants from Caer Morvan Hall followed suit and the crowd began to break up. Constable Robb came over with Mr. Goodnight. We exchanged somber greetings and John briefly explained the situation.

"Likely he strayed off," the constable said.

"Professor Carlton has been roaming these hills for weeks," H.N. said. "I doubt he lost his way."

"Anything can happen on a foggy night," the constable replied. "I warned him not to go out on the moors alone—more than once. He would'na listen." Robb sighed. "Let's have a look for the fella."

"I'll head back to the Hall and have the staff search the grounds," Mr. Goodnight offered.

The constable knuckled his forehead as if Goodnight were a lord. "Thank you, sir. That'd be welcome."

The new master of Caer Morvan jumped into his carriage. The elderly brother and sister whom I'd met before, Mr. and Miss McKenzie, took the bench and the coach rattled off over the bridge.

We broke into two groups. John and I with Uncle Arthur, H.N. with Frank Thomas and the constable.

"What about myself and Miss Neiderberger?" Mrs. Davies demanded. "Will you abandon us?"

"I thought ye'd be going back to the inn," the constable said wearily.

"I wouldn't think of it!" She poked the air in front of his chest with her cane but didn't quite dare to prod him. "You've no idea the things I've seen, Constable. Algie and I once banished a Class Four Ghoul together." She drew herself up. "Do not dismiss my contribution, sir."

I felt a new measure of respect. Class Fours were nasty.

The constable frowned.

"I'll go with them," said Finn Brody, striding up to us. He kept his webbed hand jammed into the pocket of his coat. "Dr. Gibson will see my ma back to the inn."

"We'll spread out in lines," Constable Robb said. "Keep within earshot of each other. Stay south of the river for now. Mr. Goodnight can oversee the search of the estate. If we don't find the professor in an hour, we'll broaden the radius."

It seemed a sound plan. We headed up to the moors. When the others had fanned out, I told Arthur about the lights we'd seen crossing the heath and the odd encounter with Carlton the night before.

"You think he was meeting someone?" Arthur asked.

"We don't know," John admitted. "He didn't have a lantern. But it seemed quite a coincidence."

We walked ten feet apart, calling out his name and scanning the ground for any signs of the professor's passing. The rain never ceased, though it kept to a drizzle. It was hard to imagine Carlton staying out here—even in the heat of the chase.

Both John and I were so used to Caesar's yapping that at first we ignored the distant cacophony. But the dog's cries had a frenzied edge. They were coming from over a hill to the left. When Davies's shrill voice joined the hubbub, we decided to go meet up with the others.

We hiked over the rise and found her hobbling along with Finn and Miss Neiderberger, who looked pink and flustered.

"I am sorry," she was saying. "He pulled ze leash right out of my hands!"

Mrs. Davies's mouth set in a grim line. "He's a naughty boy," she muttered. "A *very* naughty boy!"

A white dot was streaking across the moor. We picked up the pace, breasting another hill. I spotted H.N., the constable, and Frank Thomas hurrying in the same direction as Caesar. His barks resumed, reaching a fever pitch. Four large, dark birds circled in the sky. My heart sank as we hurried to the glen below.

The dog stood in the center of a circle of ancient, weathered slabs at the fringe of Portclair Forest. The very same Standing Stones where we had run into the professor. Some were flat, others with jagged tops like the teeth of an old man. When Caesar saw his mistress, he tipped his snout to the heavens and let out a mournful cry.

Like Mr. Swan, Professor Carlton lay on his back. One arm was flung above his head, the other lying across his waist. The butterfly net had fallen at his feet. But his face . . . .

Miss Neiderberger screamed, then stumbled away retching.

Finn took his hat off, gazing at the body with an ashen expression. H.N. covered her mouth with a hand. Mrs. Davies eyed the corpse with tight lips, then dashed forward and caught Caesar in her arms.

"Stay back," the constable warned the rest of us. "Weston, come with me."

"I'm a medical doctor, as well," Arthur ventured, staring at the body.

"One's enough," Robb said gruffly.

If I hadn't recognized the rubber boots and greatcoat, I wouldn't have been sure it *was* the professor. His face was a red ruin, the features nearly obliterated. My stomach twisted, yet I felt glad John would have a chance to examine him more closely. If there was any clue, I trusted Weston to find it.

"Everyone, remain where you are," I said, willing my voice to calm. "Uncle Arthur, we'll walk the perimeter. See if we find anything."

He nodded grimly. Frank Thomas had already gone to comfort Miss Neiderberger, who recovered her wits sufficiently to give Caesar's leash to her employer. He sat on his haunches, panting and looking pleased with himself.

I started a clockwise circuit around the stones, while Arthur went the opposite way. In light of the rain and tough grass that covered the moor, I doubted we would find much. Professor Carlton had probably been killed last night. Either he'd gone to meet someone—Mr. Swan's killer, perhaps—or been deliberately targeted as he wandered the moor alone. A crime of opportunity?

But why now? And why *here*?

Faint traces of intricate runes marked the granite. Each was as tall as two men put together and about three feet wide. Our guidebook said the Portclair Standing Stones were erected more than a thousand years ago, likely by the Picts. I resolved to ask H.N. about them. The author would know of any local legends associated with the stones.

A quarter of the way around, I noticed that the earth had been disturbed next to several of the stones. It was darker than the ground around it and missing the turf. Someone had been digging, then tried to cover their tracks—

"Harrison!"

Arthur's hoarse cry broke my train of thought. I hurried over to him.

He stood over one of these patches of fresh-churned earth. I followed his gaze downward, a thrill of fear tightening my belly.

"By God," he murmured. "It's the paw print of a gigantic hound!"

CHAPTER 8

There was no mistaking it this time.

Despite the weather, the impression was deep enough to have been preserved. Arthur spread his hand above the imprint, taking care not to touch it. He had large hands, but the paw was nearly twice the span.

The constable stumped over. "What d' ye have here?"

John joined him. "Muckle Black Tyke," he mouthed at me, though there was no giddiness now. He looked dead serious.

The constable stared at it for a long moment. "No animal killed the man," he said softly.

"But the face!" H.N. exclaimed. She'd ignored my command to stay put, pushing her way forward for a better view. "He was torn to pieces!"

"Buzzards did that," John said.

I thought of the dark birds I'd seen above the Standing Stones.

"The eyes were gone, meaning he was dead before the vultures came," John continued. "They can find a fresh corpse fairly quickly if the wind is right. Small predators might have been at him, too. But the cause of death was a blow to the back of the head."

"Just like Mr. Swan," the author said thoughtfully.

"Someone was digging around the stones," I said. "But the shovel is gone. I'd guess it's the same person who killed him."

"All right," the constable said, eying us. "Back to the Duck with you lot. I'll need to fetch Dr. Gibson and get his opinion. No offense intended, Dr. Weston."

"None taken," John said absently, still staring at the paw print. "He'll confirm what I've told you."

We were all soaked through at this point and more than willing to warm ourselves by the fire. John and the constable stayed with the body, while Finn went to fetch Dr. Gibson. Frank Thomas and Arthur offered to bring a cart from town to remove Professor Carlton. The Standing Stones were a popular tourist attraction and there was a track leading back to the village, which sat barely a mile distant.

The Swiss companion retired to her room, still shaken. But once we'd changed into dry clothes, Mrs. Davies and H.N. Gryffin joined me in the common room, where Cassie served us mugs of strong tea.

"I canna believe it," she said, shaking her head tearfully. "I was just speaking to him yesterday."

"What did he say to you?" I asked.

"Nothing much, missus. Just that he needed some washing done and didn't fancy the pickles on his egg sandwich. He was cross with the Cook."

"He didn't mention meeting anyone?"

"Nothing like that, missus." She lowered her voice. "The professor was very particular about things. But I canna think anyone would want to kill him for it!" She wiped an eye with her apron and returned to the kitchen.

"The murderer was searching for something," I said, blowing on my tea.

"The treasure, I imagine," H.N. replied.

"Treasure?" Mrs. Davies echoed. Caesar drowsed in her lap, exhausted from his adventure.

The author took out a flask and tipped a dram of whiskey into her tea. She offered it to Mrs. Davies, who hesitated, then held out her mug. "Oh, I suppose it's medicinal," she mumbled.

I accepted a tiny drop, mainly so I wouldn't look like a prude, but I wanted to keep my wits about me.

H.N. flipped through her leather notebook and ran a finger down the page. "Ah, here it is. The Portclair Treasure. How's your British history?"

"Shaky," I admitted.

"Well, in 1707, the Act of Union joined Scotland and England into one kingdom. It was wildly unpopular with the Scots, setting off a series of rebellions against the Protestant Queen Mary."

I felt my eyes glazing over and forced myself to pay attention. "Go on."

H.N. sipped the tea, then added a jot more whiskey from the flask.

"Mary's half-brother, Bonnie Prince Charlie, was a Catholic loyalist. He sought to claim the Scottish throne and convinced France and Spain to aid his cause. They sent ships loaded with weapons and gold. One landed at Arisaig and the treasure made it all the way to Inverness, but Charlie's forces were badly routed. About half the gold was used to fund the escape of the rebel leaders."

She closed the notebook with a little smile. "The rest vanished into the misty glens. Seven caskets of Spanish bullion worth a fortune. Over the years, rumors sprang up that it was hidden at Urquhart Castle. Others insisted it was in a cave near the Standing Stones, though no one ever found it."

She frowned. "Which would explain the print from Black

Tyke. Some of the legends claim the hound stands guard over the gold."

"So Professor Carlton was really searching for treasure!" Mrs. Davies exclaimed. "I knew that man was up to something nefarious."

"Or he interrupted someone else," I said. "And the hound was a harbinger of impending doom. Like Mr. Swan. I saw it up on a ridge the night he died."

"Well, I doubt it's one of the villagers," H.N. said. "They've lived here all their lives. Why would they be digging up there now?"

We eyed each other. The temperature in the room cooled a degree or two.

"Alibis," H.N. said briskly. "Let's have them."

"I was in my room last night," I said. "With my husband."

"And I was in *my* room," Mrs. Davies said. She glanced at the dog in her lap. "With Caesar. But I summoned Miss Neiderberger shortly after midnight to warm my feet. I have chilblains. She'll attest to it!"

"Since we don't know what time he died, that hardly exonerates either one of you," H.N. pointed out.

"What about you?" Mrs. Davies demanded haughtily.

She hesitated. Only for a fraction of a second, but I noticed it. "I was in my room. I'm afraid no one can confirm that though." She turned to me. "And husbands and wives lie for each other all the time, so I'm not writing you off either, Mrs. Weston."

I held my empty teacup out for more whiskey. H.N. gave me a thin smile and obliged.

"Fine," I said, tossing it back. "We can all lock our doors tonight."

Caesar opened an eye, then closed it again. I decided the miserable creature *was* warming to me. And, truth be told, I to him.

"What about that Welsh swimmer?" Mrs. Davies ventured. "And Mr. Doyle—"

"They arrived *after* Swan was dead." H.N. frowned. "Though the man does write detective stories."

"Oh, for God's sake," I erupted. "It's not Arthur Conan Doyle! I've known him since I was a child. He's a perfect gentleman."

A brittle silence fell.

"So how do we proceed?" Mrs. Davies wondered.

"Stay off the moor," H.N. advised dryly.

"I'm entirely serious. I came for the loch beast, but innocent people are dying!" The widow seemed genuinely upset. "We must do something."

"What about that photographer at Kinlach Cottage?" I said. "Perhaps he—"

"I can promise you Cormac Ferguson is not a killer," H.N. said fiercely.

"I wasn't accusing him," I replied. "I only thought it might be useful to look at his photographs. He's been taking pictures around the village for weeks. There might be something in them."

"Oh." She took a quick glug of whiskey. "Of course. That's a clever idea."

We all turned as John entered with Dr. Gibson. I rose to meet them.

"Professor Carlton was murdered, no doubt of that," Dr. Gibson said, covering a yawn. "He was a tall fellow. From the angle, it looks like he was bending over to look at something and the killer snuck up behind. Gave him a mighty blow to the back of the head. A spade, I reckon." He caught the serving girl's eye. "Would ye brew a pot of coffee, Cassie?"

"Can I fetch you a bite to eat, as well, doctor?"

Gibson nodded gratefully. "Haven't slept a wink," he said, knuckling his eyes. "I was called out for a difficult birth and spent the night with the lass. Happily, both mother and child are well."

"That's one piece of good news," I said, mentally drawing a line through his name on my list of suspects. "Could you tell anything else?"

"Not with the state of the body. But the damage to his face and hands did seem to be from animals."

"And what did you make of the paw print?"

Gibson looked uneasy. "It was much too large for a fox. I suppose someone's dog must have gotten loose."

"It would have to be enormous," John said. "Have you ever seen a sheepdog that size?"

The doctor reluctantly shook his head. "The villagers will say it's Muckle Black Tyke no doubt, but that's superstitious nonsense." He frowned at John. "You're a man of science, Dr. Weston. Surely you know there must be a rational explanation."

John was spared a reply by the arrival of a mutton pie and steaming cup of coffee. Dr. Gibson sat at the bar and tucked in, chatting amiably with the scullery boy, Arran, who sat next to him drying glasses with a rag.

"If the professor was murdered, you can be sure Swan was, too," I said in a low voice to John. "And so far no one except Dr. Gibson can account for themselves."

H.N. was watching us. I wondered if she knew how to read lips.

Constable Robb arrived with Finn Brody, Arthur and Frank Thomas. The constable took his hat off, regarding the assembled group with a serious look.

"I've got not one but two suspicious deaths on my hands," he said. "So I'll have to insist that none of you leave Drumnadrochit until the matter's been settled."

"We weren't planning to," H.N. protested.

"Aye." He looked at her dubiously. "I'll still need your formal statements. Who saw him last?"

No one answered. Mrs. Davies gulped down the dregs of her whiskey. H.N. scribbled in her notebook. Arthur looked around with interest, fiddling with the chain of his pocket watch.

"We all did," John replied at last.

Ursilla Brody drifted downstairs and stood leaning on her son, both still wearing black from the funeral. She had the hollow eyes of someone who can't quite fathom what's happening. I looked around. We'd all seen Carlton in the common room when he charged out into the rain.

But had one of us seen him *afterwards*?

CHAPTER 9

Once the statements were taken, the surviving guests of the Drunken Duck drifted our separate ways.

I cornered the serving maid Cassie and learned that Kinlach Cottage had originally been part of the Montague estate but fell into disrepair and was purchased by the Brodys as an artists' retreat.

"But no one ever used it as such until Mr. Ferguson came along," Cassie said. "There was a mountain o' dust. Spent two days scrubbing it, I did." She wrinkled her nose. "You wouldn't believe the moldy old things I found in there. But he wanted to keep it all. Said it gave the place character!" She laughed and shook her head.

"How long has he been there?"

"Oh, about two months now. I bring his meals, though he sometimes forgets to eat 'em. It smells something awful in there, missus."

I raised a brow.

"From all his solutions, I mean. He explained it to me, but I couldn't make head nor tail." She glanced into the kitchen, where the Cook watched us impatiently. "If that's all, missus, I ought to get back to my duties."

Kinlach Cottage sat at the north edge of town near the foot-bridge leading to Caer Morvan Hall. It was less rustic than Mr. Swan's croft house, with a freshly whitewashed exterior and a pair of dormer windows on the second floor framed by blue shutters. Clusters of lacy ferns grew along the shaded sides of the cottage, giving off a loamy scent I always associated with fresh running water.

John and I found Cormac Ferguson poring over stacks of photographic prints in the kitchen. He listened in shock as we told him what had happened and seemed happy to let us look at some of his photographs.

"I rigged up the darkroom in the back," he said.

"May we see it?" I asked.

"Certainly. I finished my exposures for the day."

He led us to a small room with heavy coverings over the windows. A table held stacks of glass negatives and wooden frames. Another had chemical baths in trays. Cassie was right—it did smell foul.

"I coat the glass negative plates with cellulose nitrate and a soluble iodide," Mr. Ferguson said. "The print itself is saturated in a mixture of fermented chloride and egg white, then dried and floated on a solution of silver nitrate—"

He talked for a while more, but I was more interested in the array of landscape prints tacked to the wall. They were taken from a vantage point that showed the near shore and wild hills beyond.

"Who's that?" I asked, pointing to a dark figure standing down at the loch. It was visible in several of the photographs, though the gradually vanishing leaves on the trees indicated that the pictures were taken over a series of weeks.

"Oh, that's Ursilla Brody. She often goes down to the loch."

"For what purpose?"

"I don't know. She likes the view, I suppose." He leaned over my shoulder. "But it gives some perspective in the foreground to have a human figure. Makes the scene more interesting."

"What does she do there?"

He cast me a sharp look. "Nothing at all, Mrs. Weston. Just stands and looks out at the water."

"Do you know what happened to Mr. Brody?"

He shook his head. "I never asked. But I gather he died when Finn was just an infant."

"I wonder if he drowned in the loch," John said.

"I don't think so. Apparently, she came with the child to Caer Morvan Hall—"

"The Hall?" I exclaimed. "She worked there?"

"Years ago. Then she inherited some money and bought the inn. But Ursilla is from the Orkneys originally."

The Orkney Islands formed an archipelago off the northeastern coast of Scotland. A wild, remote place.

"I wonder why she didn't go back," I said.

Ferguson shrugged. "I suppose she liked it here."

H.N. Gryffin must not realize that fact, else she would have pumped Ursilla for information about the Montague curse. Or perhaps she did and had been rebuffed.

"Well, thank you for your time," I said to Mr. Ferguson. "Some of these prints are very beautiful. Do you think we might buy one? It would make a fine souvenir of the trip."

"Och, I'll give it to you," he said with a smile. "A wedding gift."

"That's very kind. But how about you give us one and we'll buy another?" I suggested. "Artists must pay the bills, too."

He scratched his head. "I ken you're right about that. I'm hoping to gain membership in the Glasgow Art Club next year. If my work's good enough."

"I'm sure it will be. You have a wonderful eye for light and shadow."

He seemed pleased at this. In the end, we chose several prints. One of the Drunken Duck with Finn and Cassie standing to either side of the front door wearing awkward smiles; another that showed the moor and Caer Morvan Hall; and a third of the loch.

It was one of those that featured Mrs. Brody. I couldn't explain why, but there was something terribly lonesome about that slender figure. Her back was to the camera and I couldn't see her expression, but somehow I knew it was wistful.

It seemed odd that such a well-off, attractive woman would never remarry. Dr. Gibson was obviously keen on her. I wondered if she had loved Finn's father too much to ever give herself to another.

Cormac Ferguson promised to box up the photographs and send them over to the inn. I paused at the door as if I'd just thought of something. "You didn't happen to see the professor last night, did you?"

He gazed at me for a long moment. "I was here working all evening, Mrs. Weston."

"Of course. I just thought you might have glimpsed him out the window. I wondered if he might have been with someone else."

"In the rain and dark? No, I'm afraid I didn't see a thing."

I nodded. "Of course not. Thank you again, Mr. Ferguson."

He chewed a thumbnail and gave me a brusque nod. I didn't really suspect him, but it didn't hurt to ask.

No one, I thought ruefully, had an alibi.

"If I die," I told John as we walked back, "you mustn't mourn me forever."

His brow creased. "Well, if I die, I expect you to wear ashes and sackcloth for the rest of your days, Harry."

"Then we must both live a very long time. Or at least die on the same day. Promise?"

I held out my hand. Weston shook it.

"I'd ask what prompted this morbid train of thought," he said, "but there are so many possibilities. Two monsters on the loose and a crazed murderer to boot. Oh, and the curse, of course. I found out a bit more from the constable, if you'd like to hear it."

"And then I'll tell you about the Portclair Treasure. But you go first."

He tipped his Homburg back. "The Montague family has always been associated with both good fortune and rotten luck. The estate was bestowed on Sir Silas Montague by King James IV in 1509. Silas is the one who started the trouble. He was notoriously cruel and cold-hearted. In 1518, old Silas got one of his vassals pregnant and killed the bastard child, stabbing the poor thing and throwing it down a privy."

I pressed a hand to my mouth. "What a monster!"

"Turns out there were more infants down there. When confronted with witnesses to the crime, Silas confessed and was sent to the gallows, right here in Drumnadrochit. The estate and titles were going to be forfeit, but the king miraculously changed his mind and allowed it to pass to Godfrey, the eldest legitimate son. He built up the family's wealth but died at the age of thirty. Struck by lightning while walking on the moor during a storm."

"That *is* rotten luck," I said.

"Oh, it keeps going," John said dryly. "The Montagues managed to profit from the economic upheavals that saw similar estates fall into ruin. The family only grew richer. But every male heir died young. Every single one, Harry, for four hundred years. Which leads us to Duncan, the very last. He made it to thirty-nine, which isn't bad for a Montague, but his father died in a fire when he was eight."

"Mr. Goodnight mentioned that. It was the same tragedy that killed Mr. Swan's wife and child." I frowned. "Any connections with the loch beast or Muckle Black Tyke?"

John shook his head. "Not that I can discover. Although it was whispered that old Silas Montague struck a deal with the Devil and the infants were payment. It tainted the whole family line."

"But Duncan didn't have children himself?"

"No. He traveled as a young man, then settled at Caer Morvan Hall. The constable said he was generous to the village, building a new schoolhouse and helping those in need. Unlike his forebears, the man seemed to be well-regarded, though he never married. So perhaps the curse is finally ended."

I related what H.N. had said about the Portclair Treasure.

"It still doesn't quite fit," I said with a frown. "The story is famous. Surely others have come over the years and dug at the stones. If the gold was there, why hasn't it been found?"

"Maybe Muckle Black Tyke kills anyone who tries to steal it."

"By bashing them in the head?" I said wryly. "No, our killer is a person of flesh and blood, though I don't dispute the supernatural aspect of the case."

"Well, it wouldn't hurt to find out if anyone has died up at the stones in the last century. I'll ask the constable."

We were nearing the inn. "H.N. is lying about something," I said. "She seemed flustered when I caught her coming back after Mr. Thomas's swim. I thought she'd be raring at the bit to talk to him about the beast, but she went straight up to her room."

He nodded thoughtfully. "Well, I don't think Mrs. Davies has the strength to overpower a young man."

"Unless she crept up from behind. With the missing poker, perhaps."

We looked at each other. "Miss Neiderberger could certainly do it," John said.

"Yes, but we still don't have a solid motive." I sighed. "If we knew what Mr. Swan and Professor Carlton had in common, it would be a start. But they hardly knew each other."

"As far as we know. There must be a connection."

Back at the Drunken Duck, I learned from Mrs. Davies that H.N. Gryffin had claimed a bout of dizziness and gone to see Dr. Gibson.

"I don't trust that woman," Mrs. Davies whispered. "We must watch her closely."

I made a noncommittal noise. Her eyes darted from side to side as she opened her huge black handbag and showed me a revolver. "A gift from Algie. Thank God I had the presence of mind to bring it along."

"Have you practiced with it?" I asked.

Somehow, the thought of Mrs. Davies armed and fearful was not reassuring.

She closed the bag. "I'm an excellent shot, dear."

To my surprise, Caesar trotted over and stared up at me expectantly. I reached down and gave him an awkward pat, withdrawing all ten digits intact. The dog sighed and flopped at my feet.

"Well, don't take it out unless . . . ." I swallowed. "Just don't take it out."

"The murderer will not find us such easy prey, Mrs. Weston," she replied grimly. "Now, how about a nice game of whist?"

I begged off. John had gone to find the constable so I passed the time in our room listing the names of potential suspects, motives, and all we knew about the various curses, creatures and locations. The end result was a hopeless tangle, with arrows and lines in every direction.

Drumnadrochit seemed a perfect vortex of supernatural activity, but a key piece of the puzzle linking it all together was still missing.

My fear was that this would come in the form of a fresh corpse.

At length, John returned to report that no one had died at the Standing Stones in recent memory.

"Well, at least the treasure isn't cursed, too," I said. "That's something."

"What next?" he wondered.

I blew out a breath. "We must revisit the crime scenes, I think. See if we missed something on the first go around."

"Are you suggesting we head up to the moor?" John asked, imbuing the last word with an ominous note.

"Yes."

"Good, I was hoping you might."

We passed Arthur's door on the way out. I pressed my ear to the wood and heard the sound of a pen scratching furiously on parchment.

"We'll leave him to it," I whispered to John. "If he misses his deadline for the next Holmes story, the public will string us up."

The common room was quiet save for Frank Thomas and Miss Neiderberger, who sat talking by the fire. Finn stood behind the bar, reviewing a ledger. I noticed a fresh bandage around his hand.

"Did you hurt yourself, Mr. Brody?" I asked.

"I was cuttin' potatoes," he replied without looking up. "The knife slipped."

"Keep the wound clean," John advised.

"Tha's what Dr. Gibson said."

Finn's tone didn't encourage further inquiry. We left the Duck and started down the lane.

"Do you believe his story?" I asked John.

"I believe no one, Harry. Which one first?"

We'd reached the crossroads at the edge of town.

Kinlach Cottage sat at the end of the lane. In one direction lay the southwesterly track to the Standing Stones. In the other, the footbridge leading north toward Mr. Swan's house.

"Mr. Swan," I said at last, shivering as the rain started again.

"At least it's inside. If there's evidence, it's more likely to be preserved."

We crossed the river and followed the meandering path along the bank. Presently, the croft came into view. It looked sad, sitting dark and empty, and I thought again of Mr. Swan's dead wife and child.

"Whoever killed him had a tender heart," I said.

"Tender?" John echoed with a note of disbelief.

"Well, the killer believed he had to be disposed of, but when they staged the scene by toppling that table over, they were gentle with the photograph. If they'd been in a rage, they would have hurled it down. But they set it carefully on the ground next to the body. That tells us something."

The cottage didn't even have a lock on the door. We went inside. A bloodstain on the rug was all that remained of the old caretaker.

The upstairs had a tidy bedroom with a Gaelic Bible on the dresser and an old-fashioned box mattress stuffed with straw. The linens weren't disturbed and I guessed he'd never gone upstairs the night he was killed. Other than the bed, there was a wooden chest for clothing, a basin for washing, a small shaving mirror and a comb.

The second bedroom next door was empty save for an old chair and broken spindle.

We found nothing else of note inside and proceeded to search the yard. Mr. Swan had an outdoor privy, which made me think of horrible old Silas Montague. When I voiced this fear, John was brave enough to light a lantern and lower it into the hole. It wasn't a pleasant investigation, but he found nothing sinister lurking in the depths.

We widened the search to a tumbledown barn some distance away, poking through stacks of weather-warped boards, rusted farming implements, and old tack for horses. Then John gave a shout. I hurried over.

"The missing poker!" I exclaimed.

It had traces of blood and a few silver hairs on the pointy end. Whoever killed him had hidden it in a corner beneath a bale of mildewy hay.

"If we carry it to town in the rain, the evidence will be lost," I said. "But I don't fancy splitting up again."

Dark was falling and with it the usual fog. The hills were fuzzy outlines and I could barely discern the lights of the village across the river.

"Let's wrap it in something," John suggested.

We returned to the house and found a spare blanket in a chest at the foot of the bed. John carefully covered the bloody poker and we stepped outside.

"It proves Mr. Swan was murdered," I said. "But it also suggests that the killer didn't come with the intention of doing away with him. If they had, they would have brought their own weapon."

"Why not dispose of it somewhere farther away?"

"Perhaps they panicked." I glanced around. I could barely see ten yards now. "Which does imply that they might come back to do the job properly—"

A long, eerie cry dried the words in my throat.

CHAPTER 10

I grabbed John's arm. "What was that?"

Funny, the things one blurts in the grip of terror. It was a foolish question, but part of me hoped he would reply, "Oh, that's just a Highland owl, it sounds exactly like a hellhound. Didn't I mention them?"

Weston did no such thing. He raised the lantern, its frail light bouncing off the fog that closed in around us.

"Hush, Harry," he whispered.

We stood still for a moment, hardly breathing. Then the howl came again, low and throaty. Closer this time. The hair on my arms rose.

"Give me the lantern," I hissed.

"What for?" he hissed back.

"So you can defend us with the poker!"

He looked at the parcel in his other hand. "Oh, right."

We fumbled through this process, but I felt better when John had a foot of bare iron in his hand.

"Does iron work against Muckle Black Tyke?" I whispered.

"Don't know." He cocked his head with a slight frown. "If it's a true emissary from Hell, perhaps. But if it's merely an omen of death, the lore is inconsistent. John Dee claimed—"

I sensed a lecture coming and dug my fingers deeper into his arm.

"Ow," John muttered.

"H.N. said Duncan Montague saw a black hound before he died. That it was stalking him!" My eyes swiveled across the encroaching mist. Every shadow took on menacing dimensions.

"So there *is* a curse angle? Why didn't you say so—"

"I think we should run," I said. "Very fast."

As if in answer, a savage growl wafted through the fog, though I could scarcely tell from which direction. Then I saw the gleam of lights some distance away.

"We're closer to the Hall than the village," John said, gripping my hand. "It's our best chance."

I nodded, throat too tight to speak, and we dashed into the mist. Damp tendrils pried at my collar, the fog tearing away in shreds as we dashed headlong across the moor. I sensed a presence in pursuit, silent now save for the occasional panting rasp. My own breath tore from my lungs in white bursts. Shapes loomed ahead—dark, crouching figures that proved to be boulders or the bony, clawing branches of trees.

Adrenaline lent me a fleetness of foot I'd never suspected. Having read Mr. Darwin's *The Descent of Man* earlier that summer, I suspected that my ancestors experienced the same terrified euphoria as they fled lions across the savannas of Africa, though this thought was distant. Foremost was the urge to reach solid walls with doors that locked.

Another deep, baying howl ripped the darkness. It came from up ahead. The creature must have gotten around us somehow and was trying to sever our escape route. My fear ticked up a notch. It was *clever*—

My boot caught on a hillock, the lantern flying from my hand.

Glass shattered as our only light extinguished. John wordlessly hauled me to my feet and we stumbled onward, veering away from that dreadful sound. The terrain was rough and uneven. We were forced to slow our progress or risk tumbling over a crag.

"Can you see anything?" I whispered.

"Over there!" he pointed to a solitary spark off to the left.

We'd gone off course, but at length we reached a sloping drive paved in gravel. Caer Morvan Hall appeared suddenly out of the fog, a softly glowing sanctuary amid the sea of featureless white.

"Nearly there," John gasped, squeezing my hand, which was glued to his with sweat.

I glanced over my shoulder at the road behind. Yes, something was moving. Just beyond the edge of the fog. Low to the ground. Lithe and rippling with sleek muscle—

We sprinted the last quarter mile and pounded on the front door until Miss McKenzie appeared. She took one look at our faces and stepped back, holding it wide.

"Come in, then," she said. "Ye look in a lather."

I gibbered something about Muckle Black Tyke as she led us to a sitting room and poured two brandies. "Let me fetch the master," she said.

I nodded vigorously and took a sip. John tossed his brandy back and laid the bloody poker on the flagstone hearth. He'd had the presence of mind to conceal it inside his coat before we knocked on the door.

"That was a close one," he remarked, holding his palms to the fire.

As before, every window was covered with heavy drapes. I was glad not to see the foggy night pressing against the glass.

"What," I said, "is going *on* in this place?"

"It didn't like us nosing around," he replied. "But it didn't attack and it certainly could have. I don't believe for a second that we outran that thing."

I stared into the flames. The brandy was working its magic. I felt some steadiness return to my chilled limbs. "What does it want, John?"

"I don't know. But we're not going out there again tonight."

My gaze moved to the portrait above the fireplace. A man with fierce blue eyes and a pointy black beard stared back. It reminded me of someone, though I couldn't quite put my finger on who. I was about to ask John if he saw it, too, when the door opened and Mr. Goodnight hurried in.

"Dr. and Mrs. Weston," he said with a quizzical look. "What brings you up to Caer Morvan Hall?"

It was raining hard now, the droplets dashing against the narrow windows.

John cleared his throat. "It sounds crazy, but something chased us here."

Jack Goodnight looked genuinely baffled. "Chased you?"

"A large dog of some kind. Right to the end of the drive."

He pondered this for a moment. "We don't keep animals. There used to be kennels, but that was long ago. What did it look like? If one of my tenants let a dangerous hound loose, I'll be sure to have a word with them."

"We didn't get a clear look," I said. "But it sounded fierce."

"The creature appeared just after we found that in a barn near Mr. Swan's house," John said, pointing to the poker. "It was used to bludgeon the poor man."

Jack Goodnight stared at the poker. "By God," he muttered. "So it *was* murder."

"We were about to bring it to the constable when we heard a howl," John explained. "The Hall was closer so it seemed safer to come straight here."

"Of course." Mr. Goodnight tore his eyes from the murder weapon. He strode to the sideboard and poured a brandy. "We came to the Highlands for peace and quiet," he said, "but it doesn't seem to be in the cards."

There was a low rumble of thunder. I was about to swallow my pride—and manners—and beg him for refuge when the door flew open.

"What's going on, Jack?"

Mrs. Goodnight stepped into the drawing room, freezing when she saw us sitting there. "Oh, hello!" she said, casting a quick glance at her husband. "I didn't realize we had guests."

I rose to my feet. "We're sorry to barge in on you—"

"But I was just about to say that you're welcome to take one of the guest rooms," Mr. Goodnight said quickly, moving to block her view of the bloody poker. "The Hall's a bit drafty, but we've plenty of space. Don't we, darling?"

"Er, yes, of course," she said with a confused smile. "I'll ask Miss McKenzie to prepare a room."

"Thank you, love," Mr. Goodnight said.

She nodded with a look that said she'd like an explanation from her husband later, then swept off.

"I'd rather Evangeline doesn't know about that," Mr. Goodnight said, stowing the poker under a sofa. "She's very protective of Louisa. If my daughter saw it . . . . " He shuddered. "I heard from Mr. McKenzie that you found Professor Carlton. Was it truly another murder?"

"I'm afraid so," John said.

Mr. Goodnight shook his head. Then his gaze narrowed. "What were you doing at Swan's house anyway?"

"I'm a professional investigator," I said. "We thought we might aid the effort to find the killer."

His brows shot up. "Investigator? For whom?"

"The Society for Psychical Research," I admitted.

He laughed. "Surely you're joking."

"Not in the least." John's tone was cool. "My wife is quite respected in New York. She's solved several crimes that baffled the police."

Goodnight sobered up. "I meant no insult, Dr. Weston. But

that is to say . . . do you really believe all that nonsense about spirits and . . . curses?"

"Some of it's nonsense," I replied briskly. "Some of it isn't. It's my job to tell the difference."

He nodded slowly. "Evangeline was reluctant when I told her I wanted to buy this place. All the rumors, you know. But the price was right and I've had no cause to regret it."

His face crumpled. "The first time we took Louisa out in her pram, it was a beautiful sunny day. At first, she was fine. But then she started to cry and cry. Her face turned bright red. I thought it was just a tantrum, but when we returned to the house, she had *blisters* on her tender skin. It burned her, Dr. Weston."

John made a sympathetic noise. "I've heard of the condition."

"We tried every specialist, chased every quack cure," he said bitterly. "I spent thousands seeking a remedy. Nothing worked. I don't care about the money. I'd give anything to let Louisa play and run outside like a normal child." His shoulders slumped. "But nothing helped. Finally, we saw a doctor in Vienna who was honest with us. He said she probably wouldn't live very long. Such children develop tumors of the skin, you see. The best thing we can do is keep her away from direct sunlight."

"So you came to Scotland," I said, feeling terribly sorry for them all.

"Yes. And Louisa is doing much better. The governess is a local girl, but we kept on her nurse. She was kind enough to relocate here." He paused. "Would you like to see the nursery?"

"I'd love to," I said.

Mr. Goodnight brought us up a flight of winding stairs to the second floor and led us down a hall. He rapped his knuckles on a door at the end.

"It's Daddy," he called. "Permission to enter the kingdom, Your Majesty?"

"You may, good knight!" a merry voice called back.

"I've brought two humble pilgrims in search of bed and board. Can they come, too?"

I exchanged an amused look with John.

There was a long pause. "You bet!"

Mr. Goodnight opened the door into a land of fairytale enchantment.

CHAPTER 11

The far wall was painted with a castle, colorful pennants streaming from the towers. It had a moat and an armored knight on horseback crossing the drawbridge. A damsel with golden hair leaned from one of the high windows, waving down at him. A sky thick with sparkling stars covered the ceiling. A real telescope sat at the window, tilted up to the heavens.

Other scenes of adventure and chivalry adorned the three remaining walls. Puss in Boots wearing a feathered cap and brandishing a rapier. Little Red Riding Hood reading to a wolf in spectacles and a nightcap. Arthur and his Knights of the Round Table standing with awestruck faces around Excalibur and the Stone. Even the venerable Alice, scowling at the Mad Hatter as he sipped a cup of tea, pinky extended.

Each scene led whimsically to the next to create a panorama that wrapped around the entire room. The last of Arthur's knights was sneakily reaching for one of the cakes at Alice's Tea Party. Puss in Boots was about to skewer a wart-nosed witch as she beckoned from her gingerbread house. Hansel tugged at his sister's hand, waving a frantic warning at Riding Hood. In a wink to it all, the book she was reading was titled *A Compendium of Fairytales*.

I gaped in wonder for a moment before I noticed the child sitting at a small table in the center of the room.

"Louisa," Mr. Goodnight said. "I'd like you to meet my friends. This is Dr. and Mrs. Weston. They're staying at the Duck."

She peered at us with light green eyes that matched her mother's. "How do you do?" she said, rising to give a pretty curtsy.

John made a show of bending over her hand to kiss it. "My lady fair," he murmured.

"You're not bad at this," she said. "I might just knight you."

He placed a hand over his heart. "It would be my greatest honor."

Louisa turned to me. She had a direct, mature gaze far beyond her years. I recognized the look of a child who spent nearly all her time with adults. I'd been the same. Myrtle was seven years my senior and never bothered with me until I was old enough to boss around.

"You have freckles, too," Louisa observed. Her pale face was covered with them, like someone had dusted her in cinnamon.

I grinned. "My mother used to make me hide them with powder, but now I'm old enough to let them be."

"It's why I married her," John said seriously. "The freckles. She's also very clever."

"I'm clever." Louisa gazed up at her father. "Aren't I, Daddy?"

It didn't seem a boast. Just a statement of fact.

"The cleverest," he replied fondly.

"Would you like to see my telescope?" she asked me.

I followed the child to a cozy window seat. "Do you ever get clear nights?" I asked, as she fiddled with the eyepiece.

"Not as often as in California, but that's all right. I like nighttime best. If it's not raining, Daddy takes me out and we play croquet on the lawn. Mr. McKenzie lights all the torches so we can see."

"I suppose you often stay up late," I said, deciding she would prefer frankness.

Louisa nodded. "I read books after Mommy and Daddy go to bed." She pointed to a case that brimmed with volumes. Besides the usual nursery fare, I spotted *A Tale of Two Cities* by Charles Dickens, along with works in French and German.

"I read loads of books when I was a girl," I said.

"Which was your favorite?"

"Poe," I said, thinking of *The Murders in the Rue Morgue*.

Louisa scowled. "Mommy won't let me have those. She says they're too scary."

"So is the Brothers Grimm," I replied. "Most fairytales are downright ghoulish. Hansel and Gretel? Far worse than anything Poe could dream up."

We shared a conspiratorial look.

"That's what I said, but Mommy wouldn't listen." Louisa stared into the rainy darkness. "I wish the pixies would come back. You could see them, too!"

"Pixies?"

She nodded solemnly. If I hadn't been menaced by a hell-hound and almost capsized by a loch monster all in the span of two short days, I might have been skeptical. Louisa was clearly a child who sought refuge in imagination.

But why *couldn't* we have pixies? I thought. At least they were harmless.

"Tell me about them," I said, propping my chin on a hand.

"They only come out when it's very late and all the grown-ups have gone to sleep."

"What do they look like?"

She chewed her lip. "Like little lights. They dance on the moor."

I felt a twinge of excitement. To a child peering through a

window, a person carrying a lantern over rough ground might look like it was "dancing."

"How many do you see?"

"Only two." Her voice lowered and she cast a glance at her father, who was talking with John. "I think it's a boy and a girl."

"Oh? Why do you think that?"

She shrugged. "Who else would have to meet in secret? Maybe they're from different pixie clans and their families are feuding, like Romeo and Juliet."

I nodded. "It's the only reasonable explanation."

"Don't tell Daddy," she whispered. "He might tell me to stop watching."

I buttoned my lips. "Not a word," I whispered back, just as Mr. Goodnight approached us.

"She wasn't a *pilgrim*," Louisa declared, as he swept her into his arms. "Mrs. Weston is a selkie in disguise. Mr. Weston stole her sealskin and now she has to live with him forever and ever!"

Jack Goodnight shot us a rueful look. "Is she now?"

"It's true," I admitted. "But I don't mind so much anymore. He charmed me into falling in love with him." I frowned. "Though I do miss the sea."

"All right," Goodnight said, depositing his daughter on her huge, ruffled four-poster bed. "Even selkies and princesses have to go to bed sometime."

"I never got my knighthood," John reminded him.

Louisa bounced up and dashed to the corner, where she rummaged through a bin of costumes and props. When she turned back, she had a wooden sword in her hand.

"Kneel, sirrah," she commanded imperiously.

John dropped to one knee and received a brisk tap on each shoulder.

"I hereby dub you Sir Weston," Louisa said. "You are bound to serve the crown of Abkhazia and all its heirs from this day forth. Before God and these witnesses, do you swear to keep your oaths of fealty?"

He bowed his head. "I swear it, Lady."

"You may rise."

John stood, jaw set in noble fashion. "My blade is yours."

Louisa gave a satisfied nod and crouched down to play with an elaborate dollhouse that mirrored the castle painted on the wall. It had dozens of little people in medieval garb, cattle, dogs and cats, and even a tiny trebuchet.

It was the sort of playroom most little girls would give their eyeteeth for, yet she didn't strike me as spoiled. I think her life was too difficult for that. Yet Louisa seemed content enough as we left the room, humming to herself as she rearranged the soldiers in the bailey.

"Perhaps you think I'm too extravagant with her," Mr. Goodnight said, closing the door and leading us back down the dim corridor.

"I don't think that at all," I said. "She can't go out into the world, so you brought the world to her."

He was quiet for a moment, his face struggling to contain some strong emotion. "You do understand," he said hoarsely.

"The nursery is beautiful," I said. "Much more so than the reality beyond these walls. I hope she enjoys it for a long time."

He vented a deep breath. "So do I. But Louisa is eleven. She won't want to stay cooped up forever."

"Perhaps medicine will catch up with her by then," John said gently. "It's advancing every day. This is an age of miracles, Mr. Goodnight."

He cleared his throat, forcing a smile. "You're right, of course. We'll never give up hope."

"Who painted the murals?" I asked, aiming to distract him from his sorrow.

"Charlotte Payne. She's our nurse."

John cast him a sideways look. "That's really her name?"

"I'm afraid so."

He didn't seem to find it as amusing as we did.

"Your *nurse* did all that?" John asked in surprise.

"Impressive, eh? It's a hobby. We couldn't ask for a more devoted caretaker."

Yet his voice held a flatness that made me think he didn't like Miss Payne very much.

"I can see why you brought her along from California," I said.

He grunted, leading us down yet another long, gloomy corridor. Caer Morvan Hall was enormous. I remarked on its size and Goodnight brightened.

"It's hellish to heat, but I hope to restore the place to its former glory. Duncan Montague's father used to hold grand parties. Royalty slept here!" He said it with the thrill of a true American. "In its heyday, the Hall had a staff of forty. The McKenzies are the last of them."

"What happened to the rest?" John asked.

"Most were gone long before we came. Duncan was something of a recluse. When he died, he left all his servants generous bequests. Most chose to retire or leave for greener pastures. But I'm grateful the McKenzies stayed. They know all the quirks of the place."

"Who inherited the rest of the Montague fortune?" I asked.

"No idea. The will was sealed." He nodded towards a door at the end of yet another corridor. "That leads to the East Wing. It's been closed off since the fire. Bad memories, I imagine. I've arranged for workers to repair the damage, but we decided to settle in first."

We turned a corner and saw Mrs. Goodnight and Miss McKenzie approaching.

"I was looking all over for you, Jack," Evangeline said, an edge to her voice.

"We stopped in at the nursery."

"Oh." She seemed at a loss for words.

"Louisa made me a knight of Abkhazia," John said.

Mrs. Goodnight tensed. "She doesn't often meet new people. I hope she behaved herself."

"She was delightful," I said. "Actually, she reminded me of myself when I was a girl."

Her face softened. "Your room is ready if you care to retire. I took the liberty of laying out some spare clothing."

"You're too kind," John said.

Miss McKenzie took silent custody of us. We followed her down an endless series of hallways to a large, chilly bedchamber overlooking the front lawn. It smelled a little dank, but all the linens looked clean and fresh candles had been scattered around the room.

"The old master brought in plumbing," she said, using her own candle to light the others. "The private bath is through that door."

"Thank you, Miss McKenzie," I said with a smile.

It was not returned. She fussed with the towels, not meeting my eye. "Do you require anything else, missus?"

"Everything seems fine," John said. "Goodnight, then."

She gave a brusque nod and retreated.

"Lord, it's freezing in here," I said, rubbing my hands together.

John exhaled through his mouth. "I can see my breath."

"Do you think there's hot water?" I wondered, heading for the bath.

It had a massive clawfoot tub. I twisted the tap. A violent knocking sound rattled the pipes. After a moment, a stream of tepid water gushed forth. I held my hand beneath it, hoping it might get warmer.

"A bath, eh?" John's breath tickled the back of my neck.

"Stop," I laughed, turning to face him.

He wrapped his arms around me and we snuggled together for a moment.

"What do you think of the Goodnights?" he asked.

"They seem like decent people. I like Louisa."

"So do I. What were you two talking about?"

I pulled back to catch his eye. "She saw the lights, too. She thought they were pixies." I frowned. "From the way she described it, these clandestine meetings have been going on for a while."

"Which rules out Mrs. Davies and Miss Neiderberger since they arrived when we did."

"But not H.N. Gryffin," I added. "She's been in the village for a while. So was the professor. And that photographer, Cormac Ferguson."

"And our hosts," he pointed out.

"The Goodnights?" I sighed. "Well, we can't cross anyone off." I bent down and tested the water. "Still cold," I said glumly.

John grinned. "Then we'll just have to find another way to warm up."

CHAPTER 12

I woke in the small hours of the night drenched in sweat.

The dream faded within seconds, but my heart still banged against my chest. Not surprisingly, I'd been running from something. A faceless creature with swift paws and an empty belly.

John slept beside me, his breathing deep and even. Thank God he wasn't a snorer. I kicked the heavy quilt off my feet, pulse slowing. The skies had cleared and a shaft of moonlight spilled into the chamber.

Ancient houses like Caer Morvan were never silent—not entirely. Their own slumber was restless, filled with creaks and rustles and the sigh of the wind against the eaves. Long centuries of damp and cold warped their bones.

Mice gnawed at their flesh.

Spiders skittered across their skin.

"Stop it, Harry," I whispered. "If an eleven-year-old child is brave enough to live here, you can make it through a single night."

Still, the empty vastness of the place made me glad I wasn't alone.

I wondered why the McKenzies had stayed. They could easily have taken the money Duncan Montague left them and moved down to the village. But maybe Caer Morvan Hall was the only home they'd ever known.

I lay there for a bit, contemplating the odd series of events since we'd arrived. In the shifting moonshadows, a wild thought occurred to me. My last case had involved psychic abilities in a young woman. Could the eruption of supernatural happenings derive from a single source?

A lonely child who spent all her time daydreaming about magical creatures?

I dismissed the thought almost as soon as it came. Louisa Goodnight had not crept out of her nursery and bonked anyone on the head. It seemed unlikely that the murders had no connection to the loch beast and the hound—which Duncan Montague had been fearful of, thus linking it all back to the curse.

But Duncan was dead. He'd left no legitimate heirs. If Muckle Black Tyke's purpose was to torment the family, why was it still hanging around?

Someone believed there was a treasure hidden at the Portclair Standing Stones. The digging was clear evidence of that. Did old Swan know something about it? And had the professor simply been in the wrong place at the wrong time?

Perhaps the lights were two people working together to find the gold—and eliminating anyone who got in their way. If the hound did guard the treasure, they might have riled it up. Now it was bent on punishing anyone who walked the moor at night.

It seemed to work, though it didn't explain why no one had found the treasure before. Or why Swan hadn't just dug it up himself if he knew where it was.

The timing of the Goodnights' arrival was suspicious, but Jack Goodnight was already a very rich man. His reason for coming here seemed perfectly plausible. It was obvious the man loved his daughter deeply.

I shifted position, plumping my pillow, and tried to go back to sleep. The house continued to settle and creak, but my rational mind sorted through these various rumblings, dismissing them as harmless. At last, my eyes grew heavy. I was on the verge of drifting into the black when a new sound snapped me to instant wakefulness.

It was different from the rest. Not loud, but with a furtive quality. Another minute and I might not have heard it at all.

Clouds covered the moon. My eyes opened wide in the darkness, ears straining.

The chamber was silent for a long stretch. Then the sound came again. Like a gas jet being turned on.

I shook John's shoulder. "Wake up," I hissed in his ear.

He mumbled something sleepily and I was forced to pinch him.

"Plum cake!" he exclaimed, sitting up with a jolt like a vampire rising from its coffin. "What?!"

"Hush!" I fumbled at the bedside table. *Where were the matches?*

I felt him rubbing his arm. "Something bit me," he grumbled crossly. "Bedbugs—"

"That was me," I whispered, groping across the table and knocking the candle to the floor. With a soft curse, I brushed the bare boards with a fingertip. "Drat, it rolled under the bed."

"Why," he asked in a level tone, "did you bite me, Harry?"

"I didn't bite you. I pinched you. We're not alone!"

The sound came again, like the dry rustle of leaves. It triggered an instinctive revulsion. I pulled my legs up to my chest, burying them under the goosedown quilt.

"Did you hear that?" I demanded.

"Not really—"

"Just wait."

We sat in the darkness. Blood pounded in my ears.

"Probably a mouse," John said, stifling a yawn.

"I've been listening to the mice for an hour. It wasn't a mouse."

"I'll fetch a candle." He swung his legs to the floor.

I heard his bare feet cross the room. He gave a yelp and my heart stopped.

"Kicked a footstool," he said though gritted teeth. "Hang on. Weren't there matches over here?"

He walked to the hearth. The scrape of sulphur. Light bloomed. I caught a glimpse of an empty room, the edges lost to shadow. When the flame reached his fingers, John dropped the match with another quiet yelp. Darkness fell—thicker this time since my night vision was ruined by the flare of light.

"See, nothing here," John said.

"Light a candle," I whispered. "Light them all."

"Yes, my lady." He struck another match and touched it to the candelabra on the mantel.

The light slowly spread to the far walls. I let out a pent-up breath.

"That's odd," John said, bending down.

"What?" My eyes were jerking in the sockets, devouring every inch of the chamber.

"There's a rope dangling down the chimney."

I stared at his back. "A rope?"

He reached into the hearth and tugged at something. "It must be tied up at the top. Who the devil would do such a thing?"

"That might have been what I heard. The slither of it dropping down." I frowned and crawled out from the safety of the covers, setting my feet on the cold floor.

"Much too tight for a person to fit," he said, sticking his head inside the fireplace. "Flue's open. Feh!"

He withdrew his head as soot and ash drifted down.

"I'll call Miss McKenzie," I said, turning to reach for the bellpull next to the bed.

The blood-curdling shriek snapped his head around. My skin started to tingle. Heat rushed to my face.

"Don't move, Harry."

Weston's voice was taut as a tripwire.

I didn't reply. Not in words, at least. I think a small bit of air escaped my throat. The rest was locked firmly in my chest.

A large, mottled snake coiled around the bellpull. It must have been under the bed. Probably slithered past my bare feet on its journey. A forked tongue flicked out.

"No sudden movements," John warned—unnecessarily.

From the corner of my eye, I sensed him inching forward.

The snake regarded me with shiny black eyes. Its head was about six inches from my reaching hand.

My sister Myrtle had written a monograph on the poisonous reptiles of Southeast Asia. I recognized this one. The hood named it a king cobra. Approximately fifteen feet in length. Sufficient venom yield to paralyze an elephant. Highly intelligent, though not especially aggressive.

Unless provoked.

How I regretted that scream.

"Stay back," I croaked, turning my head very slowly.

John stopped. He looked as terrified as I'd ever seen him.

"You're not to do anything at all, do you hear?"

He nodded.

I let out a breath and lowered my hand. The hood flared. The tongue forked out again.

I was about to take a shuffling step when the door flew open. The snake reared back to strike. A gunshot echoed through the room. I stumbled backwards as Mr. Goodnight raised his pistol again, firing at the bellpull. He wore a dressing gown, his eyes wide, though he gripped the pistol with steady hands.

John ran over to me, shielding me with his bulk, but I could see the cobra was already dead.

"What the devil!" Jack Goodnight exclaimed, poking it with the toe of his slipper. "Are you unharmed, Mrs. Weston?"

I gave a shaky nod.

"Someone *sent* that thing down the chimney!" John erupted. He was in a towering fury, all his fear channeling itself into sudden rage.

Goodnight took in the rope, his face pale. "Outside," he snapped.

We all ran down the stairs to the front door. He flung it open but there was no sign of anyone. Jack Goodnight didn't bother dressing. He seized a coat from a stand and plunged out into the night. John looked loathe to leave me and settled for watching him through the open door. Our host raced down the west wing, studying the ground beneath our window. He returned a minute later with a grim expression.

"Ladder marks. But whoever did it is gone."

"Who even knew we were here?" I asked John.

He shook his head. "No one."

We retreated back inside the Hall. Once Goodnight turned the bolt, John seized his hand, shaking it vigorously. "I'd beat you bloody for firing a pistol in the direction of my wife, but you saved her life, sir," he said quietly. "Thank you."

I frowned, but Jack Goodnight seemed to understand the spirit in which this was intended. He nodded. "I'd feel the same. And you have my word that I wouldn't have tried it if I weren't a crack shot," he said. "I grew up dispatching rattlers in the desert." His brows creased. "But that was no rattlesnake. I've never seen the like."

"King cobra," I said dryly. "*Not* native to these parts."

"Someone wants you dead," he said, looking at us each in turn. His lips thinned. "And they tried it under *my* roof. You have my sincerest apologies—"

I waved this away. "It's hardly your fault, Mr. Goodnight."

"Still. If there are any resources at my disposal that would be of help in getting to the bottom of this, you have only to ask."

"I wouldn't mind speaking with Mr. and Miss McKenzie," I said.

"Of course. I mean to question them anyway." He scowled. "All of the servants. If there was an accomplice in this house, I'll see they're caught and punished."

We turned as Mrs. Goodnight came flying down the stairs with one of the other women I recognized from the day we first met them on the lawn. The nurse, Miss Payne. Both wore dressing gowns.

"What on earth happened?" Mrs. Goodnight demanded. "We heard gunshots!"

Her husband squared his shoulders. "A snake got inside. It was about to bite Mrs. Weston."

She drew her gown tight across her chest. "A snake?" she repeated in disbelief.

"It's dead," he said. "But someone let it into the house."

The two women exchanged a shocked look. "What do you mean, *someone?*" Mrs. Goodnight said.

"Rouse the servants," he said brusquely.

"But it's four o'clock in the morning—"

"I don't care," he snapped. "Gather them in the kitchen. I'll question them myself."

"Are you all right, Mrs. Weston?" she asked, eyeing me with concern.

"Perfectly fine. Your husband's quick actions saved the day."

Had the shoe been on the other foot, I would have given John a warm smile or some gesture of affection. Mrs. Goodnight merely nodded. "I'm glad," she said.

"I hope Louisa wasn't too frightened by it all," John said.

"She's with her governess, Miss Parker. I'll make up some story." We stared at each other awkwardly. "Well, I'm relieved you're all right." Evangeline Goodnight swept away without a second glance at her husband, the nurse at her side.

"I'd like to change before we question them," I said.

I was still in a flannel nightdress, with no shoes on, and the chill had seeped into my bones.

"Yes, of course," Goodnight said. "I'll see a fire's lit in the drawing room. We can meet there in a quarter hour." He paused. "Er, do you think it's safe now? I'll give you the pistol if you want it."

"I believe the immediate danger has passed," I said. "The killer's rather elaborate plot failed. I doubt they've cooked up another so quickly."

Though it might have worked, I amended silently, had we both been fast asleep. Cobras liked warm nesting places. If it had crept under the covers and surprised us . . . .

"She's right," John said, holding out a hand for the pistol. "But I'll take it anyway."

We went back upstairs. I made John fetch our clothes from the Dead Cobra Room and we donned warmer attire in the chamber next door. My woolen dress was still unpleasantly damp.

"There's something peculiar," I mused, tugging a stocking over my frozen toes.

John had recovered sufficiently to shoot me an ironic look. "Peculiar? How so?"

I nudged him with a boot. "Well, my scream brought Mr. Goodnight. Thank the Good Lord. But Mrs. Goodnight only said something about the gunshots." I gave a crooked smile. "So where was she at four o'clock in the morning?"

CHAPTER 13

"Ooooh, the wife," John said, tucking the pistol into the waist of his trousers. "But does she make sense with the rest of it?"

"Not really," I admitted. "It's just a thought."

"But worth looking into if she wasn't in bed with her husband."

I forced myself to return to the bedchamber and examined the rope still dangling into the fireplace. It yielded few clues.

"Manila hemp," I reported to John. "Common everywhere, from sailing ships to hangman's knots."

"But the snake isn't," he replied. "Where could someone get a cobra in Scotland?"

"An excellent question." I threw open the window and peered around. "Well, there's the ladder."

It had been left lying on its side around the corner of the house. I saw a pile of planks and other building materials.

"If they knew it was here, they must be familiar with Caer Morvan Hall," John said.

We went downstairs and waited in the drawing room where a promised fire had been lit. It took the icy edge off, though I dragged my chair nearer to the flames. Mr. Goodnight told us that he'd had workers in to examine the roof of the East Wing. They'd left the ladder and rope in a shed.

"I can get a list of everyone who was here from the foreman," he said. "This was about two weeks ago. They're supposed to come back and start work once I've had the plumbers draw up an estimate."

John thanked him. I doubted the killer's name would be on it, though it couldn't hurt.

Mr. Goodnight went to fetch the McKenzies. They came in looking anxious.

"No one is accusing you of anything," I said straight off, hoping to set them at ease. "We just wondered if you might have seen or heard something out of the ordinary."

They both shook their heads.

"We were both abed, weren't we, Edith?" Mr. McKenzie said, hands twisting nervously in his lap.

His sister nodded. "I swept the hearths and brought the mistress her tea. Then I said my prayers and readied for bed."

"Your mistress? You mean Mrs. Goodnight?"

"Aye. She likes it with a touch o' honey and just a drop o' milk."

I turned to Mr. Goodnight. "Are your rooms near to ours? It would be helpful to pinpoint everyone's movements."

He shifted in his chair. "My wife and I keep separate bedchambers," he said in a cool tone. "Hers is farther down the corridor."

"Oh, I see."

It wasn't all that unusual, though I couldn't imagine wanting such an arrangement myself. It did explain why she didn't hear the scream.

I decided to change tack. "Have you ever seen lights on the moor?"

Miss McKenzie flinched, the tiniest of movements. Then her features smoothed. "No, missus."

Goodnight was frowning at her. He must have seen it, too. "Speak up, Miss McKenzie," he said sternly.

"I haven't myself, sir," she amended reluctantly. "Though others claim to have seen the fairylights. I ken they're just old stories."

"And you, Mr. McKenzie?"

Her brother lifted his chin. "No, sir."

I was dying to ask them about the Montagues, but I doubted Goodnight would take kindly to it. He seemed intent on quelling the rumors about Caer Morvan Hall.

"Very well," I said. "If you think of anything, please inform your employer."

Miss McKenzie curtsied with a mixture of relief and irritation. The pair of them left the room together. There weren't many more to speak with. A young scullery maid who stammered her replies in sheer terror. A stableboy and the cook. The young governess, Miss Parker.

None had seen or heard a thing.

"That's the trouble with attempted murders in the middle of the night," John remarked when we were alone. "Everyone's *abed*."

"And successful murders," I added. "Our killer prefers the cover of darkness."

"Killers plural, if there really are two of them."

The sun was well up by now. My eyes felt gritty and I was grateful when Mrs. Goodnight came to offer us breakfast. We dined in a cavernous room that could have seated sixty, huddled at one end of an enormous table. With the heavy drapes covering the windows, it might easily still have been the middle of the night.

But the arrangement allowed Louisa to join us and her cheerful chatter lightened everyone's mood. She'd been told that a huge rat infiltrated our chamber in the night and Daddy shot it with his pistol.

"You're a hero!" she beamed, planting a kiss on his cheek.

Goodnight smiled wanly. "Almost big as a dragon it was, my little dove."

"Did it spit fire?" she asked, eyes wide.

For all her blazing intelligence, Louisa still had the will to believe in magic.

I cast a fond look at my husband. They weren't so very different.

"Nearly ten feet across the room," John declared, right on cue. "Set the drapes alight." He heaved a sigh. "If that evil wizard hadn't stolen my sword, I would have dealt with it myself. But now I have to go on a quest to get it back."

She leapt to her feet. "I'll give you a special talisman to help!"

Louisa darted from the room, blonde hair flying behind her.

"Perhaps she'll be a writer someday," I said, thinking of Arthur with a twinge of guilt. He must be worried sick.

"It wouldn't surprise me," Jack Goodnight said. "She can spin a yarn, all right."

"The nursery is wonderful," I said to the nurse, Miss Payne, who sat next to Evangeline.

She blushed. "Thank you. It's a work in progress."

"Isn't she talented?" Mrs. Goodnight said with the first genuine smile I'd seen on her face. "And she didn't even go to school for it."

"My grandfather was a painter," she said. "I suppose I inherited his passion for art. But it's very hard to make a living at it. Nursing seemed a safer path."

"Well, I'm glad you've found an outlet," I said. "It would be a waste otherwise. Louisa's a lucky girl."

"She helped me design it," Nurse Payne said enthusiastically. "You should have seen the room when we first arrived. It had the most dreadful mustard wallpaper. We tore it all down and made sketches. Really, Louisa should get most of the credit. I just did what she asked me to."

"More than that, I think," I replied with a laugh. "The figures are perfect. Just as I remember them from the books."

"She already wants me to paint over and start fresh," Nurse Payne said with a rueful shake of her head. "Her tastes are always evolving. Now she's fallen in love with Dickens. David Copperfield and Nicholas Nickleby—"

Louisa ran into the dining hall and pressed a gift into John's hand.

"It's a magic amulet," she said. "It'll make you invisible so you can get your sword back!"

He regarded the bit of oval cardboard on a cord with a look of awe. It had sequins clumsily stuck on with glue.

"The Amulet of Koth! Hidden for so many centuries . . . ." John shook his head. "I cannot accept this, Lady. It's too valuable."

"You must," she said, hanging it around his neck. "Else all is lost, Sir Weston."

He closed his eyes and drew a deep breath. "Thank you, Lady. I shall not fail."

She lowered her voice and glanced around furtively. "But beware the Neebles. They lurk in the Dread Forest and are immune to the amulet's power."

"The Neebles." His jaw tightened. "I nearly lost an arm to one on my last quest."

"Sing a lullaby and they'll fall asleep. It's their only weakness."

"Thank you again, Lady. You are as wise as you are beautiful."

She snatched a scone from the basket and took a huge bite. "Good luck, Sir Weston," she mumbled through a mouthful of crumbs.

"No speaking with your mouth full," her governess admonished.

Louisa cast her a haughty look and dashed away.

"You can keep that if you like," Mrs. Goodnight said with a laugh. "She has dozens of magic charms."

"Keep it?" John replied in mock indignation. "It's a gift from the Princess of Abkhazia. You'd have to pry it from my dead fingers."

No one laughed. John snatched up his coffee and drank it down so quickly he ended up choking. I had to pat his back, after which we all finished our meals in silence.

"Mr. McKenzie is bringing the carriage around," Mr. Goodnight said, laying his napkin on the table. "We'll go straight to the constable."

John stopped in the drawing room to retrieve the bloody poker we'd found at Swan's house. Once outside, I examined the ladder impressions. The legs had sunk deep into the earth. In daylight, I could also see faint footprints leading away.

"They're different than the heel impression I saw at Swan's house," I said to John. "That was broad like a rubber boot."

"Professor Carlton wore rubber boots," he pointed out.

"If the print hadn't been obliterated, I'd try to compare them. But this looks more like a man's dress shoe."

We both glanced over at Goodnight, who stood waiting at the carriage.

"Like his?" John said, his voice turning cold.

"Don't jump to conclusions," I said quickly. "Why would he have saved me if he did it?"

"To deflect suspicion from himself."

"No, he wouldn't have had time to clamber down from the roof, clean himself up, put on a nightdress, and then burst into the room. It was only a matter of two minutes or so from the time I first heard the rope fall to his arrival."

John's shoulders relaxed a fraction. "I suppose you're right."

He swept a hand through his hair. "But someone tried to kill you, Harry. I know it's not the first time, but by God, when I get my hands on them . . . ." He trailed off, fists balling.

Weston was normally good-natured to a fault. I rather enjoyed the sight of him fire-eyed and snorting like one of Louisa's dragons.

"Not just me," I said. "You, too." My own resolve hardened. "We'll solve this one, John. It's only a matter of time."

"That's the problem," he muttered. "I'd almost say the hell with it and go home, but we've been put under house arrest by the constable." He scratched his jaw. "Inn arrest?"

"A directive we've already ignored," I said, taking his arm and steering for the carriage. "We have to tell him about the cobra. God only knows what's happened in our absence."

These words proved prescient. When we arrived at the constable's residence, his wife informed us that he wasn't at home.

"Where's he gone?" Mr. Goodnight asked irritably. "We've had a very serious incident up at the Hall."

She regarded us with a stony expression. "There's been another death, sir. One of them lot staying at the Duck."

"Which one?" I demanded, fighting the urge to seize her apron.

"Don't know. But they've all gone up there."

"Where?" John demanded.

Her gaze moved past his shoulder to a forested peak overlooking the village.

"Craigmonie," she replied.

CHAPTER 14

M r. McKenzie drove the coach as close as we could get by the road, after which we hiked up a steep incline to Craigmonie. The peak held the traces of an Iron Age fort, but we didn't make it that far before we spotted Dr. Gibson, Constable Robb, and the photographer Cormac Ferguson standing over something I presumed to be the body.

It must have tumbled down from above. My breath rasped in my throat as we clambered the last few yards up the hillside. John knew what I was thinking. He clasped my hand as we drew closer.

"It's not him, Harry," he said. "It can't be."

Uncle Arthur had been a stolid presence in my life since I was a little girl, always bringing toffee and a warm smile when he visited our home. He had a child of his own now. My chest tightened at the thought that he might never hold his daughter again.

Then I saw who it was and filled with shameful relief.

H.N. Gryffin lay against a boulder, her neck twisted at an awkward angle. The outcrop had stopped her from rolling the rest of the way down. She must have died instantly—after the terror of plummeting from the cliff above. She wore the elegant silk walking dress I'd seen in the common room that first night when we arrived. One shoe had fallen off and sat a short distance from the body.

The constable watched us approach with obvious relief. "Dr. and Mrs. Weston! I feared . . . ." He cleared his throat. "I'm glad to see you well." He took his hat off. "Mr. Goodnight."

"May I?" John said, crouching next to the body. The eyes were half-open and staring glassily.

Dr. Gibson nodded. John touched her hand. "Still warm," he murmured.

"I only came to get some photographs of the glen," Cormac Ferguson burst out. "I'd set up my equipment on the crag and then I saw her down here." He covered his face. "Jesus Christ."

"I'd deem it death by misadventure," Dr. Gibson said wearily. "But in light of the professor and Mr. Swan that seems doubtful."

"Any idea what she was doing up there?" I asked, gazing at the crag above.

"No, but I mean to find out," the constable said grimly.

"We put the professor in the icehouse while his next of kin are notified," Dr. Gibson said. "I suppose we can make room for one more."

"Have you been up there yet?"

The constable shook his head. "We just arrived a few minutes ago." He cast a sideways glance at the photographer. "Mr. Ferguson summoned us."

"This maniac's been busy," Goodnight muttered. "He set a cobra on the Westons at the Hall last night."

The constable blanched. "Did you say *cobra*?"

We related the story during the steep climb to the top of Craigmonie. Like the Standing Stones, it was a well-known spot, with sweeping views of the village and Urquhart Bay. By the time we reached the summit, my legs were trembling from exhaustion. I paused to catch my breath, locking eyes with a red squirrel that scolded us from a branch of a gnarled Scots pine.

I wondered if it had witnessed poor H.N.'s demise.

Cormac Ferguson's tripod was still standing on the ledge, along with the case for his photographic equipment. Of course, he could easily have set it up after shoving her over the cliff.

I clambered over exposed roots and peered down. H.N. was clearly visible below, though you had to lean out a bit.

"She must have been . . . meeting someone," I puffed. "I can't imagine her hiking up here for the view, as nice as it is."

Smoke trailed from the chimney of the Drunken Duck. The valley below looked like a postcard, with green fields and the blue-gray waters of the loch in the distance. But if Ferguson *was* innocent, the killer was likely down there somewhere. Hiding in plain sight.

"When did you arrive?" I asked him.

"About an hour ago," he replied.

"Had you seen her today?"

"No. Cassie brought over some breakfast. Then I packed my things and hiked over. I'd been waiting for a clear day." He scowled at me. "I already told all this to the constable. What business is it of yours, anyway?"

"My wife was almost killed last night," John reminded him stiffly. "I'd say we have a vested interest in finding who did it."

Ferguson looked abashed. "I'm sorry. It's just . . . I can't believe Hatty's dead!"

His shock seemed genuine, though that meant little.

"She went to see you yesterday, didn't she?" I asked Dr. Gibson.

"Eh? Oh yes, she stopped by my office complaining of vertigo."

"Perhaps she had a bout o' dizziness and lost her footing," the constable said hopefully.

"Did you find anything wrong with her?" John wondered.

"Not a thing. I gave her a nerve tonic and sent her on her way."

"What was in it?"

Gibson gave a dry chuckle. "Iron mixed with blackberry juice and sugar. It's what I give the patients with no real illness."

We searched the hilltop, but her killer had failed to drop a monogrammed handkerchief or other useful clue. Craigmonie was a lonely spot. The perfect place for a murder, I thought grimly. One little push and over she went. The village was much too far for anyone to hear the scream.

"I'd like to pay my respects to her again," I said, "We only met a few days ago, but I considered Miss Gryffin a friend. Is that all right?"

The constable shrugged. "I've no objection."

We made our way back to where she'd fallen. The men stood a little way apart as I crouched down and took her hand. Like John said, it was still warm and pliable.

"I'm sorry, H.N.," I whispered. "You deserved better. And I hope you don't mind what I'm about to do, but it might help catch whoever did this."

I caught John's eye and shot him a meaningful look.

"What's that?" he exclaimed, pointing into the distance.

The others turned and I seized the opportunity to quickly squeeze her coat pockets.

"Do ye see something?" the constable demanded.

"I thought . . . a flash," John replied. "Never mind, it's gone now."

By the time they turned back, I was rising to my feet. Dr. Gibson offered to wait with the body until it could be removed. The rest of us started the hike back down, with John and Goodnight helping Ferguson carry his equipment.

A great tawny owl fluttered from branch to branch, then silently glided off into Portclair Forest. When we reached the waiting carriage, John gave Constable Robb the poker from Mr.

Swan's cottage. The constable examined it with an unhappy expression.

"Am I free to go?" Ferguson asked.

"For now," the constable replied. "But it's time I call in the lads from Inverness. They'll want a word with you."

He swallowed hard. "Of course. Thank you, constable."

"Three now," he grumbled as we rode to the Drunken Duck.

"And one attempted," John added.

The constable scowled. "It all started with that rumor about the loch beast. This was a peaceful place before . . . . " He trailed off, avoiding our eyes. "A peaceful place," he muttered.

"We have reason to believe there are two people involved," I said, describing the twin lanterns that had been seen on the moor.

"As if one's not bad enough," he replied wearily. "I'll bear it in mind, Mrs. Weston."

Back at the inn, the pool of suspects had dwindled rapidly. Mrs. Davies gasped when we entered the common room, sending Caesar into a fit of furious yapping.

"You're alive!" she cried, tears in her eyes. "Algie said you were, but I feared the worst."

Even Miss Neiderberger smiled.

Arthur leapt to his feet and pulled us both into a warm embrace. "Where on earth have you been? I was up at daybreak searching the heath."

"Settle down," the constable barked. "Who here saw Mrs. Gryffin this morning?"

Finn and Ursilla Brody stood behind the bar. They exchanged a worried glance.

"I did," Mrs. Davies replied warily. "At breakfast. She left in an awful hurry." Her hand shot to her mouth. "She's not . . . Is she?"

The constable nodded. "Fell from the top of Craigmonie." He glanced at John and me. "The Westons spent the night up at the

Hall and just came back, so they're off the hook. What about the rest of you?"

Miss Neiderberger paled. "I took Caesar on a long walk," she said. "But we did not go anywhere near Craigmonie."

"We were both here," Finn said, putting a protective arm around his mother's shoulders.

"For the whole morning?" the constable prodded.

"I took my usual walk down to the loch," Ursilla said.

"She was hardly gone half an hour!" Finn exclaimed.

"What time was this?" The constable took out a pad.

"I don't know," Ursilla said. "Shortly after breakfast."

"It could have been anyone in the village," Finn muttered. "Why don't you question *them*?"

"I intend to," the constable said evenly. "Where's Cassie?"

"In the kitchen helping the Cook wash up."

"Do you require my presence?" Mr. Goodnight asked. "I'd rather not leave my wife and daughter alone."

"You're free to go, sir," the constable replied.

I could see that Mrs. Davies was dying to corner me, but I suddenly felt so tired, I could hardly keep my eyes open.

"I'm going to our room," I said.

"I'll be up in a minute," John said. He took Arthur's arm and drew him over to the fireplace. I guessed he was relating the story of the cobra.

I'd only meant to bathe and change out of my rumpled dress, but the bed looked very tempting. I lay down on top of the covers and instantly fell asleep.

CHAPTER 15

The shadows were lengthening when I finally awoke. I wandered down to the common room and was surprised to find that only Mrs. Davies was there, the cane resting across her knees.

"Where did everyone go?" I asked, settling into a chair.

"To meet the policemen from Inverness. There was a devil of a time getting the poor woman down from the crag." She poked her stick at me. "Why did you stay at Caer Morvan Hall last night? I tried to pry it out of your husband, but he gallivanted off with the rest of them before I had the chance."

I met her challenging stare. "We were chased there," I said. "After discovering the missing poker in Mr. Swan's barn."

She leaned forward, the firelight gleaming on her dyed-brown curls. "Chased by whom? Or should I say, *what?*"

Could Mrs. Davies have hiked up to Craigmonie? She exaggerated her infirmities, but still, I thought not. And there was no real reason to hide the truth. I drew a deep breath and launched into the tale of our misadventures at the Hall. She listened in silence.

"You must be getting too near the truth," Mrs. Davies said when I'd finished.

"I wish it were so," I replied ruefully. "But things seem more muddled than ever."

"I don't like that photographer. The one who supposedly found her." The widow's eyes narrowed. "I overheard the serving wench telling the constable that the pair of them had an argument this morning."

I perked up. "Really?"

Her voice took a conspiratorial note. "They were standing out back by the well. The girl couldn't make out what they said, but it was heated. H.N. stomped off in a huff. Ferguson stood there for a moment, then headed off in the direction of Kinlach Cottage. But he could easily have changed his mind and followed her."

"I ought to go question Mr. Ferguson again."

She opened her purse and took out the revolver. "Do you want my gun?"

"Put that away," I hissed. "No, I don't want your gun. I've already shot someone accidentally once."

Mrs. Davies stowed it away, casting me an appraising look. "Did you?"

"John," I admitted. "Though he wasn't my husband yet."

She laughed. "Well, he still married you. That's true love."

I frowned. The words tickled my memory. "Ferguson told us that Ursilla Brody worked at the Hall once. She was in several of his photographs, standing down at the loch. Has she ever mentioned Finn's father to you?"

Mrs. Davies shook her head. "It would be rude to inquire. I assumed her to be a widow."

"As did I. But I wonder—"

The door banged open and John strode into the inn. "You're up!" he said.

"And feeling sharp again," I replied with a smile, as he bent down to kiss my cheek. "Any news?"

"Two policeman arrived from Inverness. They're with Constable Robb questioning the townsfolk. Any breakthroughs?"

"Not yet." I turned to Mrs. Davies. "But I do have a question for you. When you saw H.N., did she have her notebook? It wasn't with the body."

"So that's what you were looking for," John murmured.

Mrs. Davies thought for a moment. "No, I didn't see it. And she was always jotting notes." She sniffed. "Spying on us all."

I felt a stab of excitement. "If she was meeting someone she didn't entirely trust and the notebook held a vital clue, she might have left it behind as a precaution."

"Would she be so foolish as to meet a suspected murderer alone?" John ventured. "On a cliff?"

"She might if she didn't realize they'd done it. She might have thought they had information."

"Or she was trying to blackmail them!" Mrs. Davies whispered.

"Anything is possible. But the fact remains that her notebook is missing."

"The constable already searched her room," John said. "He told me nothing was found."

"Because she hid it somewhere." I chewed my lip.

"Let's have a look ourselves," John suggested.

"I'm coming with you," Mrs. Davies declared, levering herself up with the cane.

"Where's Miss Neiderberger?" I asked. "And Caesar?"

"With that Welshman," she replied, a disapproving note in her voice. "Caesar required a walk and Mr. Thomas insisted on going along for protection."

Mrs. Davies was already striding for the staircase and we had no choice but to follow. H.N.'s room was unlocked. I felt guilty rummaging through her things, but it was in the service of catching whoever had murdered her.

Mrs. Davies turned up some racy French negligee, which she hastily stuffed back into the dresser. There were several copies of H.N. Gryffin's books but no notebook.

We checked all the usual places. Beneath the feather mattress. Under the rug. Inside her cosmetics case. John even tapped the walls looking for false compartments.

"We're overlooking the obvious," I said with a sigh. "She had it with her and the killer removed it after pushing her over the edge. Or before."

"I suppose it could have been in a pocket," Mrs. Davies conceded.

John had gone stock still. I recognized the look in his eye.

"What is it?" I demanded.

He picked up one of her books and began to madly flip the pages. "In *The Secret Chamber at Mont Morrone Abbey*, the devious Count Strozza steals the letters from Lady Mary's lover so she thinks he was lost at sea. He hides them in the dungeon of the abbey."

"The abbey had a dungeon?" I frowned.

"Just bear with me, Harry." John ran his finger down a page. "Here we are. Chapter Nineteen. *Strozza caressed the cold stone with a fingertip, the hollows of his lean face appearing cadaverous in the flickering candlelight. His features contorted in jealousy. A desperate passion driven by congenital madness—*"

"Get on with it," I muttered.

John cleared his throat and skipped the next page. "*He lifted the flagstone and there bestowed the marriage proposal from the feckless Lord Dudley. It nestled among the dessicated bones of Strozza's previous fiancé. The count's lips spread in a cruel smile. 'You will succumb to my suit, Lady Mary,' he whispered. 'Or I will see you both dead!'*"

"Sounds like a dreadful fellow," Mrs. Davies remarked.

"Those Italians are a hot-blooded lot." She leaned over his shoulder. "What happens next?"

"Mary flings herself from the battlements," John said, closing the slender volume. "After the count tries to despoil her virtue."

"The abbey had battlements?" I asked.

"Tower. Whatever you call it. Anyway, Lord Dudley arrives just in time to witness her suicide. It turns out he *was* in a shipwreck, but he managed to cling to a bit of flotsam and swim to shore. He beats his breast and shouts his grief to the heavens, et cetera. Then him and Strozza skewer each other in a duel."

"My word!" Mrs. Davies said.

"And this all relates how?" I asked.

"Well, I doubt there's a dungeon under the Duck . . . ." John paused. "Though nothing would surprise me at this point." He handed the book to Mrs. Davies, who tucked it surreptitiously into her handbag. "But the inn certainly has a cellar. Let's find out what's down there."

We crept to the main floor and I ran to the kitchen, peering inside.

"All clear," I hissed.

The fat tabby was curled up in its favorite spot on the windowsill. Out in the yard, I saw the cook chatting with two women from the village. I imagined there was a great deal to gossip about and hoped she'd stay out there for a while.

The cat's tail twitched as we slunk through the kitchen, but it didn't deign to open its eyes. We descended into a large root cellar.

"No flagstones," John said in disappointment. "But I still say it's hidden down here. Where else could she be certain no one would find it?"

"Let's just hope we don't stumble over another body," I muttered.

Mrs. Davies gave a dry chuckle. "There's scarcely anyone left to murder at this point, dear."

I eyed her cane for a moment—stout oak with a silver handle that could do some damage—then bravely turned my back on her and set to searching. It was dim and cool below the main level of the inn. Nets of onions dangled from hooks on the ceiling, along with sacks of carrots and potatoes. I saw a few of Mrs. Brody's traps that were designed to capture mice without harming them, but no signs of vermin.

Again, some connection tingled in my memory. It was frustratingly elusive. I waded deeper into the cellar, poking through odds and ends of discarded furniture. A spiderweb whacked my face and I tore the clinging, sticky shreds away with a small noise of disgust.

On the transatlantic crossing—for which our wealthy friend Edward Dovington had bought a lavish first-class berth—I'd had visions of strolling hand-in-hand with my new husband across the heath. The wind tousling John's curls as he laughed and swept me into a kiss, followed by a candlelit supper and . . . all sorts of pleasant activities.

Instead, I was now searching for a dead woman's diary whilst attempting to extract what felt like an egg sac from my ear.

After coming upon not one but *two* other corpses, and nearly dying a painful, lingering death myself.

Not to mention the near mauling on the moor.

"Is it me?" I whispered aloud, squinting into a barrel that reeked of sour ale. "Or John? Because these sorts of things don't happen to normal—"

His cry of triumph pulled me out of my wallowing. I hurried over.

"Found it!" John said, brandishing the journal. "And another one, too."

He held up a second volume that looked ancient. It was bound in red leather and tied up with a black ribbon.

"Well done, Dr. Weston," Mrs. Davies said. "We must examine both in the light."

We turned for the stairs. The glow from the kitchen was blotted out by a dark silhouette looming above. Then it leaned down and I saw it was Finn Brody.

"What are ye doin' down there?" he demanded.

"Dr. Weston offered to make a poultice for my foot," Mrs. Davies replied smoothly. "The cook was absent so we took it upon ourselves to seek out the ingredients."

Finn scowled. "The cellar's off limits to guests."

"We're terribly sorry," John said, snatching two carrots from a bundle with one hand, as the other jammed both books into the back of his pants. "This is all I need!"

"Carrots?" Finn echoed dubiously.

"And brandy. An old family recipe."

His blue eyes regarded us without expression for a long moment. Then he retreated into the kitchen. I half-expected the cellar door to slam, followed by the sound of a bolt, but he returned a second later with a lit candle, holding it out to guide our path.

"Watch yer step," Finn warned Mrs. Davies. "The stairs are steep."

She made a great show of limping to the top, with me supporting her. If I had any doubts about her ability to lie convincingly, these were set to rest by her performance. Finn seemed to expect her to collapse at any moment for he hovered at her side with an anxious look.

It was understandable considering the number of newly vacant rooms at the inn. But I wondered if he didn't suspect what we'd been up to.

"Has Miss Neiderberger returned?" Mrs. Davies asked.

Finn shook his head.

"I have been abandoned it seems," she said with a cluck of the tongue. "Dr. Weston, would you see me to my room?"

"Do ye need to cook those?" Finn asked, glancing at the carrots.

"No, they would lose their efficacy," John said briskly. "I'll just brew the remedy upstairs."

We started across the common room.

"Don't ye need brandy?" Finn called out.

John made a face, then turned back. "Of course. You've saved me a trip."

He grabbed the offered bottle and we made our way up to Mrs. Davies's room. It smelled strongly of the lavender sachets she'd strewn about.

"Wards off evil spirits," she explained. "Shall we have a drink?"

"Oh, why not?" I replied with a sigh. "Perhaps it will get the juices flowing."

Brandy was dispensed. Then we all sat down and opened H.N. Gryffin's diary.

CHAPTER 16

The first half of the journal was filled with all the notes H.N. had taken since arriving at Drumnadrochit.

Tales of selkies and kelpies. Muckle Black Tyke and the Montague Curse. We skipped over most of it, including the portion on the Portclair Treasure, since we already knew about that.

The final pages were more interesting.

She'd written: *Swan?! What did he see?*

Professor Carlton's name appeared underneath, alongside a reference to the Standing Stones.

The next section was devoted to logging the comings and goings of her fellow guests at the Duck, with dates and times.

"She *was* spying," Mrs. Davies said with a snort.

The following page had only the words: *He fell for it!*

"Who?" Mrs. Davies wondered. "And fell for what?"

I blew out a frustrated breath. "Of course, H.N. was taking notes for herself. She knew much more than she wrote down."

John turned the page. They held the cryptic words: *Poor Ursilla. Does it run in the blood?*

The revelation came to me in a rush. I felt a perfect fool.

"Finn is Duncan Montague's son," I said. "The black hair and blue eyes. I saw a portrait of Duncan at Caer Morvan Hall. It looked familiar, but I couldn't place it. But take away the beard and I suspect they'd be the spitting image of each other."

"Oh, my!" Mrs. Davies covered her mouth. "Do you think the boy knows?"

"He must. I imagine it's an open secret in the village."

"Does it run in the blood," Mrs. Davies murmured. She turned to me with wide eyes. "Do you think she meant *murder*?"

On the next page, H.N. had written a list of names.

Finn and Ursilla Brody
Jack & Evangeline Goodnight
The McKenzies
Mrs. Davies
Miss Neiderberger
Cormac Ferguson
~~The Westons~~
~~Dr. Martin Gibson~~
~~Cassie/Cook~~
Mystery accomplice?

"Why am *I* there?" Mrs. Davies demanded. "And *not* crossed off?"

"They could be potential victims," I said weakly.

She huffed. "They're suspects and we both know it."

"The culprit might be a villager we've never met," John said.

"Do you really believe that?" Mrs. Davies asked.

There was an awkward silence.

"No," I admitted. "I think it's someone on that list. Or more than one."

"Let's see the other book," John suggested. "Perhaps it will shed some light."

I untied the black ribbons from the second journal, revealing a faint heraldic shield stamped into the leather, with the words *Non vox sed votum.*

"That's the Montague crest," he exclaimed. "I saw it at the Hall."

The book was very old with brittle, yellowing pages. The spelling was atrocious, the penmanship spidery and faded. But when I saw the date—1520—and author's name, my heart beat faster.

"How did H.N. get her hands on this?" I asked in astonishment.

While I puzzled over the Middle English dialect, John related the sordid tale to Mrs. Davies—how Sir Silas Montague had murdered his bastard children by throwing them down a privy.

Godfrey was his eldest son. He'd inherited the estate and died at the age of thirty when he was struck by lightning on the moor.

It took some time to decipher, but I render Godfrey Montague's diary here faithfully, with only minor corrections to make the text comprehensible.

The first portion was relatively carefree, chronicling the life of a young laird. Its pages were devoted to horses, dogs, and pretty lasses.

But somewhere in the middle, the journal took a darker turn.

June the 16th. They took Father away at dawn. Mother refuses to eat or speak. The servants despise us all, I think. It is only the hard winter that keeps them from fleeing back to their hovels.

But I cannot indulge such dyre thoughts. I am the master of Caer Morvan now and must be strong. I knelt in the chapel, seeking solace, but a Black Wynd blew out all the candles.

What will become of us?

June the 22ⁿᵈ· I was permitted to see Father on the eve before the gallows cart came. He paced the cell liked a caged wolf. Raging with Grayte Furie at the King. Then a sudden calme came upon him. He said he knew a way to save our name from ruin and ordered me to do as he bade.

When he set forth what it was, I wept and refused him. Father said I must, for my Mother and Sisters' sake. If I failed, he would return with the Sluagh and wreake a Terrible Vengeance upon me.

He called for quill and parchment and bade me write it all down.

This is madness.

June the 23ʳᵈ. The cowards in the village pelted him with stones, but he said no word against them. When the Vile Crymes were read, Mother fainted. I am glad the girls were not made to watch.

June the 26ᵗʰ. I gave the gravedigger a silver coin to keep silent. He crossed himself and spat thrice on the ground, making the sign to ward against evil. But he is afraid of me now. If silver does not hold his tongue, I hope his terror will.

July the 13th. It is done. God help me, it is done.

July the 21st. The King withdrew his Writ of Attainder. The Montague lands and title have come to me. All believe he showed mercie, but I know the truth. I can scarcely hold the quill, my hand trembles so. From whence does this power derive? It is foul magick, I fear, but I cannot take it back now. I cannot—

The rest was smeared in a blot of ink.

"In Celtic folklore, the Sluagh is a host of unforgiven dead,"

John explained. "They fly in a whirlwind of darkness to steal souls. As a young man already facing an awful situation, Godfrey would have been terrified of this threat."

When I turned the page, a slip of paper fell out. It immediately fell to pieces when John unfolded it. The paper was stained with a brownish substance and some of the words were lost. We lined up the edges. From what I could tell, it looked like a recipe.

> . . . *place in an earthenware vessel with zimat, nitre, salt, and long peppers, the whole well-powdered. Leave in this vessel for a fortnight, then expose to full sunlight during the dog-days until it becomes quite dry. If the sun is not strong enough, put it in an oven with fern and vervain.*
>
> *"Next make a candle from tallow of the corpse, virgin wax, sesame, and ponie. Once lit, those in every place into which you go with this baneful instrument shall . . .*

Again, the ink had run and I couldn't make out what it said.

"Tallow of the corpse?" Mrs. Davies said. "That's revolting!"

"What's zimat?" I wondered. "Or ponie?"

"Horse dung," John muttered. He looked up with an expression of excitement. "I know what this is!"

"I'm afraid to ask," I said with a sigh. "But I suppose I must. What are we dealing with now? A warlock? Some kind of magic potion?"

"In a way." He had an unseemly glint in his eye. "I must admit, I never thought I'd come across a real one. I've read about them, of course—"

"Spit it out, young man," Mrs. Davies said crisply. "Night is falling. If there's a demonic entity coming for us, I'll need adequate time to prepare."

He drew a breath. "It's a Hand of Glory!"

Silence greeted this statement.

"A what?" I prompted.

"Hand of Glory, Harry!" John rolled his eyes. "Surely you've heard of them."

"I have," Mrs. Davies said. "In vague terms. It's the pickled appendage of a man who's died on the gibbet."

"Precisely," John agreed. "But not just any man. A murderer —preferably one who committed a really heinous crime."

"Like Silas Montague," I said, thinking of the dead babies the townsfolk had discovered.

No wonder his poor wife had fainted.

John picked up the stained scrap of parchment. "This *is* a recipe. And unless I miss my guess, it's where the Montague curse began."

"So Silas ordered his son to cut his hand off and pickle it?" I ventured. "To what end?"

"They're potent talismans, Harry. Very potent. But they carry a price. If the Hand was passed down through the generations, it would explain the Montagues' singular run of both good fortune and untimely death."

"So the murderer isn't looking for the Portclair Treasure," Mrs. Davies said. "They're looking for *that*."

"What does a Hand of Glory do exactly?" I asked John.

"Traditionally, when you place a lit candle in the hand, one made from the fat of the corpse itself, it renders immobile anyone who sees it."

"I suppose that could be useful," I said. "But it doesn't seem enough to kill three people over. Our murderer is getting desperate."

"I agree. This one must be special."

"I wonder why Duncan didn't use it to save himself from Black Tyke?"

"Maybe he couldn't." John sighed. "Until we know more about this particular Hand of Glory, it's impossible to know what they intend to do with it."

I gazed at the family motto. *Non vox sed votum.*

"Your Latin's better than mine," I said. "What does that mean?"

"The literal translation is 'Not a voice but a wish.' Essentially, not words but deeds."

I frowned. "What if it *is* meant literally?"

"You mean . . . the Hand of Glory grants its owner a wish?" Mrs. Davies said tentatively.

John whacked the table, making us both jump. "Now that would be worth killing for!"

"It does seem to be a key piece of the puzzle," I said. "And whether it works or not is immaterial. If the killer or killers think it does . . . ."

"The question remains," Mrs. Davies said. "How did H.N. come by this diary? And where is the Hand of Glory now?"

"Still hidden, I suspect. Maybe Duncan realized it was evil and didn't want anyone else to suffer as he had. So he stashed it somewhere. Then he died and the secret was lost."

"How does Muckle Black Tyke fit?" John wondered.

"I suppose it could be guarding the location. Anyone who comes too close gets scared off. But it makes sense that Mr. Swan might have known where it was. He was the groundskeeper. Served at least two generations of Montagues."

More pieces slipped into place. "Let's say they looked everywhere with no luck. So they finally decided to turn the screws on Swan and went to his cottage. He sent them to the Standing Stones, where Professor Carlton happened to come upon them digging the next night. They had to get rid of him."

"But why kill Swan if he told them where it was?"

"We can only speculate. Either they meant to kill him all along or the confrontation escalated. I suspect the latter since the killer seized the poker from Swan's fireplace. They also took care not to break the photograph of his wife and child afterwards, which suggests remorse."

"But Swan lied," John said.

I nodded. "If he was loyal to Duncan, he must have realized how cursed the thing was."

"And H.N.?"

"She might have been meeting the very person she stole Godfrey's diary from." I frowned. "Yet she trusted them enough to go alone to Craigmonie. I wonder why?"

"She clearly thought the killer was someone else," John said grimly. "And it cost her her life."

I opened H.N.'s notebook and studied the list again. "How long has Miss Neiderberger been in your service?" I asked Mrs. Davies.

"About six months."

"That's not very long."

The widow blanched. "She came with impeccable references. You don't think . . . .?"

"I rule no one out, Mrs. Davies."

"Except for me, I assume," she said, eyes narrowing.

"Naturally," I lied.

John rose and paced to the window. "We thought it all started with Mr. Swan, but it really goes back to the death of Duncan Montague. He must have been in possession of Godfrey's diary. Someone else got hold of it, confirming the existence of the Hand, but not where Duncan had hidden it."

"Ursilla Brody is the obvious choice," Mrs. Davies said. "She was Duncan's *paramour*. And young Finn would feel entitled to the Hand, despite his low birth."

"True enough. They're at the top of the list." I scanned it. "The Goodnights came months after Duncan died and have no connections to Scotland that we're aware of."

"That doesn't rule out the servants who stayed on at Caer Morvan," John said. "Miss McKenzie didn't seem well-pleased to have us there. And frankly, it doesn't make sense that they remained. They're both in their sixties. Duncan left them a bequest. They could have chosen to retire comfortably, but they didn't."

"True enough. But we can attest that no one at the Hall could have killed H.N. We were with them all morning, the staff included." I ran a finger down the list. "I can't see much motive for Dr. Gibson. He knew Duncan, but he was attending a birth when Professor Carlton was killed. That's easily confirmed."

"What about the Brodys?" Mrs. Davies said. "If it is them, we're mice in a trap!"

I slapped my forehead. "The mice! That was it!"

"What was what?" John asked.

It had been tickling my brain since we were down in the cellar.

"If someone was keeping a large snake, they'd have to feed it, wouldn't they? There's traps all over this inn, but they're always empty. Cook claimed the cat keeps them under control, but that thing is fat and lazy. I've never seen it stir itself once."

"It might hunt at night," John said. "But I see your point."

"Even if the killer isn't someone from the inn, they'd need a confederate to remove the mice," Mrs. Davies put in. "The kitchen is fairly busy. Young Finn caught us down in the cellar within minutes." She thumped her cane on the floor. "Another piece of damning evidence!"

"Still, we've no real proof it's the Brodys," I conceded. "It's all circumstantial. We can't just accuse them. If we're wrong—or even if we're right—they'll toss us out on our ear." I smiled. "And I've grown oddly fond of the Duck."

"Which leaves us where?" John asked, scratching his head.

"Still in the dark, but with far more than we had before. I think we must speak with the photographer, Cormac Ferguson, straight away and find out what he argued with H.N. about."

"I'll keep a close eye on the Neiderberger woman when she returns," Mrs. Davies said, clutching her handbag. "Don't be gone too long."

I nodded. The thrill of the chase was mounting in my blood. We were getting close to the truth.

But so, I feared, was our quarry.

If the Hand of Glory did grant wishes, what would happen if a deranged killer found it first?

CHAPTER 17

Wₑ left Mrs. Davies in the common room on the assumption that no one would make an attempt on her life with Cassie, the cook, and the scullery boy Arran just a few feet away.

Or vice versa, if the widow was up to no good.

John retained custody of both journal and diary. I had a thought about how to use them, but first I wanted to pry the truth from Cormac Ferguson.

"He found H.N. Gryffin's body," I said as we walked through the village. "As a photographer, he had the perfect excuse to roam the moor. He's also Scottish and might have heard about the Hand of Glory somehow. He has no alibi for either Mr. Swan or Professor Carlton. Plus he's been here the longest. Two months, Cassie said."

"So he lured H.N. up to Craigmonie?"

"When I mentioned questioning Ferguson, she was quite passionate in her claim that he couldn't possibly be the killer. I think at the very least they were having a romantic affair."

I reminded John of the negligee in H.N.'s room and my

abrupt encounter with her after Mr. Thomas's ill-fated swim in the loch.

"She seemed flustered. I wonder if she was coming from a liaison with Ferguson. She had the look."

"What look is that?" he asked with amusement.

"Bright eyes. Flushed cheeks." I scowled at him. "Like I ought to look right now, seeing as this is our honeymoon."

"I promise to make it up to you," he said with a slow smile that did much to improve my mood.

We approached Kinlach Cottage with apprehension. I was glad John had brought Mr. Goodnight's pistol.

No one answered when we knocked on the door. After a moment, John opened it. The remains of lunch sat on the table, reminding me that I hadn't eaten since Caer Morvan Hall.

"Hello?" I ventured. "Mr. Ferguson?"

He didn't seem to be at home.

"Let's check the darkroom," John suggested.

Sweat slicked my palms as I opened the door. The heavy window coverings reminded me of the Hall. Ferguson had rigged up a combination of blankets and what looked like an old animal hide rug. It was stuffy inside, the air thick with chemicals.

"I can hardly see a thing," John muttered.

Dusk had fallen. A bit of light spilled through the kitchen windows behind us, but the room was thick with shadows. I ventured past the trays of solution and stacks of glass negative plates.

A large sea chest sat in the corner. It must have come with the cottage. One of the "moldy old things" Cassie had mentioned.

I girded myself and flung the lid wide.

It was empty.

"What the hell are you doing here?"

We spun around.

Cormac Ferguson glared at us from the doorway. "Do ye make it a habit of breaking into people's homes?"

"We feared something had happened to you," I said quickly. "We didn't touch anything."

He didn't seem mollified. "If I'd been exposing negatives, you would've ruined them."

"We apologize, Mr. Ferguson," John said, one hand in his pocket. "No harm done?"

He gave a gruff nod as we returned to the kitchen.

"Where were you?" I asked.

"At the privy." He laughed. "What, ye think there's plumbing in this place?" His laughter suddenly died. "Why," he asked the ceiling, "am I answering *your* questions? You're lucky I don't fetch the constable—"

"Then we can dispense with the pleasantries," John said in a cool tone. "We know you argued with H.N. Griffin this morning. And that you were more than friendly acquaintances."

Ferguson's jaw tightened. "Who told ye that?"

"She did," I replied.

It was just a guess, but his shoulders slumped. "I told her to keep quiet," he muttered. "It was just a fling!"

"Did she see it that way?"

He sank into a chair and stared at the floor. "She'd promised to pay off my debts. Why else do ye think I'd bother with a woman old enough to be my mother? That's what we fought about. She said she needed more time. That she was about to come into plenty o' money, but it might take a while."

He looked around the room. "I've done some good work here, but I miss Glasgow. I told her I was leavin'. She didn't take it well."

He gazed at us pleadingly. "But I didn't kill her! I've no idea who did."

"Did she mention a Hand of Glory?" I asked.

John shot me a sharp look.

138

"A what?" Ferguson echoed in evident bewilderment.

"Never mind. So she gave no indication of who she might be meeting?"

"None. She stormed off. It was a sunny day for once. I thought I'd get a last series of the loch and village from Craigmonie." He swallowed. "I'll admit, when I saw her lying down below, I considered packing my equipment and quietly returning to the cottage. Let someone else find her." His mouth twisted. "But I couldn't do it. I heard what happened to Carlton. The vultures."

Ferguson cleared his throat. "It wasn't right to leave her like that. So I fetched the constable." He gave a mirthless laugh. "Now I'm stuck here. If I leave, they'll think me guilty for certain."

I regarded him for a moment. He was a bit of a cad, but I believed his story.

"When did she tell you about us?" he asked with a frown. "Hetty was a heavy drinker, but she knew how to guard her tongue, even in her cups."

"She didn't," I admitted with a smile. "But we appreciate your candor, Mr. Ferguson."

He scowled. "I suppose you'll tell the constable now."

"Perhaps not," John said. "If you behave yourself."

He nodded fervently. "I hope you catch whoever did it to her. And the rest, too." A thought occurred to him. "Do ye think I'm in any danger?"

"Only if the killer thinks you know something."

"Well, that's a comfort," he replied bitterly.

We left Ferguson sitting at the table with his head in his hands.

"I thought we were keeping the Hand of Glory quiet for now," John said as we headed back toward the village.

"It's our last card," I replied. "I think we must play it, John."

He squinted at me. "Make ourselves the bait, you mean?"

"It's time to stir things up. Bring this mess to a boil. If we go around trumpeting our discovery to everyone on that list, it might draw the guilty parties into the open."

He nodded uneasily. "I can't think of anything better. But it's a mighty risk, Harry."

"Do you think the policemen from Inverness will solve it?"

John chuckled. "Not a chance."

"Then what choice do we have?"

"There's always a choice," he pointed out. "We could give the journal and diary to the constable and be done with it."

The thought was tempting. But I knew I couldn't walk away from this one.

"I'm an agent with the Society for Psychical Research. This is an extremely dangerous artifact, John. It should be locked away in the Society's vault. In the wrong hands . . . ." I shook my head. "Can you think of the *right* hands? No pun intended. But this thing seems to bring out the worst in everyone."

"A vile talisman taken from a vile man," John agreed. He cast me a sideways look. "What would you wish for?"

"I don't know." I took his arm. "A long, happy life with you, I suppose."

"There!" He shook his head with a laugh. "You've gone and wasted it!"

I frowned. "What would *you* wish for?"

"A Golden Goose. One that grants wishes. Then I'd get an unlimited number."

I elbowed his ribs. "What about the dying young part?"

"I'd use a wish to fix that."

"Somehow, I don't think this curse is so easily outwitted," I said dryly.

"You're right." He pulled me closer. "Good thing we have your wish already."

"Where's Dr. Gibson's practice?" I asked.

He pointed to a whitewashed stone cottage some distance away, this one much larger than Kinlach.

"Let's pay him a visit," I said. "The doctor attends all the births around here. I wonder what he has to say about Finn Brody."

We passed a stable that smelled pleasantly of horses and hay, and ventured up a neat brick path to the front door. Dr. Gibson answered John's knock with a guarded look.

"Dr. Weston," he said. "What can I do for you?"

"We've discovered some new information and hoped you could confirm it," John said.

"Er, certainly." He stepped back from the door and we entered a cozy sitting room lined with medical journals.

"It's about the Brodys," I said, deciding to be direct. "Duncan was Finn's father, wasn't he?"

Dr. Gibson frowned. "How does that bear on anything?"

"A great deal, I should imagine," I replied. "It's a matter of inheritance, you see. A certain valuable object."

"Duncan Montague's will was sealed," he replied evenly. "You'd have to talk to the estate lawyers if you want to know about that."

"I doubt this object would have been listed," John said. "It's the pickled hand of Sir Silas Montague."

Gibson laughed uneasily. "If this is some kind of joke—"

"It's no joke," I said. "Show him what we found."

John took out the diary. Dr. Gibson studied it. "It does appear authentic," he said. "Where did you get this?"

"H.N. Griffin had it."

I showed him the fragmented instructions for the Hand of Glory. He scanned them with a frown. "You don't actually believe this object still exists three hundred and seventy years later?"

"We're certain of it," John replied. "May I?"

The doctor returned the scraps of paper. "This is . . . bizarre."

"We don't deny that," I replied. "But it can be no coincidence that it was in Miss Gryffin's possession just before she died. So, doctor, was Finn Duncan Montague's son?"

He nodded heavily. "Yes. But he'd never . . . that is to say, he's nothing like his father, Mrs. Weston. Or any of the rest of them, if the rumors are true. Finn's a kind-hearted lad. He wouldn't harm—"

"A mouse?" I finished, shooting John a look.

"Yes," Gibson said with a touch of defiance. "I've known them both for almost two decades. They're entirely incapable of what you're implying."

"Well, someone's capable," John said. "These deaths are quite real, doctor."

He let out a breath. "Please, sit down. I'll tell you about the Brodys. And Duncan Montague."

We took chairs by the hearth as he explained that Duncan had returned from a voyage to the Orkney Islands nineteen years before with a new housekeeper—Ursilla Brody. A short time later, Dr. Gibson was called to attend a birth at Caer Morvan Hall.

It was all kept quiet. The villagers were told she was a widow with a newborn whom Duncan had taken pity on. Only Swan and the McKenzies knew the truth.

"Did Finn have webbed fingers as an infant?" I asked.

"Aye. Ursilla said her grandfather had it, too. I offered to perform a procedure to cut the excess skin away, but I warned her that the risk of infection was high. She said she didn't care and refused to chance it. He was healthy in all other respects."

Gibson smiled. "Finn's self-conscious about it, but he's a bonny lad. He's caught Cassie's eye and I suspect the feeling is mutual."

"How did Duncan feel about his son?" John asked.

"He doted on the boy."

"Did Ursilla love her employer?" I asked, thinking of the way she stood at the shore like a woman pining for someone.

Gibson gave a dry laugh. "I wouldn't call it love. He adored both mother and child, but she refused to marry him. He finally decided it was torment to keep her under his roof and bought her the inn."

"You knew him well?" John asked.

"I was his physician. He confided in me, up to a point." Gibson filled his pipe with tobacco and lit it with a taper from the fire. "Duncan Montague was a strange man. He could be cold as a February frost, but he had the Montague passion running in his veins when it came to Ursilla."

"Did he ever mention the curse?"

"Aye. He grew obsessed with it in his later years. I tried to talk sense into him, but he wouldn't listen."

"Perhaps he was right," John ventured. "All the previous heirs did die young."

Gibson cast him a weary look. "Most people back then died at an age that would be considered young today, Dr. Weston. Between wars and plagues, the average life expectancy in the 16th and 17th centuries was about fifty. And that's a generous estimate."

"But every single Montague?" John persisted. "You must admit that defies the odds."

Gibson shrugged and exhaled a stream of smoke. "In any event, I warned him that the preoccupation would take a toll on his health and it did. Duncan was jumping at shadows by the end."

"Muckle Black Tyke, you mean?" I said.

A reluctant nod. "He stopped going for walks on the moor."

"Did you attend the death?" John wondered.

"I hadn't seen him that last week. An old friend from my regiment came to visit. He was staying with me the morning Duncan was found."

"Where did he die?"

"Out at the end of the drive. The McKenzies summoned me."

"I thought Duncan was afraid to leave the Hall," I said.

Gibson shrugged. "Well, I can confirm that it was heart failure. No one murdered him if that's what you're asking. In my opinion, the curse was a self-fulling prophecy. He worked himself into a lather over it all and his heart finally gave out."

He gave us a hard look. "You're barking up the wrong tree with the Brodys. They already have all they could want. Ursilla gained her freedom, and they both own the Drunken Duck. The inn is all they care about. She was heartbroken when old Swan died. He was always kind to her."

"What about the McKenzies? Did they dislike her?"

"I wouldn't know. They keep to themselves."

We stood.

"Thank you, Dr. Gibson," I said. "You've been a great help."

He scratched his head. "I don't see how, but you're welcome, Mrs. Weston. Will ye be staying in Drumnadrochit?"

"The constable has given us no choice. It seems we're all stuck here until the killer is found."

"Then let's hope Robb makes some headway." He gestured with his pipe. "But mark my words, it isn't Finn Brody."

The men shook hands and we took our leave.

"Duncan Montague must have been meeting someone," I said, as we set off down the lonely lane that led back to the Drunken Duck. "Why else would he risk the moor?"

"I still say his son is the likeliest culprit," John replied. "Or Ursilla Brody. The pair of them could be the lanterns."

"Maybe." I frowned. "But the ones I saw were coming from opposite directions. Wouldn't they be leaving the Duck together?"

"At least we know what they've been searching for."

In daylight, Drumnadrochit was a cheerful place, with

chickens pecking in the yards, children at play, and goodwives in white aprons hanging washing out to dry.

But on a moonless night like this one, with nary a streetlamp to be seen, the houses seemed much farther apart, the pools of darkness between them thick as cobwebs.

I nearly shrieked when a tall figure materialized out of the shadows.

"Uncle Arthur!" I said, clutching my chest.

He was panting and wild-eyed. "I went to look for you," he gasped. "But I saw something else!"

"The loch monster?" John suggested, while Arthur caught his breath. "Muckle Black Tyke? Pixies?"

"No," Arthur wheezed. "A man running across the moor. Without a stitch of clothing!"

CHAPTER 18

I t seems that poor Arthur, having been left in the lurch yet again, had taken it upon himself to mount a search for us. He was at the footbridge when he spotted a pale form in the hills above.

"Naked as the day he was born," Arthur explained, sipping his brandy. "It was dark, but I could tell that well enough."

We were back at the Duck in our accustomed places by the fire.

Mrs. Davies occupied the best armchair. The elusive Miss Neiderberger sat at her side, knitting a red sweater for Caesar. Apparently, there had been some excitement involving the cat. Despite his obesity and evident lassitude, Teddy had emerged victorious. Caesar licked his wounds in a basket at Mrs. Davies's feet, the offending feline having been banished to the kitchen.

"Naked, you say?" Mrs. Davies remarked. "That's peculiar."

"Probably a village boy on a dare," Frank Thomas suggested. The Welsh swimmer leaned against the hearth.

Miss Neiderberger smiled up at him. "My brothers did such things," she ventured. "Zey were wild."

"And here I thought you came from a respectable family," Mrs. Davies admonished.

Miss Neiderberger blushed and buried her face in the knitting. I watched the needles click and clack in her strong fingers.

"Or it could be an escaped lunatic," John suggested. "Any asylums around here?"

I took a long swallow of the Duck's strong ale. "Other than the one we're currently in?"

"There are no asylums outside of Inverness, Dr. Weston," a soft voice said over my shoulder.

It was Ursilla Brody. She must have heard my flippant remark.

"Are you all right there, Harry?" John asked with a twinkle in his eye.

I set the mug down, still coughing. "Swallowed funny."

Ursilla smiled. How very black her eyes were. Not like Finn's at all.

"I realize you're all in an awkward position," she said. "Ordered by the constable to remain here. If there's anything we can do to make your stay more comfortable, just say the word."

"You've been very accommodating already," I said. "But thank you."

The others murmured their thanks. Ursilla drifted away. She was still wearing a dark mourning dress and it made her white skin look even paler. She was quite beautiful, but there was a strangeness to Mrs. Brody I couldn't quite put my finger on.

"Where's Finn?" I asked in a low voice. "Has anyone seen him?"

"Not since he caught us in the root cellar," Mrs. Davies whispered back.

"I find that suspicious," Arthur muttered through his mustache.

Everyone present knew about the Hand of Glory. We'd also

apprised them of what we learned from Cormac Ferguson and Dr. Gibson.

"It's just like Count Strozza," Mrs. Davis said, brandishing *The Secret Chamber at Mont Morrone Abbey*. "Congenital madness!"

"Keep your voice down," I hissed, glancing at Ursilla.

The innkeeper was chatting with one of the villagers at the bar, but she kept turning our way.

I made a surreptitious motion at the scullery boy, Arran. He trotted over.

"Where's Master Finn?" I asked casually. "I wanted to ask him about something."

"Off delivering barrels of the Duck's ale to the Prince o' Wales Inn in Achnahannet. It's down past Strone Point." His chest puffed with pride. "Ours is the best in the glen."

"When's he expected back?"

The door opened at that moment and Finn strode inside. "See to the horses, Arran," he called out.

The scullery boy darted off. Finn noticed us staring and gave a puzzled wave with his good hand. The other, as always, was jammed in his pocket.

We must have looked unhinged, all grinning and waving back with false heartiness. He nodded uncertainly and approached his mother, whispering in her ear. The two of them went up the stairs.

"It's too late to do anything except search the moor again," I said. "And that doesn't appeal to me."

"Nor I," Frank Thomas agreed. "In Wales, we call it the *gwyllgi*. A great black mastiff with eyes of flame." A log in the fire popped with a hiss of sparking embers. His voice lowered. "One of the *Cwn Annwfn*. Dogs of the otherworld."

Miss Neiderberger shivered. Caesar whined and stuck his nose beneath his tail.

"A potent legend," Arthur said thoughtfully.

"What would Sherlock Holmes make of it?" I teased him.

"Holmes would discover a rational explanation," Arthur replied with a smile. "But I fear poor Watson would be entirely credulous." He shot to his feet. "I think I'll try to get a little writing done. Jot down some ideas." He waved a hand. "You know where my room is. Give a shout if anything happens."

Uncle Arthur strode for the stairs with his distinctive energetic gait.

"I, too, shall retire," Mrs. Davies declared. "Let us pray we all live to see the dawn."

She scooped Caesar from his basket and trudged for the stairs. After a furtive glance at Frank Thomas, Miss Neiderberger gathered her knitting and followed suit.

"Poor Ilsa," Frank said when they were gone. "That woman is a dragon!"

"Mrs. Davies?" John said. "I wouldn't want to work for her, that's for sure."

"Have you gotten to know Miss Neiderberger?" I asked.

"A lovely lass," Frank said wistfully. "Strong as an ox, too. She dragged one of those rowboats up onto the shore all by herself."

"She was out on the loch?" I said in surprise. "When?"

"This morning. I caught up to her on the shore, but she hardly needed my assistance."

Suspicion bloomed. "Wasn't she scared of the beast?"

With all the other goings on, I'd scarcely given a thought to the creature lurking in the dark waters of Loch Ness.

"She says it's a kelpie," Frank replied. "And that they're not dangerous unless you provoke them."

John and I exchanged a look.

"Miss Neiderberger said that?"

She'd struck me as a pragmatic sort. Hardworking, disciplined and efficient in the tradition of her Teutonic ancestors. But Miss Neiderberger, it seemed, had a vivid imagination.

Or she was simply lying.

"That's what everyone in the village says," Frank replied with a shrug. "T'was a water horse that rocked the boat and nearly tugged me under."

"The legend is common to a number of lochs in Scotland," John said. "On land, they look like horses. But mount one's back and it will carry you straight into the depths."

Frank Thomas shuddered. "Well, I'm off to bed, too."

We followed him up the stairs and locked our door.

"Someone's not what they seem," I said. "But who?"

"Plenty of motives," John replied. "If the Hand of Glory grants a wish, it could be anything at all."

I undressed and got into bed. "H.N. Gryffin was at the top of my list. I thought she might be designing a diabolical mystery just to see if we could solve it. To prove she was more clever than everyone. But it wasn't her."

"Unless she was one of the conspirators and they had a falling out on the crag."

I leaned over to blow out the candle, then hesitated.

"Would you look under the bed, John?"

He didn't laugh at me. "Of course."

Weston leaned down and yanked the quilt up. "Nothing but dust."

"Could you close the chimney flue, too?"

"Already did, Harry."

I kissed him. "I knew I married you for a reason."

He slipped Goodnight's pistol beneath his pillow. "Just in case."

We were both too tired to do more than spoon. I feared that every little noise would set me on edge, but the Drunken Duck didn't have the same oppressive aura as Caer Morvan Hall. Within a minute, I fell fast asleep.

I WOKE AT DAWN FEELING REFRESHED AND READY TO FACE whatever ghastly events the day brought.

John was still sleeping. I donned a pearl gray walking dress and washed my face. I didn't feel hungry yet. It was a lovely morning and I decided a brisk walk would do me good.

Only the scullery boy, Arran, was stirring when I went downstairs. He was coming out of the kitchen with a dreamy look and jumped when I bid him good morning. I told him my destination in case I never returned, and set off for Temple Pier.

As I'd hoped, a figure stood at the shore, gazing out at the peaceful loch.

"Good morning, Mrs. Brody," I said with a smile.

Her head jerked around in surprise. "Oh, Mrs. Weston! Good morning."

Mist hung over the water and wreathed the pines on the opposite shore. High, tattered clouds moved slowly overhead, painting the scene in stark shades of gray. Across the bay, Urquhart Castle sat on a high promontory of Strone Point.

"I keep meaning to visit the ruins," I said.

"Most of the guests do. So much history." She said it with a touch of bitterness. "Men fighting men over a patch of bloody ground."

"The Wars of Scottish Independence, you mean?"

She nodded. "It was the only Highland castle to hold out against the English invaders, though it did fall eventually. When the soldiers of William of Orange were besieged by the Jacobites, the English blew up the gatehouse when they retreated. Local folk quarried much of the stone that remained." She pointed. "That tall bit near the water is Grant Tower. It was damaged later in a storm, but most of it's still there."

We were silent for a moment. The wind tugged strands of blonde hair loose from her bonnet, sweeping them across her pale face.

"I'm very sorry about Mr. Swan," I said. "You seemed close to him."

She stared out at the loch. "He was a good man. I canna believe someone wanted to harm him." Her jaw hardened. "Or the others. Why is there so much cruelty in the world?"

I had no answer for that. "Do you have any ideas at all about who it was?"

I thought I saw a flicker in her eyes, but she shook her head. "None, Mrs. Weston."

"What if I told you that the Montague family had a dark secret?"

She cast me a sharp glance. "It would'na surprise me. I suppose you speak of the curse."

"More than that. I think we've discovered the source of it."

I told her about Godfrey's diary. Her face went perfectly still, her eyes unfocused.

"A wish?" she whispered.

"We could be wrong about that. But I do believe this Hand of Glory is a powerful talisman."

The strangest expression flitted across her features. Longing and dread mingled. Then she blinked and turned to me with a level gaze. "I knew nothing o' that," Ursilla said. "Nor does my son, I'm sure."

"You worked at the Hall—"

"Aye." Anger flashed in her black eyes. "For a brief spell. Once I left, I never returned. I want nothing to do with the Montagues." She adjusted her bonnet. "I must be getting back to the Duck, Mrs. Weston."

Ursilla gave me a brief nod and hurried up the road. I stared after her slender figure until it vanished around a bend.

She *was* hiding something, yet I sensed it was a secret still buried. She hadn't scoffed at the Hand of Glory the way Dr. Gibson did. No, she'd believed me without question.

But she hadn't known until I told her.

Something else nagged at me. The talisman didn't grant unlimited wishes. If it did, the heirs would use it to live long, prosperous lives. Of course, it might give two, or three, or any number. But I suspected it was one only. The chance to have your heart's desire—and then pay the price down the road. It would take great strength of will not to use that wish up the moment the Hand fell into one's possession.

Duncan Montague had been madly in love with her, but she refused to marry him. He'd bought her the inn, perhaps in the hope that she'd change her mind. But if he'd had a wish left, he surely would have used it to make Ursilla his wife and Finn his legitimate heir.

So what had Duncan used his wish for?

Back at the Duck, I spotted John through the window. He was seated at a table in the common room and seemed to be muttering to himself. He raked a hand through his hair, tugging it in the way he had when he was at wit's end. I felt a twinge of guilt as I hurried through the door.

"Harry!" he exclaimed, jumping to his feet.

"I took a walk down to the loch," I said. "Didn't Arran tell you?"

He shook his head. "I haven't seen him."

"I'm sorry, I should have left a note."

"Yes, you should have," he agreed with a scowl. "I thought we were sticking together."

"We are," I said in a placating tone, kissing his cheek. "But it's barely half a mile and broad daylight. Did you see Ursilla come in?"

He nodded at the kitchen. "She hauled Finn in there. She had a rather dire expression and I was worried . . . never mind. What happened?"

I related our encounter at the loch and my speculation about Duncan's wish.

"That's a good point," John said, smiling up at Cassie as she delivered two plates of eggs, kippers and buttered toast. "We need to learn more about him."

"I think it's time we pay another visit to Caer Morvan Hall," I said, lowering my voice. "We haven't ruled out the Goodnights. Or the McKenzies. And the servants would have known Montague since he was a child. Dr. Gibson said they were in on the secret of Finn's birth. I bet they know plenty of other things, too."

Uncle Arthur was shut up in his room writing. Cassie said he'd had breakfast sent up and seemed intent on his work, so John and I decided to leave him be. John collected Mr. Goodnight's revolver from our room.

It seemed prudent to bring it on the long walk across the moor—and returning the gun provided the perfect excuse to turn up without an invitation.

CHAPTER 19

A cold wind swept down from the north as we crossed the footbridge and started up the track to the Hall.

"Should we tell Jack Goodnight about the Hand of Glory and Godfrey's diary?" John wondered. "Everyone else knows."

I'd already given the matter some thought. "If he's the killer, he already knows about it. If he's not, we run the risk of having the door slammed in our faces. Mr. Goodnight isn't like the gang at the Duck. He claims he doesn't believe in any of it."

"Then how do we convince him to let us talk to the McKenzies?"

"Maybe we can use the treasure story instead. Leave out the supernatural aspect for now. We'll say all the talk is that there's Spanish gold buried somewhere and the murderer is hunting for it. Some are claiming Duncan found it."

"That's thin."

"I suppose it is," I admitted. "What if we say H.N. wrote it all down in her notebook? See how he reacts to that?"

John rubbed his hands for warmth. "It's worth a try."

We crossed the moor without incident. It was about nine in the morning when the hulking stone manor came into view. It had an oddly lopsided aspect with lights glowing in one wing and the other half in darkness.

Miss McKenzie admitted us to Caer Morvan Hall. She wore a long black dress and her eyes looked bloodshot. The housekeeper's lips tightened when she saw us, but she gave a curtsey and went to fetch Mr. Goodnight.

The master of the Hall appeared a minute later, looking dapper in a morning coat and polished black boots. He greeted us with a guarded smile.

"I brought your pistol back," John said, handing it to him.

"Thank you, but you needn't have." He gazed at us expectantly.

"There have been some new developments," I said. "We thought you ought to know."

He tensed. "Have the police found who killed those people?"

"I'm afraid not. But Miss Gryffin, she's the one who fell from Craigmonie, had a notebook. We found it."

He waited. I saw no alarm in his expression.

"She'd been investigating various rumors and seemed to believe there might be a connection to Sir Duncan Montague," John added.

Now Goodnight did look surprised. "Montague?"

"I know it sounds crazy," John said. "But if you'd permit us to speak with the McKenzies one last time, it might help."

"Oughtn't Constable Robb be the one to question them?"

John held his gaze. "I wouldn't say this to one of the locals, but you're a fellow American. They do things differently over here, sir. The constable seems like a good fellow, but he's a bit old and set in his ways." John squared his shoulders. "In light of what happened to my wife, I'd like to handle the matter myself."

They exchanged one of those secret-handshake looks men give each other.

"I understand, Dr. Weston," Goodnight said. "Come on in. We'll settle this ourselves."

John waggled a brow at me when Goodnight turned away. I wanted to kiss him. My husband could be almost childlike in his enthusiasms. It was easy to forget that he was also as wily and devious as they come.

Goodnight led us to the same drawing room as the last time.

"How did you settle on Caer Morvan Hall?" I asked.

"One of Louisa's doctors put me onto it. He'd read in the papers about Duncan Montague dying. End of a noble line and all that. The place piqued my interest. It had everything I was looking for. Quiet and remote, with plenty of room for Louisa to run around indoors. It's not often one of the these grand old homes goes up for sale."

We all sat down by the fire.

"So what's this about a treasure?' Mr. Goodnight asked, a gleam in his eye.

John related the story of the vanished chests of bullion sent to aid King James in his bid for the Scottish throne.

"Someone was digging at the Standing Stones," he said. "Miss Gryffin seemed to think it might even be on your property."

Goodnight laughed. "Well, if it is, I haven't found it yet. But it's funny, my own little empire does come from gold." He glanced up at the Montague portraits hanging on the walls. "Those boys were born with a silver spoon, but not me." His chest puffed out a little. "We Goodnights earned what we have. My father was one of the miners who got in early, back in forty-eight. Made his fortune in the Sierra Nevada. It was a wild ride. Millionaires made overnight. Then the hordes descended. The seams were played out by the fifties, but he was smart and invested in the railroads. I expanded it to real estate."

"And made a bundle," a woman's voice remarked dryly. "Jack never tires of telling that story."

Evangeline Goodnight stood in the doorway. He cast his wife a cool glance, which she ignored.

"Mr. and Mrs. Weston. I didn't realize you'd paid us another visit."

"We just arrived," I said.

She frowned. "Any word from the village? Jack told me what happened when he brought you back to town. That poor woman. It seems we have a lunatic roaming the Highlands."

"Nothing concrete," I said. "Won't you join us?"

She looked flustered. "Actually, I had plans to visit Inverness this afternoon. I so rarely escape these walls, you see. I'd been planning the outing for weeks."

Goodnight frowned. "You make it sound like a prison, Evangeline."

She turned to him with an icy expression. "At least I'm free to go into the city. See the sights. Poor Louisa is the one behind bars."

"That's hardly my fault," he objected, flushing.

She glanced at us. Her tone softened. "I didn't say it was. I'm sorry, Jack. It's just . . . all her friends were in California. She has no one here."

"She has us!"

"It's not the same and you know it." Mrs. Goodnight gathered herself. "I'm sorry," she said again to no one in particular.

The scene was more than a little awkward. "Don't let us keep you," I said with a smile. "We were just returning your husband's revolver. We don't mean to stay long."

Jack Goodnight didn't bother to correct this assertion. He eyed his wife with a mixture of regret and exasperation.

"If you're sure." Her smile faded as Nurse Payne joined her. The nurse was dressed for an outing, with a fancy hat and fur-trimmed coat.

"Oh, hello," the nurse said to us in surprise, turning to her employer. "Are you ready, Eva?"

"Let me just fetch my purse." Mrs. Goodnight gave us a little wave.

The warm friendship between the two women was obvious in the way Charlotte Payne leaned in as they departed. I couldn't help but notice the contrast with Mrs. Davies and Miss Neiderberger.

"Don't mind my wife," Jack Goodnight said when they were both gone. "She chafes at the confinement. I suppose it's natural. Our lives were completely different before. But she'll get used to it in time."

"I'm sure she will," John said.

An uncomfortable silence descended.

"So, er, this treasure," Mr. Goodnight said. "You think that's the motive?"

He sounded relieved that it was something he could understand.

"Most likely," I agreed. "There are various rumors. The Standing Stones. Portclair Forest. The Hall, of course."

"And the castle," John reminded me.

"Urquhart?" Goodnight asked.

I nodded. "That ruin at Strone Point."

He nodded thoughtfully. "Yes, I've ridden past it in the coach. Well, shall I summon the McKenzies?" Goodnight slapped his knee. "Dammit, Evangeline will have taken Mr. McKenzie to drive the coach. I'll see if I can catch them."

He leapt to his feet and ran from the room. I leaned towards John. "They *do* have marital troubles," I whispered across the cavernous drawing room.

"Do you think they're really going to Inverness?" he whispered back.

"No idea." I jumped up and ran to the window. "The coach is already at the end of the drive," I reported.

"Footsteps," John hissed.

I flung myself back into the armchair and donned an attitude of nonchalance, though my heart was racing.

The door opened. Mr. Goodnight entered with a stone-faced Miss McKenzie.

"I'm afraid we just missed Mr. McKenzie," he said. "But you may pose your questions to his sister." He gestured to a chair. "Sit down."

The elderly servant obeyed. She adjusted her skirts and folded her hands in her lap.

"We'd like to know more about Duncan Montague," John said.

She frowned. This was clearly not what she'd expected. "What do ye wish to know?"

"Just what he was like," I said. "You can speak frankly, Miss McKenzie. We promise to keep whatever you have to say confidential."

She looked at Mr. Goodnight, who nodded. "My brother and I came to Caer Morvan shortly after Sir Duncan was born. He was a fanciful child, rather like Miss Louisa. He loved stories."

"Was there any one in particular he liked best?"

She smiled. "Aye. *Legends of the Sea Folk*. It had the same tales my own mother told us. Master Duncan knew every one by heart. O' course, he outgrew all that eventually. Got itchy feet and decided to travel, see the world. He left the Hall when he was eighteen and we hardly saw him for six years. Then he came back."

"With Ursilla Brody."

Her face grew guarded. "That's right. She didn't stay long. I don't think she liked working here very much."

"Did anything unusual happen after he returned?"

She stared at me. "Like what?"

"I don't know. Did he gain any new lands or titles? Recover from a life-threatening illness? Just anything that sticks in your head."

"I can't think of anything, Mum."

"All right. I understand he left you and your brother a bequest."

"Yes, Mum. The master was very generous to think of us."

"Do you know who else he named in his will? Besides the other servants, I mean."

"Oh, I wouldn't be privy to that sort of thing."

"Of course. We shall move on. Were you and your brother present when the fire occurred?"

Her hands tightened in her lap. "Yes, Mum."

"What do you remember of that day?"

"It was Christmas Eve. The master then was Duncan's father, Sir Preston Montague. He liked to entertain. About two dozen guests were expected. The staff was busy making the Hall ready."

"But no one had arrived yet?"

She shook her head. "Thank the Lord, no. They weren't due until after Boxing Day. Christmas was for family only."

"When did it start?"

"Late that night. I was abed when I heard the shouts. I woke and smelled smoke."

"That must have been frightening."

"Yes, Mum. I pulled on my dressing gown and ran into the hallway. Started banging on doors. We all hurried outside. Flames were leapin' from the windows of the East Wing." She drew a deep breath. "The men fetched buckets and made a line from the well, but the fire was burnin' something fierce by then."

"When did you realize Sir Preston was still inside?"

"Not right away. It was chaos, Mum. Then Mr. Swan came out with young Duncan in his arms. The boy was only six. They were both coughin' and covered in soot. I learned later that Swan tried to reach his wife and child but couldn't get through the flames, so he went back for Master Duncan. T'was very brave. He nearly died bringin' him out."

"Why were Mr. Swan and his family staying at the Hall? I thought he was the groundskeeper."

"He wasn't then. Swan was just a footman. He moved out to the cottage later. I think he couldn't stand to be in the Hall, Mum."

"Why stay at all?"

She sighed. "I canna say for sure. He kept to himself. But him and Duncan were very close after. They'd both lost people dear to 'em, see? I imagine he felt a bond to the boy."

"Where did Sir Preston die?"

"In his bedroom." She frowned. "He always locked himself in at night with a key. It had broken off in the lock. He must have panicked and twisted it too hard. Couldn't get out before the fire took him."

I shared a quick look with John. That sounded like the curse at work—or something even more sinister.

"How did it start?" John asked.

"Must have been the Christmas tree."

"Wouldn't that have been in the main entry hall?" I asked.

"Aye. We called that one the Big Tree. But there was also a Little Tree upstairs. It was in a library near the old nursery. Young Duncan liked to read his books there by the light of it." She smiled sadly. "He called it the Pixie Tree on account o' the twinkling candles."

A chill touched me. "Wouldn't they have been extinguished when he went to bed?"

"Of course, Mum. Mrs. Swan was always careful to put the candles out before goin' to bed. She was Duncan's governess." Miss McKenzie shook head. "She must have missed one that night because the police said the fire started in the second-floor library."

"Why was Mrs. Swan sleeping upstairs and not in the servants' quarters?"

"Young Duncan had night terrors. He'd often wake up

screamin' like a banshee. So Lord Montague—Preston, that is, Duncan's father—he finally moved Mrs. Swan and her own daughter into the room next door to the nursery. It was an unusual arrangement, but I s'pose it gave him peace o' mind."

"But not Mr. Swan?"

"No, Mum, that'd be improper. He kept to their room below stairs."

"Wasn't that awkward for the family?"

"I couldn't say, Mum," she muttered.

"Why the child, too?" John asked.

Her jaw set and this time she held my gaze firmly. "Mrs. Swan insisted on it."

It took me an instant to understand her meaning. "Oh," I said. "Yes, I see."

Preston Montague had more in common with his ancestors than the title and money. The man was a pig and everyone at the Hall knew it.

"Did anyone ever suspect the fire had been set deliberately?" I asked.

She looked shocked, but something in her face made me suspect the question had indeed arisen.

"I can't think of anyone who would have done such a thing, Mum."

"That's not what I asked though, is it?""

She looked down at her lap. "Oh, there's always gossip. But nothing ever came of that. It was ruled a careless accident and that's what I believe it was."

"What gossip?" Mr. Goodnight demanded.

"Truly, sir, I canna even recall what they said. It was all nonsense." Her lips tightened and I doubted we'd get more out of her on that score.

"One last question. I suppose everything in the nursery burned?"

She nodded. "To ash. Except for the book I told ye about.

Legends of the Sea Folk. Duncan had it clutched to his chest when Mr. Swan brought him out."

"Do you have any idea where it is now?"

I was surprised when she answered promptly.

"Miss Louisa has it."

"You gave it to my daughter?" Jack Goodnight asked with an unhappy expression.

"She found it somewhere, sir. I'm sorry. I didna want to take it from her. She liked the stories."

His frown deepened. "I hope you didn't tell her where it came from."

Miss McKenzie looked worried. "Of course not, sir. I just said it belonged to the old master. That's all, sir."

He nodded curtly. "Thank you, Miss McKenzie, you're dismissed."

She gripped her skirts, gave him a curtsy, and left the room.

"I'm not sure I follow your line of questioning, " Mr. Goodnight said. "The fire was twenty years ago. And if Duncan's connected somehow, the man's been dead for nine months."

"Just following every lead," I replied vaguely. "But I think we'd better speak with Louisa, don't you?"

CHAPTER 20

"How goes your quest, Sir Weston?" Louisa asked eagerly as we entered the nursery.

She wore a blue satin frock and a tiara encrusted with what looked like real diamonds. Three dolls in matching pink ruffles sat around the low table, which was set for a tea party.

"I managed to get past the Neebles, Lady. But I still must brave the Mountain of Misery where the ice giants roam. The wizard's castle sits at the pinnacle."

She thrust an empty teacup at him. "Drink some hot cocoa before you go, for strength."

John bowed and pretended to sip from it. "Thank you, Lady."

"Louisa," Mr. Goodnight said with false cheer. "Do you have a book called *Legends of the Sea Folk*?"

She scampered to the bookcase and pulled out a slender volume. "Right here, Daddy."

"May I see it?"

Something in his voice tipped the child off. "You won't take it away, will you?" she asked, clutching it to her chest the way little Duncan Montague must have when he was rescued from Caer Morvan Hall.

Mr. Goodnight held out a hand. "Just let me see it."

Her smile died, but she reluctantly came over and gave him the book.

The cover was moth-eaten cloth, the binding coming loose. I could barely discern the title.

"Where did you get this?" her father asked, eyeing the book with distaste.

A secretive looked crossed Louisa's face. "Oh, I found it lying around somewhere. Can't quite remember—"

"Don't lie to me, young lady," he said sternly. "Were you in the East Wing?"

Louisa scuffed her shoes on the carpet. "Only once!" she burst out. "I was curious, Daddy."

"I told you not to go in there," he chastised in a more gentle tone. "It's dangerous. We don't know how sound the walls are. You could have been hurt."

"There was nothing, anyway," she muttered, still not meeting her father's eye. "Just that."

"I'm afraid I can't let you keep it," he said.

Her face fell. "Why not? I like the stories! They're not scary, not really."

Jack Goodnight frowned. "Still—"

"If we live here, I ought to know the history, don't you think?" She got up on tiptoes and pecked his cheek. "Please, Daddy?"

I could see Goodnight wavering. He sighed. "I'll read it myself first. Then I'll decide."

Louisa clearly interpreted this as a victory. "Oh, thank you, Daddy!" She turned to me. "Mrs. Weston, do you remember how I called you a selkie when you came before?"

I smiled. "Yes, I do."

"I read about them in there." She cast a covetous glance at the book. "Selkies are nice. Not like mean old kelpies that want to eat you up." Her cheeks flushed. "Er, I mean, they don't always. They're just pretty black horses that like water."

Her father couldn't help but laugh. He swept her into a hug. "No promises, Princess. I'll have to discuss it with Mother and Miss Parker first."

Louisa scowled. "They never let me have *anything* good."

"Miss Parker?" John asked.

"The governess," Jack Goodnight said. "It's her day off."

I remembered him saying they'd hired a local girl from one of the nearby villages.

"Wash up for lunch," he said to Louisa. "Then we'll see."

She gave a glum nod and watched us leave.

"Might I have a look at that?" I asked Mr. Goodnight in the hall.

He handed the book over. The first page had Duncan's name written in childish block printing.

"I wonder how she got through the door to the East Wing," Mr. Goodnight murmured. "It's always locked."

"Who has the keys?" John asked.

"The McKenzies. I'll have a word with them." His jaw set. "They know Louisa is a precocious child. If they did leave it unlocked . . . Of course, I had workers in to look around last month. They were in and out of the wing for several days. It might have happened then."

I quickly scanned the pages. They bore the signs of hard use. Grubby fingerprints and small tears. As Louisa said, the tales were centered around kelpies and selkies, with the hero—or victim—generally being a fisherman. Nothing about Muckle Black Tyke or the darker lore of Britain.

I returned the book. "This might seem an odd request, but would you mind terribly if we had a look around the East Wing ourselves?"

Goodnight considered it, then gave a shrug. "I suppose it's all right. I'd like to ensure it's locked anyway. But I wasn't merely trying to frighten Louisa. The ceiling of Sir Preston's bedchamber came down. The head carpenter claimed the rest is structurally sound, but I'd feel responsible if something happened. I think I'd best accompany you. And we'll remain on the ground floor."

"Sounds fair enough," John said.

In short order, Mr. Goodnight had secured the keys from the McKenzies. They both insisted it had been locked after the workers left, so he concluded that Louisa must have crept inside at some point during the inspection.

Caer Morvan Hall was laid out on the axis of a central corridor. The door to the East Wing was sandwiched in a passageway between the formal dining room and back parlor.

"The upstairs held the family's sleeping quarters and several guest rooms," Mr. Goodnight explained as he turned the key in the lock. "Downstairs was the old staff quarters in the rear, and a library and breakfast room in the front."

He threw open the door and we stepped into the East Wing. Everything not made of stone had been gutted. Ancient soot streaked the walls and ceiling. Overlapping footprints were clear in the dust, presumably the workers.

Mr. Goodnight lit a candle. Not a beam of light penetrated the boards over the broken windows.

We passed a crossing passage he identified as leading to the servants' quarters.

"The McKenzies lived there, along with the rest of the staff," he said. Goodnight pointed to another door opposite that led directly outside. "They all got out that way. It was the entrance for deliveries. The Hall used to have a second kitchen."

We passed a wide staircase leading up into darkness. John moved ahead, venturing inside a high-ceilinged chamber with blackened wooden paneling. It was empty except for a rectangular shape wrapped in a dingy sheet that sat propped against one wall.

Of course, my husband beelined for it.

"What's that?" I asked, though part of me had already guessed.

Maybe it was the deeper chill in the air. Or the way the shrouded object seemed to repel the frail glow of the candle.

Mr. Goodnight looked uncomfortable. "One of the portraits. It's the only thing I know of that survived the fire unscathed."

"Can we see it?" John asked, his fingertips already resting on the sheet.

Goodnight hesitated. "If you must," he grumbled.

John unwrapped the painting, sending whorls of dust dancing in the still air. The portrait was in the dark, medieval style with light cast only upon the subject's face. A man, perhaps thirty years of age. His head was turned away to a three-quarters profile, yet his gaze rested squarely on the viewer. The features were unremarkable, neither handsome nor ugly, but the gray eyes held a knowing, evil light. Unlike the later Montagues, his hair and whiskers were a fiery red.

"Sir Silas Montague, I presume," I said softly.

Mr. Goodnight nodded. "Someone stored it in here. I didn't care much for it, so I decided to let it be."

I thought of the Montague heirs. None were what you'd call kind-looking, though Silas was certainly the worst of the bunch.

"Why did you keep any of them?" I wondered.

John let the sheet fall and a palpable sense of relief came over me.

Mr. Goodnight exhaled a foggy breath. "I don't rightly know. They were hanging in the drawing room when we arrived. They seemed a part of this place. And then we just got used to them." He shook his head. "But I'll admit, this one did disturb me. Unlike my daughter, I'm not prone to whimsy. It just struck me as odd that it survived the inferno. That's all."

He turned abruptly and strode for the door. We hurried to catch up.

"There's nothing more to see." Goodnight gave us a rueful look. "I keep meaning to get rid of it, but it's from the damned fifteen-hundreds. Probably worth a bundle. Maybe I'll donate it to a museum." He laughed. "Get my name on a little brass plaque!"

We exited through the door to the main body of the house. Goodnight locked it securely behind us.

"Thank you for coming. Her Highness will be watched more closely after this." He licked his lips. "I can't say I like the thought of my daughter poking around in there."

"Nor do I," I said. "You shouldn't wait to dispose of that painting." I took out one of my business cards. "This has the address of the London Branch of the S.P.R. They'd be happy to take it off your hands."

He regained some of his jaunty aspect. "The famous curse? I'll bear it in mind, Mrs. Weston." Goodnight slipped the card into a pocket. "I hate to make you head back to the inn on foot, but Evangeline took the coach. It's no trouble if you prefer to wait for them to return. I have work to do in my office, but you're welcome to stay for lunch."

John and I exchanged a quick look. It would be hours before they returned.

"We'll walk," I said. "It's still daylight."

"Are you sure?" Goodnight frowned. "I'd lend you horses but we only keep the four."

"We'll manage," John said. "But thank you for the offer."

They shook hands. "Good luck with your investigation," Mr. Goodnight said. "As I said before, I'm glad to be of help in any way."

We thanked him and started down the drive.

"I hope he takes my advice," I said. "That painting gave me a funny feeling when I looked at it."

"Me, too. Did you believe him? About keeping the portraits?"

"I don't know. I suppose it's plausible. We might be chasing ghosts here, John."

He arched a brow.

"Not in the literal sense," I amended. "No one's ever claimed the Montagues come back from the grave. But the fire *is* troubling."

"It sounds like the poor Swan family was caught up in the curse. I don't believe for a second that the key to Montague's bedroom broke off in the lock by happenstance. He was just the right age for the payment to come due."

We reached the spot where I'd seen a dark form pacing the mist. I suppressed a shudder. But there was no fog today. The sun shone brightly, casting swift cloud-shadows on the rolling heath before us. There was nowhere for the beast to hide and I relaxed a little.

"Maybe." I clutched my hat down against the brisk wind. "I still think Miss McKenzie was hiding something. When I asked if anything unusual had happened after Duncan returned to the Hall, she answered a tad too quickly."

"Could she have been thinking of Finn's birth? The affair with Ursilla Brody?"

"That's possible, though I'm not sure it really fits the bill. All the Montague men were rakes so it's nothing out of the ordinary."

We strode along in companionable silence for a few minutes, each chewing over what we'd learned. Drumnadrochit drew nearer, nestled in the glen below, and beyond it the choppy waters of Loch Ness. I was glad to have Caer Morvan Hall at my back. Louisa was the only truly cheerful thing about the place. It was no wonder she sought solace in stories of knights and wizards, kelpies and selkies . . . .

"And the book of Scottish folktales?" John said out of the blue.

I smiled to myself. Our brains often ran along parallel tracks.

"Duncan had a vivid imagination. Sometimes you outgrow it, like Miss McKenzie said."

"And sometimes you don't." He grinned. "I'm a case in point, Harry. I always liked ghost stories the best."

"And you certainly haven't outgrown them," I agreed with a laugh. "Not even the real ones."

"Especially the real ones—" He cried out and spun to the side.

I thought he'd tripped over a hillock until I saw the dark, wet patch blooming on his sleeve. A distant crack echoed through the hills. An instant later, my husband was carrying me to the ground. We landed hard, John on top.

"Hold still," he hissed through gritted teeth.

I could hardly breathe under his weight. "What. . . ."

"Someone's shooting at us," John answered grimly.

CHAPTER 21

I swore like a sailor. "How bad is it, John?"

"They missed. It's just a graze." He shifted slightly and I drew a deep breath. "Keep your head down."

"Just a graze! You're bleeding all over me. And . . . *obviously.*"

Our eyes locked. His still looked clear and remarkably calm, but the wetness soaking my dress was worrisome.

"There's a tree not too far off. Maybe we can wiggle over there."

"Where are they shooting from?" I asked.

"The angle makes it that ridge." He nodded his head in the direction of a distant crag.

Another pop echoed through the valley. A bullet struck the dirt about four feet away.

"Scratch that," he hissed. "Run!"

We both rose to a crouch and crabbed our way toward the trees. Another bullet whizzed past, much closer this time. I risked a glance over my shoulder but saw nothing. Then we reached the shelter of the branches. It was a Scots Pine with twisting branches near the base that gave easy footholds. John clambered up and pulled me after him with his good arm. We climbed until we were completely veiled by the sweet-smelling needles.

"They know where we went," I said, trying to catch my breath. "I imagine they'll come along shortly."

"Whoever it is, they're a damned good shot," John replied. One hand gripped his shoulder. Blood welled between his fingers.

I unwrapped my red scarf and tied it tight around his arm above the elbow. "Do you feel dizzy?"

"A bit." His teeth were chattering. "Not so bad."

I leaned into the crook of the tree and started chafing his hands. "You're cold as ice!"

"Mr. Goodnight's the one who boasted of his s-skills with a p-pistol," John stammered.

"Save the speculation for later," I said gently. "We need to get you out of here."

I pushed a branch aside. The moor seemed empty, but I knew whoever it was had simply shouldered the rifle and set out on foot to corner us. Drumnadrochit looked close, perhaps another mile, but it might as well as have been on the moon for all we could reach it.

In a way, we'd been lucky. The tree was the last one on the barren track leading from Caer Morven Hall into town. Any farther and we'd have been . . . sitting ducks.

My lips parted to emit a mirthless laugh when a howl sliced through the moaning wind. Somewhere off to the left. Much nearer than the town.

"You've got to be joking," I muttered.

"Wonder which one'll get us first?" John asked with a wan smile.

I let the branch fall into place and pressed back against the sticky bark. "Do you think hellhounds can climb trees, John?"

He was quiet, giving this serious consideration. "Bears do. And big cats, of course."

"Wonderful."

"I'm not saying it c-can. Just that it's theoretically possible."

I bit my lip. "Should we make a dash for it?"

John shook his head. "We're safer up here. Maybe the hound will scare the shooter away."

We waited for a tense fifteen minutes or so. I listened to the wind whistle and sigh across the moor, sharing my meager warmth with my husband. No more shots came. A lone cricket chirped in the grass below.

"Harry," he said at last in a drowsy voice that frightened me.

"What, John?"

"They're not coming." He forced himself to sit up straight. "I think we'd better chance it while I can still—"

I pressed a hand to his mouth and shook my head. Then I slowly looked down. John followed my gaze.

The thick branches blocked the view, but there were gaps. Something crouched at the base of the pine. Jet black but with a slight sheen.

The cricket had stopped chirping. Even the incessant wind had died.

Later, when I pondered what had drawn my attention, I concluded it was the uncanny silence.

We both kept stock still. The thing rose and began to pace, flashes of darkness against the tawny grass. Could it smell the wound? John had his injured arm resting lightly on a branch. I watched a single drop of blood form at the tip of his ring finger. My gut clenched. I leaned forward to catch it in my own cupped hand just as the crimson droplet broke free.

An instant too late.

Of course, it made no sound, but I fancied I could hear the tiny splash as it struck the earth.

The hound gave a low snarl, followed by intense snuffling.

I closed my eyes and braced myself for the deadly leap into

the tree. The crackle of branches and warm breath on my neck. If it even breathed at all.

Then the cricket struck up a tune again. I cracked one eye.

"It's gone," John said wearily. "Saw it lope off."

"Truly?"

He nodded.

The mile to Drumnadrochit took us nearly an hour. John was exhausted and I insisted on stopping to let him rest at various points along the way. The sun was nearly gone by the time we staggered into the yard. Mrs. Davies gave a little shriek as I burst into the common room, yelling for Dr. Gibson.

"The fiend has struck again!" she exclaimed, as Miss Neiderberger helped me deposit John in a chair. "What happened?"

"Someone shot at us on the moor," I said. "Help me get his coat off."

In the end, we cut the sleeve away with a pair of scissors because some of the blood had dried and adhered the cloth to his wound. I exhaled with relief when I saw it was indeed shallow. Ursilla Brody had already run to fetch the doctor and he appeared within a few minutes, black bag in hand.

Finn, I noted, didn't seem to be present at the inn.

"Boil some water, Cassie," Gibson instructed the serving lass. "I'll need plenty of it."

She nodded, wide-eyed, and ran into the kitchen.

"Mrs. Brody, brighten the lamps, if you please."

She obeyed, her movements mechanical

"Did you catch a glimpse of the shooter?" Dr. Gibson said as he examined the wound.

"Wash your hands before you dress it," John muttered. He sat with his head tipped back against the chair, gripping the arm.

Gibson chuckled. "I intend to, *doctor*. You do know our sort makes the worst patients?"

John gave a faint smile.

"No, I didn't see him," I replied, glancing at Mrs. Davies and Miss Neiderberger. "Or her."

"I hope you're not suggesting I could have done it," Mrs. Davies replied tartly.

"Nothing of the sort. Only that we have no idea who's behind this."

"Don't we?" she muttered, eyeing Ursilla Brody.

The innkeeper flushed and kept her gaze on the ground.

"And where is your son?" Mrs. Davies demanded. "Why isn't he—"

"I'm right here," Finn Brody growled from the doorway. His black hair was damp, his peacoat hanging open. The normal hand clenched in a fist at his side. It was missing the bandage, I noticed.

"If yer implyin' something, just come out and say it. I'm tired o' all the whispers and innuendo!"

Mrs. Davies opened her mouth and closed it again.

"No one is implying anything, Mr. Brody," I said. "But my husband's been shot. We're all understandably on edge."

Finn turned to John and Dr. Gibson, the anger draining from his face. "Jesus, how bad is it?"

"Minor, actually," Gibson said, drying his hands on a towel. "Mrs. Weston's tourniquet prevented serious blood loss. But I think Dr. Weston was very lucky." He bandaged the arm. "With rest you'll be fine."

Finn looked grim. "I'm fetchin' my shotgun and getting some of the lads together. This has gone on long enough."

He stormed away. Mrs. Davies sniffed. "Well, I feel much safer now."

"What do ye have against my son?" Ursilla asked. "What has he ever t' ye?"

"Not a thing," Mrs. Davies said, thumping her cane. "Come, Miss Neiderberger!"

The two women departed, Miss Neiderberger casting us all

an apologetic look over her shoulder. Dr. Gibson helped me get John upstairs to our room, where he put on a clean shirt and lay down.

"Thank you," he murmured. "I'll just have a little nap."

"Don't let him out tonight," Gibson warned. "He must keep that bandage clean and dry."

John slept for several hours. I stayed at his side, flipping through H.N.'s notebook, but she'd kept her theories to herself. I wondered if she'd solved it and that's why she was killed.

If we knew who she'd taken Godfrey's diary from, we'd have our killer. As an October gale rattled the glass windowpanes, I read the passages written in that spidery hand again.

I knelt in the chapel, seeking solace, but a Grayte and Terrible Wind blew out all the candles...

Did we indeed face a demonic entity? My very first case had involved such a creature, though I didn't believe in it at the time. But I had come a long way since then.

It was All Hallow's Eve, I realized. The time when the boundary between this world and the next grows thin. When witches and wulvers and all manner of things walk the darkness.

Just the sort of night a Hand of Glory might be found by someone who had made blood sacrifices of their own.

I laid a hand on my husband's uninjured shoulder.

"John?" I whispered, heart pounding. "I think you'd better wake up."

CHAPTER 22

It was around nine o'clock when the clamor of voices below drew us down to the common room.

Finn and Ursilla Brody stood with Arthur, Frank Thomas, and Miss Neiderberger. A village man who looked familiar twisted a cap in his hands, glancing at the door.

"What's happened?" I asked.

"Arran's gone missing," Finn replied. "No one's seen the boy all day. I thought he'd run home, but his da says he never turned up for supper."

I felt a stab of worry. "I saw him early this morning," I said. "Just after dawn. He was downstairs. I gave him a message for my husband."

"Which I never received," John added. "I didn't see him when I came into the common room."

"It's normally Arran's day off," Finn said. "Will ye stay here while we mount a search? Just in case he turns up?"

"Of course," I replied.

They broke into pairs. More villagers waited outside the inn. I watched through the window as they fanned out toward the moor.

"I have a bad feeling about this," I fretted. "Arran seemed startled when I saw him this morning. If it was his day off, he wasn't even supposed to be here. Then we went to Caer Morvan and it all slipped my mind. I didn't even think of him until just now. But maybe if I'd mentioned it earlier—"

"You couldn't have known," John said. "If something has happened, it might help to figure out why. What could the boy have known?"

Something brushed my leg. The orange cat, Teddy, was sitting on his haunches, gazing up at me. I stroked his ears and was rewarded with a purr. A spark of memory ignited.

"Do you remember what Mrs. Davies said? That whoever was taking the mice from the traps must have had a confederate at the inn?"

John nodded.

"We assumed it was one of the Brodys. But what if it was Arran?"

"The scullery boy," John said slowly.

"I doubt he had any clue what they wanted the mice for. They probably slipped him some coins and made up an excuse to keep it quiet." My gut tensed. "But the child would be a loose end, John."

He banged a fist on his thigh. "If we could only figure out where the damned Hand of Glory is hidden, we might have a chance."

"Well, it's not at the inn or Caer Morvan Hall. I'm certain our killer would have thoroughly searched both places."

"We're overlooking the obvious," John said glumly. "Duncan could have just tossed it into the loch. That's what I would have done if I didn't want anyone to find it."

I shook my head. "A cursed object of that power wouldn't be so easily disposed of, John. Remember the Swooning Shadow?"

Laugh if you will, but we'd nearly died recovering a jar of

lindenberry jam that proved to be infested with the spirit of a dead Norseman. The jam was eight hundred years old but remained surprisingly delicious, according to its victims. The ones who hadn't gone stark raving mad, at least.

Several had attempted to dispose of the jam—by fire, iron, and one notable instance, a thousand-foot plunge from a cliff— but it kept reappearing in the larder to lie in wait for the next peckish victim. In the end (after a series of misadventures I won't relate here) we used tongs to put the jar in a sack and deliver it to the offices of the Society for Psychical Research on Pearl Street in Lower Manhattan, where it was safely deposited in the underground vault.

"Aye," John said in a painful Scottish accent. "The Swoonin' Shadow. Like a bad penny, that was."

"I wouldn't be surprised if other Montagues tried the same thing," I said. "But the connection is even stronger since it runs through a direct bloodline. If Duncan had simply thrown it away, I bet the Hand would reappear to tempt the next in line. Which would be Finn, despite his illegitimacy."

"What if he has the Hand already?"

"I suppose it's possible. Even that he hasn't used it yet."

"Black Tyke might have allowed him to have it since he's technically a Montague." John leaned back in his chair. "It's not at the Standing Stones. We know that much."

I stared at him. "Say that again."

"Er, we know that much?"

"No, the first part."

"It's not at the auld Standing Stones?"

He pronounced it as they did in the village. *Standing Stoons.*

"John," I said, suddenly electrified. "I might have it!"

He sat up straight. "Go on, Harry."

"Well, something always troubled me about Swan's death. Someone went to his house and demanded to know where it was hidden. Threatened him, no doubt. We assumed that he sent them to the Standing Stones because that's where the killer was digging when Professor Carlton was killed. Clearly, Swan *did* reveal new information."

"And they murdered him anyway."

"Yes. Nothing was found at the Stones—the attempt on our own lives at Caer Morvan Hall proves that. If the killer *had* found the Hand, they could have just quietly used it. Or hidden it away themselves until it all blew over. But they've grown ever more desperate."

"Sound logic," he said.

"Back to Mr. Swan. We then made another assumption: that he'd lied to his killer. But what if he didn't?" My heart beat faster. "What if he told them the truth, but they misheard because of his thick Scottish burr?"

"So the Hand is . . . ?"

"At Strone Point. The castle, John!"

His eyes gleamed. "It makes sense. The Hand of Glory might even feel at home there, what with the blood-soaked history of the place. If Duncan stored it carefully, the thing might stay put. For a while at least."

I nodded. "Another Scot wouldn't have made that mistake. But an American very well might."

His lips thinned. "One from California, perhaps?"

"Or a German," I added. "Neiderberger. Though my money's on Goodnight."

John regarded me gravely. "He has good reason to want that wish, Harry."

I remembered the look in Goodnight's eye when he said he'd give anything to see his daughter run outdoors in the sunshine.

"I know," I said. "But it still doesn't excuse murder."

John squinted. "Did we ever mention Strone Point to him?"

I thought back to the previous afternoon. Our time at Caer Morvan Hall was a bit blurry. I recalled the events that followed much more vividly. The rifle shot and being treed by the hound.

"No, you did," he said after a moment. "I'm sure of it. We talked to Miss McKenzie, and then his wife came in. There was that awkward bit where we all sat there staring at each other. We were discussing all the places the treasure might be. He changed the subject and ran off to look for Mr. McKenzie. But it could have sparked a new train of thought. There's no time to lose!"

"Are you sure you're up to this?" I asked dubiously. "You lost a fair amount of blood today."

"The castle's not far. I can make it."

I hesitated. "Maybe we should wait for one of the search parties to return."

"And what if we arrive too late? The only way to prove it now is to catch them in the act."

He was right, but I still didn't like it.

"John—"

"Be right back," he cried, heading for the stairs.

He reappeared a moment later with Louisa's "amulet" dangling from his hand. John hung it around his neck. "For good luck," he said.

We were donning our coats when Mrs. Davies appeared at the foot of the stairs, clutching Caesar to her breast. His face was even more scrunched than usual, jammed as it was against her powdered décolletage. The dog cast us a sheepish look, tail thumping against his mistress's arm.

"Where are you two off to?" she demanded. "Did they find that boy?"

"Not yet," I replied. "We thought we'd join the search."

"But your arm, Dr. Weston!"

"It's just a scratch," he said with a smile.

Her gaze narrowed. "You were shot. But go on. Leave me all alone here. A defenseless old woman."

"Where's Miss Neiderberger?" I asked with a sigh.

"Haven't a clue," she huffed. "She won't be getting a reference from me, I can tell you that!"

We shuffled towards the door. Then I had a thought.

"Do you still have your gun?" I asked Mrs. Davies.

"Right in here." She patted her handbag.

"Do you think we might have it?"

I expected her to refuse, but she promptly reached into her purse.

"Oh, you can certainly have it, Mrs. Weston," she said with a sinister smile, gripping the pearl handle.

Caesar's beady eyes fixed on us. His tail stopped wagging.

I tensed, but Mrs. Davies sailed over and pressed the gun into John's hand. "There you are, dear. Your wife said you're the better shot."

"Perhaps you should wait in your room," John said, stowing the gun in his pocket. "I'm sure someone will return soon."

"But who will it be?" she asked in a funereal tone. "Salvation? Or a ruthless, bloodthirsty—"

"We really must go!" I sang, closing the door in her face.

John flipped up his collar as we hurried along the road leading down to the loch and then southward to Urquhart Castle. A chill wind was blowing across the water, driving ragged streamers of cloud before it.

"Goodnight must have accomplices," John said. "The McKenzies?"

"Maybe. I'm still working that part out."

The possibility of more than one killer made a mess of everyone's alibis. No one except for John and myself was clear for every single murder.

"You're assuming it's a man, but maybe it's Mrs. Goodnight," Weston ventured. "She seemed thick with the nurse. They could be plotting together."

"I won't rule it out. But women simply don't have the same freedom of movement as men do. If she was seen prowling the village or moor, people would remark on it."

"She could have done it at night," John persisted. "They sleep in separate bedrooms."

"But he's the one who heard that the Hall was for sale. Who dragged the whole family to Scotland. Can you really picture Evangeline Goodnight digging holes at the Standing Stones and then bonking Professor Carlton on the head with a shovel?"

"Why not? You always say women can do anything that men can do."

"And better," I replied with a grin. "But somehow she doesn't seem the type."

"What is the type?"

"Neiderberger."

He scoffed. "Too obvious."

"So you're saying it was Evangeline and the nurse, eh?"

"They left Caer Morvan Hall not long before we were shot at on the moor. They could have laid in wait for us, if Mr. McKenzie was also an accomplice."

"Why would he help them?"

"Money."

"Enough to cover up all those deaths?" I sighed. "Well, greed has driven people to even worse things, I suppose. But I still say it's Jack Goodnight. Somehow, he must have found out about the Hand."

The faint lapping of waves came from the darkness. We'd reached Urquhart Bay. The loch sat on the left, with the castle ruins a short distance ahead. We regarded the jagged silhouette.

"So what's the plan?" John asked.

"We'll have to wing it."

"You say that every time, Harry."

"Do you have a better one?"

"Not really."

"I could be dead wrong. It's all just a theory."

In fact, it was a very slender thread on which to dangle the entire case. A single misheard syllable.

John took Mrs. Davies' gun out of his pocket. "Let's find out," he said.

CHAPTER 23

We crept silently toward the ruins. Urquhart Castle sat on a slab of rock above the loch, about six hundred feet long by two hundred wide, with the castle walls following this natural contour. The keep itself was roofless except for Grant Tower. It stood sentinel above a steep drop at the edge closest to Loch Ness.

The ruin was accessed by means of a modern walkway that crossed a deep, regular depression in the hillside that must have been a moat before the castle's destruction. Beneath were the remains of a stone bridge. I recalled what Ursilla said about the English soldiers blowing up the gatehouse on their way out.

We crept across the wooden walkway. Chunks of the outer curtain wall had collapsed, but the damage was at the top. The thick wall still stood, concealing whatever lay behind it.

John cocked the pistol. We passed through the old portcullis and turned a corner into an open bailey. The tower lay before us on a bluff overlooking the loch. Half was crumbling, the crenelations at the top broken off like rotten teeth. The other half stood about forty feet high. It was a bright moon that night, but the tower cast a long shadow across the grassy hilltop.

I saw no one. The arrow slits were dark. Yet something told me we weren't alone. The air felt heavy somehow. Thick and crackling.

John touched my arm and pointed.

A faint glimmer of light came from the area just below the castle on the loch side. It must have been part of the main keep once, though only the enclosing walls had survived. As we approached, I heard the scrape of someone digging in rocky earth.

The light grew brighter. I spotted the lantern first. It sat on the ground, partly shuttered and placed so it would be invisible from the road. A form hunched over a hole, the pick discarded at its side. Then the face angled our way and I saw it was Jack Goodnight.

We'd arrived just in time. He was struggling to lift a lacquered box about a foot long and half as wide. It resembled a tiny coffin and seemed heavy, for he dropped it with a grunt. We emerged from the darkness just as he threw the lid wide.

"Don't!" John cried.

Goodnight spun around. He held the Hand of Glory.

It was a singularly hideous object. The digits were long and shriveled, stiff yet curled slightly inward. Each had a dirt-crusted nail at the tip, but they were torn as though old Silas had clawed at the rope around his throat.

In the old days, if a crime was especially heinous, the hangman would sometimes use a short rope so the condemned man dangled there, slowly suffocating, instead of falling far enough to break his neck.

I remembered Godfrey's words: *I'm glad the girls were not made to watch.*

The back of the hand was brownish-gray, but between the creases of the fingers the pickled skin remained a stark white. It looked more like the burnt talons of a bird than anything that had once been part of a human being.

"Stay back!" Goodnight warned, brandishing the Hand of Glory.

John and I halted ten feet away.

"We know why you're doing this," I said. "To save your daughter. But you'll leave her an orphan, Mr. Goodnight. That thing is unspeakably tainted—"

"Don't pretend to understand," he spat, taking a step backwards. "You can't know what it's like to have a child who won't live to see the age of twenty! It's almost worse than if she'd died an infant."

"You can't know that for certain," John said firmly. "She seems to be doing well. I saw no signs of cancer—"

"Not yet." He gave a miserable laugh. "But that's only because we keep her hidden away. It's no life for anyone, let alone an intelligent, charming young girl."

"Surely you can find a compromise," I said. "There are other places besides Caer Morvan Hall."

Goodnight shook his head. The box lay at his feet. "No! I don't care if I die as long as Louisa has a chance to live the life she's meant to."

I felt John tense beside me. "I'm sorry," he said, raising the gun, "but we can't let you do this."

Goodnight cast him a look of pure anguish. "Then shoot me, Weston."

John swallowed. He tightened his grip on the gun. "Don't think I won't!"

But I could see the emotions warring in his face. My husband wasn't the sort to kill a man in cold blood. He was too kind-hearted. I wished now that I'd kept the gun, though I'm not sure what I would have done either.

"Please, sir, just put it down," John pleaded.

He started to lower the pistol, adjusting his aim to injure, when Goodnight moved faster than I thought possible. He snatched up a candle from the box and thrust it into the leathery palm. The fingers closed tight. He had no time to strike a match—but he didn't need to. A livid flame erupted from the wick.

My limbs instantly turned to lead. I gasped in shock. It felt like being immersed in an ice bath from the neck down.

John stood unmoving next to me, his arm extended, finger resting on the trigger.

"Shoot him," I hissed.

"I . . . I can't!" John spluttered.

My head was the only thing capable of movement and even that was stiff. One of John's legs was bent, frozen in mid-stride.

Half-remembered phrases whirled in my head.

. . . *lit candle . . . tallow from the corpse . . . renders immobile anyone who sees it . . . .*

In our preoccupation with the wish, we'd overlooked the essential property of *every* Hand of Glory.

Goodnight stared at us in evident surprise. Then he walked forward and tentatively reached out and poked John in the chest. My husband toppled like a felled tree. His head bounced against the rocky turf and he lay still. I studied him, frantic. It was impossible to tell if he was breathing, but I didn't see any blood.

Goodnight gave a startled laugh. Then he squeezed his eyes shut, lips moving silently.

I couldn't be sure with the leaping shadows cast by the candle, but it seemed to me that the Hand twitched, those ragged nails digging deeper into the mottled flesh.

"It's done," he murmured, echoing the fateful words of Godfrey Montague. "God help me, it's done."

"Just put it back in the box now," I begged. "We won't say anything, I swear it!"

Goodnight stared at me. "With all the blood on my hands? Come now, Mrs. Weston. We both know that's a lie."

"But you felt remorse after Swan, didn't you? The photograph . . . ."

Goodnight gave a reluctant nod. "His poor dead child was around Louisa's age. It tugged at my heartstrings. So I set the picture next to the body." He scowled. "It didn't occur to me anyone would notice that. But Swan was an accident! I didn't mean to . . . . He made me angry."

Jack Goodnight began to pace, the Hand of Glory still clenched in his fist. "Swan pretended he didn't know at first. I'd already looked everywhere. It wasn't at the Hall. So I finally confronted him. He babbled some words at me."

His gaze unfocused. "I don't know quite what came over me, Mrs. Weston. I seized the poker and . . . . " The hotelier exhaled an unsteady breath. "As he lay dying, he whispered it again. I thought he said the Hand was at the Standing Stones."

"Where Professor Carlton came across you the following night."

Goodnight shook his head with a mirthless chuckle. Something in his demeanor made me think he was relieved to confess it all to someone. And I was the perfect captive audience.

"Who'd imagine a fella'd be out roaming the moor with a butterfly net in the wee hours?" he asked me. "Carlton demanded to know what I was up to. I had no choice!"

"Your daughter saw you," I said. "Out on the heath. She thought the lights were pixies."

He looked stricken. "Louisa can't know. She can never know!"

John groaned. His eyelids fluttered. I felt a surge of relief.

Goodnight looked down. His face hardened. "I spared your lives once, but I can't afford to do it again. I'm sorry, terribly sorry—"

A faint growl from the darkness made his eyes widen. "What was that?"

"Blow out the candle," I hissed. "Please, Mr. Goodnight!"

Sweat erupted on my brow. Every instinct screamed at me to run, but I couldn't move a muscle.

I flashed back to the moor. The thing that had stalked us in the fog. That had prowled beneath the Scots Pine, snuffling at the drop of John's blood.

"It's here for the Hand," I gabbled. "Muckle Black—

"Shut up," Goodnight snapped.

His head cocked, listening. The shadows danced and swayed in the wind. He thrust the Hand of Glory out before him like some talisman, but I knew it couldn't save us now. Its power was used up. The wish expended.

And Jack Goodnight would be paying the price sooner than he imagined.

"You're not a Montague!" I whispered. "Dammit, you've made a terrible mistake—"

"I told you to be quiet." He backed away, glancing nervously over his shoulder.

"You can't just leave us here like this. For God's sake—"

My protests trailed off. From the blackness cast by Grant Tower, I heard a new sound.

The soft padding of paws.

CHAPTER 24

G oodnight propped the Hand of Glory against the tower wall. He pried the pistol from John's stiff fingers.

"If you think bullets will stop the hound, you're even crazier than I thought," I said. "It's spectral, you fool. And it wants the Hand of Glory back. Shooting at it will just make it angrier!"

Goodnight cocked the pistol. "I'll take my chances," he said bravely.

A strange calm had settled over him. I caught a glimpse of the iron-willed builder who'd carved a luxury resort from the California desert, steamrolling anyone who got in his way. The gun was steady in his hand, aimed over my left shoulder.

But this was a fight Jack Goodnight could only lose.

John and I were blameless, though the creature might not see it that way. Once its bloodlust was up . . . .

It made matters worse that the approach was coming from my rear. I twisted my head as far as it would go, skin prickling.

"Do you see anything?" I hissed.

"Not yet," Goodnight replied.

The wind ruffled his short brown hair. I wished it would

blow out the candle and release us, but the Hand of Glory seemed impervious. It crouched against the battlement like an evil toad.

"What's happening?" John demanded, suddenly alert.

"Hush," I whispered. "Pretend you're dead."

"I feel like I am. Can't move at all." His head craned up at me. "You look funny."

I'd been frozen with one hand stretched before me, the fingers spread into claws.

"Stop talking."

"Why?"

Goodnight shot us an exasperated look.

"Because—"

The gunshot was deafening. An instant later, a great dark shape sprang past me, bowling Goodnight over. He shrieked as slavering jaws snapped shut an inch from his face.

Black Tuck was even bigger than my feverish imaginings had pictured, closer to the size of a lion than a dog. Its coat was black as coal and rippled with lithe muscle. Its eyes looked like red lanterns. They burned with unearthly rage.

It pinned Goodnight's shoulders with its forepaws. He seemed beyond screaming. His mouth worked soundlessly as Tuck lifted its muzzle and howled. Then it burst into a frenzy of savage barks. I could almost feel the thing's hot breath. Frothing saliva splattered Goodnight's face, which had gone the color of ash. His eyes rolled up in his head and he fainted dead away.

Muckle Black Tuck lowered its massive head. I expected it to tear his throat out, but it just sniffed him.

"Down!" a woman's voice cried.

The hound gave a last snarl and backed away, sitting on its haunches and regarding us with a baleful eye.

Ursilla Brody strode into the light. She held an arm up, shielding her eyes from the candle that still gleamed against the tower. Her gaze settled on Jack Goodnight.

"You were right," she said to the hound. "It *was* him."

Black Tyke chuffed. It had a satisfied air.

"You control the hound?" I said in bafflement. "But how?"

Ursilla laughed softly, keeping her back to the paralyzing candle. "Control? I wouldn't go that far." She sighed. "I don't suppose we can keep it secret anymore. If only . . . ." She shook her head. "But he insisted on saving you both."

"*Saving* us?" John ventured.

The hound stood. The shadows surged forth to embrace that dark pelt. It melted away with very little fuss, revealing her son, Finn Brody, on hands and knees. His black hair was a bit tousled, his blue gaze guarded, but he was otherwise himself.

I should add that he was entirely in the nude.

Ursilla tossed him a bundle of clothes. Finn rose to his feet and pulled them on. He cleared his throat.

"I hope I didn't scare ye too badly," he said, cheeks flushing.

"Scare us?" I echoed. "You stalked us across the moor!"

"I was just tryin' to keep ye away from the Hall. I'd seen Goodnight in a few places he oughtn't have been. After the killings started, I grew suspicious."

"And what were *you* doing out there? We saw a pawprint by the Standing Stones." I glanced at the Hand of Glory. "Looking for *that*, I suppose."

Finn eyed it with disgust. "Lord, no. I did'na even know about it. I was lookin' for . . . ." He cast a quick look at his mother. "Something else. None o' your business."

"You don't want the wish?" I said, frowning. "Oh, and er, if you could blow that candle out, I'd be most grateful."

He stared at me. "What wish?"

"Nothing," Ursilla said quickly.

Finn turned to his mother. "What's she talkin' about, ma?"

Ursilla didn't reply, but her face was taut with apprehension. Clearly, she hadn't told her son all of it.

He pointed to the Hand. "That ugly thing grants a wish? Bloody hell, let me use it then—"

"No!" She burst out. "I won't allow it!"

"Why not?" Finn demanded.

"Because it's cursed." John's voice drifted up from the ground. "Trust me, whatever it is you want, it's not worth it."

"Ye don't know what it is I want," Finn said coldly.

Ursilla drew him some distance away. The pitch of their discussion said they were arguing, though I couldn't make it out.

"How's your head?" I whispered to John.

"Sore. Why am I the one who always gets bonked?" He stared up at the sky, one leg partly raised.

"At least you're relatively comfortable," I said. "I'm stuck like this!"

He eyed my beseeching hand. "You look like a statue. Stick a torch in your fingers and you could pass for Lady Liberty."

"It's strange that our heads can move but the rest feels like blocks of cement."

"Why do you think it doesn't affect Finn?"

"He's a Montague. And it didn't affect Goodnight because he was holding the Hand." I glanced at the prone form of the hotelier. "He confessed to me, though we didn't make it to the end before Finn came."

"I didn't see that one coming. With the hound, I mean. Did you?"

"Totally in the dark," I admitted.

"How does he do it?" John wondered. "Change like that? Finn's no werewolf. I've seen him polishing the silver. Plus it's only a quarter moon."

"He's something else," I agreed. "But we really ought to be thanking him. His intentions were good. I suppose he couldn't admit to the constable that he'd seen Goodnight creeping about the moor. Not when he was in hound form himself."

"No," John agreed. "That wouldn't go over well in a small village."

I frowned. "What do you think they'll do with us? Now that we know?"

"Hush," John said. "They're coming back!"

Finn looked furious. I braced myself but he stalked past us to the unconscious form of Jack Goodnight.

"You killed Jacob Swan," he growled. "And half the guests at the Duck." His fists balled. "I ought to do the same to you."

Ursilla hurried to her son and laid a hand on his shoulder. "We'll fetch the constable. He'll go to prison for the rest of his days. You're not a murderer and we both know it."

I let out a sigh of relief.

Finn shook his mother off. "There's a first for everything—"

He suddenly cried out in pain. A split second later, I heard the crack of a rifle. Finn swore through clenched teeth and sank to the ground. Red bloomed on his trouser leg.

Ursilla shielded him with her body, but there was no second shot.

I heard footsteps approaching.

"Who's there?" she screamed into the dark.

Her head twisted back and forth in a panic, but her body remained motionless. When she rushed to aid her son, she must have let her guard down and glanced at the candle.

Like John and me, Ursilla Brody had fallen under its spell.

But I knew who was here.

It was the person who had killed H.N. Gryffin.

Goodnight couldn't have pushed her from the cliff. We were with him all that morning.

Like the pebble that triggers the avalanche, the rest of it slid into place.

I thought of the cobra and who might have access to such an exotic creature.

The shooter on the moor.

The person who knew Arran well enough to talk the boy into taking mice from the traps.

Only one person in the village fit that particular profile.

"You," I hissed as they stepped into the light.

CHAPTER 25

D r. Gibson wore a rifle slung over one shoulder. His brow creased as he stared at Ursilla. "What are you doing here? You weren't supposed to be here."

"You shot my son," she said in disbelief. "How could you?"

"He'll live." Gibson sounded unconcerned. "I was a sniper in the Highland Regiment. I hit what I aim for."

"You missed me on the moor," John said angrily.

"True enough. I was aiming for your heart." Gibson chuckled. "But you were a lot farther away, Weston. Count yourself lucky it was a windy afternoon." He shot an annoyed look at Finn. "And that *he* showed up. I would've finished you both otherwise."

The candle still burned in the Hand of Glory, but it had no discernible effect on him. The doctor made no effort to shield his face. If anything, he seemed amused—and entirely unsurprised—by our plight.

I studied his features. Finn Brody resembled his father, Duncan Montague, but Dr. Gibson's flaming red hair and pitiless gray eyes belonged to old Silas. I was a fool for not seeing it before.

"You're a Montague," I said.

Finn swore. His face was tight with pain. "I'll kill ye for this," he grated. "Mark me—"

Gibson pointed the rifle at him and he fell silent.

"Duncan was my half brother," the doctor admitted. "His father bedded my mother when she worked as a chambermaid at the Hall. The old goat kept coming to her room even after I was born." Gibson's lip curled. "On those nights, he made me sleep on the floor at the foot of the bed. I grew up listening to him grunt and groan on top of her."

So Sir Preston was a monster, too. I felt a moment's pity for Gibson, despite all he'd done, but this was short-lived as the implications dawned.

"It was *you* who set the fire at the Hall."

His face went blank. It was horrible to behold. Like a mask had fallen—or rather, been discarded, and the real Dr. Gibson was revealed beneath. Still just a man, but with some essential piece missing.

"Thought I'd feel bad about it," he said slowly. "I played with Swan's daughter sometimes. Didn't mean for her to die. But it's funny, I felt nothing afterwards. Nothing at all. I realized I could do anything I wanted. Get away with anything."

"And no one suspected?"

"Aye, but they couldn't prove it. Only my mother knew the truth. She quit her post and moved us to Inverness when I was seven. The life of a bastard's not easy, but I was smart. Did well enough with my studies that I earned a scholarship to attend college and then medical school." He laughed. "When I returned to Drumnadrochit with a different name, no one had a clue who I was."

"You came back to finish your revenge," John said.

He swaggered over to John and crouched down. My gut tightened as he poked the bandaged arm.

"Hard as a plank you are!" he exclaimed. "But I guess you can still feel pain."

John glared and Gibson patted his cheek. "As to your question, that was my intention at first. To find a way to destroy Sir Preston's son." He turned to Ursilla, his features softening a fraction. "But then I saw you standing down by the loch, the sun on your hair. I was smitten."

She eyed him with revulsion. "How could you do this? Finn is your nephew!"

"Half nephew. And the boy will live." His gaze returned to John and me. The emptiness there chilled me. "As for you two—"

"You were very clever," I said. "Using Mr. Goodnight to do your dirty work."

Gibson nodded absently. His attention had shifted to the sinister object at the base of the tower. He strolled over and picked up the Hand of Glory, staring at it in wonder.

"When Duncan told me about this, I didn't believe him at first. But then he confessed the rest of it." His hungry gaze fixed on Ursilla. "He stole you away, but he never managed to win your heart." An unpleasant chuckle. "Duncan died a broken man if it's any consolation. I imagine the curse would have caught up with him eventually. I just hastened matters along."

"How did you rope Mr. Goodnight into it all?" I asked, hoping to keep him talking long enough that I could figure some way out of this.

"It took some searching. With Duncan gone, I needed just the right man to be the new master of Caer Morvan. Someone desperate enough to do as they were told and not ask too many questions. A colleague in the States had heard about Louisa's condition. I sent him a newspaper clipping about the Hall and suggested a new clime might do the trick. Goodnight took the bait. After that, it was easy enough to convince him to mount a search for the Hand."

"You couldn't do it yourself because the servants were still there."

"Aye. The McKenzies would have noticed me snooping about. I expected the Hand would be somewhere inside the Hall, so I made sure Goodnight bought it with all the furnishings intact. I already had Godfrey's diary proving that it existed, but there was no sign of the Hand itself."

"So H.N. Gryffin stole Godfrey's diary from *you*," I said.

His mouth twisted. "The woman got onto me somehow. She faked a bout of dizziness to get into my office. I examined her and told her she was fine. Then Finn turned up banging at my door with a nasty cut on his hand. The lad was leaking like a sieve."

I remembered seeing Finn that morning with a bandage. He'd said he got it slicing potatoes. I'd been suspicious at the time, but he was telling the truth.

"I was only gone a moment," Gibson continued, "but she must have rifled through my desk and taken Godfrey's diary. By the time I'd finished with Finn, she was gone. It wasn't until later that I realized the diary had vanished. It didn't take long to guess who'd nicked it."

"So you lured her up to Craigmonie."

He laughed. "That's the funny part. I didn't even have to. She sent *me* a note asking me to meet her on the crag."

"How much had she pieced together?" I asked.

"Most of it. The only thing she got wrong was the murderer. She'd followed up and confirmed that I was off delivering a baby boy the night Carlton was killed." He glanced down at Jack Goodnight, who was still out cold. "I hadn't planned it that way. Didn't even realize Jack had run into the professor at the Standing Stones. But it worked out quite well." He gave a wolfish grin. "A bit of serendipity, Mrs. Weston."

I scowled. "So you pushed H.N. over the edge?"

"After a bit o' chitchat. She thought it was young Finn

behind it all. Ye should have seen the look of surprise on her face. I was on my way down when that photographer showed up. Luckily, I glimpsed him on the path before he saw me. I hid and took a back path down to the village, then waited for the summons that she'd been found."

"You volunteered to stay behind at Craigmonie so you could search the body," John muttered.

He nodded approvingly, like a teacher with a prize pupil. "I thought I'd better get rid of the diary. Of course, turned out she didn't have it with her, but I didn't need it anymore. The diary only confirmed what Duncan told me. Otherwise, it was useless."

He raised the Hand of Glory, studying it from various angles. "What a wondrous thing this is," he murmured. "I could be King with this. I could open the gates of Hell or make a volcano erupt halfway around the world." His voice trembled slightly. "I could—"

"And the snake?" I said quickly. "I suppose your friend from the regiment brought it."

"Eh? That's right." Gibson blinked and gave another pleased nod. "I meant to kill Duncan once he told me where he'd hidden the Hand of Glory. Then I learned he was about to do something rash so I stepped up the timetable. It needed to look like natural causes. I considered various poisons. Then it came to me! Snakebite."

"But no adder native to Britain is poisonous enough to guarantee death."

That much I knew from a monograph on snake venom my sister had written.

"Precisely." Goodnight approached, leering in the candlelight. My bile rose as he lowered his face to mine.

"But I had an old friend from my army days," he whispered in my ear. "He stayed behind in India after the rest of us went home. I'd saved his life and he owed me. I asked him to bring me a viper." Laughter gusted. His breath had a nauseating meaty smell. "Said it was for medical research."

"An elaborate plot." I kept my voice calm. Something told me fear would only make him worse.

Gibson stepped back, clearly relishing my discomfort. "I'm a patient man, Mrs. Weston. Of course, the bite mark on Duncan's ankle was nasty, but since I was the one the constable called to determine cause of death, it was simple enough to cover it up and say he died of a heart attack."

"But Duncan hadn't told you where the Hand of Glory was."

"No." Gibson frowned. "I asked him to meet me at the end of the drive. It wasn't easy to lure him out, but I claimed to have found a remedy for the curse. That did the trick. The damned creature escaped its sack before I meant to loose it. That was my only mistake, but it was a bad one." A careless shrug. "If he'd lived long enough to reveal where it was, all those people would still be alive."

"Not your only mistake," I said, unable to keep the anger from my voice. "There *was* someone who might have incriminated you. The scullery boy at the Duck. You convinced him to bring you the mice to feed your snake."

A muscle in his jaw twitched. "Arran kept his mouth shut, but he would have let it slip to someone eventually."

"*You* gave me those traps!" Ursilla burst out. "I thought you were being kind. Oh, those poor little creatures."

She seemed more upset about the mice than the boy, but I chalked it up to shock.

Gibson regarded us. "The night you went up to the Hall, I was set to meet Goodnight on the moor anyway. He was nervous about all you'd discovered. I told him I'd take care of it." The doctor sighed. "I imagine he panicked when he heard you scream. Thought he'd better play the hero so you weren't suspicious."

He eyed the pick on the ground. I had a sudden flash of

Professor Carlton lying there with his head bashed in. "Well, that about wraps it all up."

"Not quite," I said desperately. "If you mean to dispose of us, you might as well tell us what your wish is. The one you were willing to murder for."

His gaze turned to Ursilla Brody. "I tried to court you," he said accusingly. "But you wouldn't have me."

She stared at him with naked hatred. "Because I sensed it in you, Martin. The selfishness and cruelty." Her lip curled. "You're no better than the rest of them."

"Worse in some ways," Finn added through clenched jaws. He started dragging himself toward the doctor. Gibson raised the Hand of Glory.

"Don't," he warned. "This can still get worse, boy."

"She'll never be what you want," Finn snapped. A lock of dark hair had tumbled across his forehead. His eyes held a savage gleam.

"Ah, but she will." Gibson gazed into the wavering candle flame. "With this, I can make her worship the ground I walk on. She'll be a proper wife to me until the end of our days. Devoted to my every whim. And you'll be my son." He gave a nasty smile. "I don't care what you are. In fact, it might come in handy. See, you'll be my slave, too. My own pet doggie."

Finn gave a snarl of inarticulate fury. Ursilla's face had gone dead. Empty of emotion. I could only imagine the life she was envisioning for both of them—herself most of all.

"When I'm done, you won't remember a thing. Only that I saved you both from Jack Goodnight after he killed the Westons." Gibson's gray eyes narrowed. "But give me any more trouble and ye'll have to join them in a shallow grave."

I wondered how I could ever have thought him kindly. His face had an avid, greedy expression as he clutched the Hand. In that moment, he was the spitting image of his distant ancestor,

Silas Montague. Gibson's eyes closed, lips moving to whisper his wish.

Ursilla gave a quiet sob. Finn sat in a pool of blood, but he started hauling himself forward again, fingers digging into the rocky earth. Shadows writhed around him. I suspected he was trying to change, but the pain of his injury was preventing it. He was still a dozen feet away. I knew he'd never stop Gibson in time.

I drew a deep breath and howled at the top of my lungs, doing my best impression of Muckle Black Tuck. It was all I could think of.

Gibson's eyes flew open. Anger flashed across his face.

"Martin?"

The noise had roused Jack Goodnight. His eyes looked bleary, but he pushed himself to sit. I watched a rapid calculus cross the doctor's face. He glanced again at the pick, wondering if he should dispose of Goodnight now. Then his head tilted as a new thought occurred.

"Jack!" he exclaimed. "I thought you were dead."

Goodnight looked around wildly. "It was here! It tried to kill me!"

"The hound?" Gibson cocked a brow. "Well, it's gone now," he said, offering his free hand.

Jack Goodnight took it. He noticed Finn and Ursilla with alarm. "When did they get here?"

"Everything's fine," Gibson said smoothly. "But I could use your help now. One last task and then it's all over, Jack. You can go back to your family."

Goodnight's face crumpled. "Four more?" he whispered brokenly. "I don't know, Martin."

"Not four. Just two. The Westons. They'll ruin us, Jack. There's no choice."

"What about the Brodys?"

"I'll take care of them." He gestured with the Hand of Glory. "This will make it right."

"He'll kill you, too, once it's done, ye stupid twat," Finn said, eying them both with fury.

"Shut up," Gibson snapped. He turned back to Goodnight. "We're partners. I've always played fair with you, haven't I? You got your wish, didn't you? Well, it's time to finish this."

Goodnight gave a reluctant nod.

"We can't shoot them," Gibson said in a reasonable tone. "I fired the rifle once and got away with it, but twice more? Someone might hear. Better it looks like they drowned in the loch."

My stomach sank. Had I been given the choice, I would have taken the rifle without hesitation.

"Doesn't matter if they can swim," Gibson continued. "In this condition, they'll sink like stones."

"Which one first?" Goodnight wondered.

"The husband. Just throw him over the side."

"Now, wait a minute," John protested, as Goodnight walked over and grabbed him under the arms.

"Please, Martin," Ursilla begged. "Don't do this. I'll marry ye! Do whatever ye say!"

"It's too late for that. I want to see it in your eyes when you look at me. The love you never gave to Duncan." He barked a laugh. "You despise me now and we both know it. But that'll change."

"Get your hands off him!" I shouted at the American, feeling the blood rush to my face.

"Don't worry, you'll be joining him next," Gibson assured me.

Goodnight dragged John over to a low, crumbling stone wall. I heard grunts of effort as he maneuvered him into position.

"By God, he's heavy," Goodnight wheezed. "It's like wrestling a log!"

"Just roll him over the side," Gibson called. "The woman'll be easier."

Goodnight nodded and gave my husband a shove with one boot. I watched him vanish into the dark and waited for a terrible splash.

In that moment, when all seemed lost, I recalled our idle conversation after visiting Gibson's house. The pledge to both die on the same day. How had it come to this? I'd failed miserably. In hindsight, the truth was obvious. But now it was too late—

"Dammit," Goodnight said after an agonizing minute. "He caught on a bush. Something's hooked around a branch."

I exhaled a shaky breath. The taste of salt on my tongue made me realize my cheeks were damp with tears.

"Climb down and knock him loose," Gibson said impatiently.

"I can't. The slope's too steep." He leaned farther over the edge.

The doctor unhooked the rifle from his shoulder and started to reload it. "We'll just have to risk a gunshot then—"

A sound pierced the darkness.

One I had once despised, but which now came as heavenly music to my ears. It was canine, though not the fearful baying of Muckle Black Tuck.

This was a high-pitched yapping.

An instant later, Caesar burst from the shadows of Grant Tower.

CHAPTER 26

The Pekingese had fire in his eyes. His ears streamed back in the wind, but the rest of him was stuffed into a red sweater with a festive holly pattern. It made a tinkling noise and I realized Miss Neiderberger had sewn bells on the garment.

Caesar ran forward with a brave growl and sank his teeth into Dr. Gibson's ankle.

The doctor let out a stream of curses, shaking his leg. Caesar was flung violently from side to side, but he had a firm hold on the trousers and refused to let go.

Gibson hopped closer. If he'd thrown the Hand of Glory away he could have dislodged the dog with ease, but he was unwilling to relinquish his prize.

"Get off me, you little devil!" Gibson shouted.

I saw a chance and started whipping my head around like a madwoman. The movement unbalanced my frozen limbs and I slowly descended on the doctor like a falling coatrack. I bounced off Gibson and hit the ground. He stumbled backwards with a shriek.

I saw with satisfaction that the candle had set his hair alight.

Gibson finally dropped the Hand of Glory and swatted at

the flames engulfing his head. With a cry, he flung himself over the stone wall. There was the crackle of a body tumbling through shrubbery, followed by a faint splash.

The grotesque talisman lay next to my cheek. I watched, heart pounding, as the apelike fingers unfurled. The candle slid from its grasp. It guttered, then went out.

As soon as the flame extinguished, the fetters of the spell dropped away. Life returned to my body in a rush. I pushed myself up and ran to the stone wall, pins and needles pricking my feet. It was too dark below to see anything.

"John!" I shouted. "Are you still down there?"

I will confess to you, Faithful Reader—though I never have to my husband or another soul—that if no answer had come, I might have gone back for the Hand of Glory and used the wish myself, curse be damned. Life without Weston was not worth living.

But this fateful choice never came to pass.

"Harry?" he called back.

I whispered a silent prayer of thanks. "What are you caught on?"

"A sort of twig. It looks flimsy . . . . Uh-oh."

I heard a loud crack.

"John! Speak to me!"

His voice drifted up. "It's all right! The twig snapped, but I grabbed hold of some roots. It's lovely to move again. Er, do you think someone might help me?"

I turned back to the tower. Ursilla had been liberated, as well. She was tying a makeshift tourniquet around her son's leg. Mrs. Davies stood next to them, heaping praises on the hero.

"*Who's* a good boy?" she trilled. "Is it *you*? Are *you* my good boy?"

Caesar barked and gave me a canine grin.

Jack Goodnight had been apprehended by Miss Neiderberger, who held him by the collar. Blood dripped from his nose. He struggled against her iron grip, but when he saw Uncle Arthur and Frank Thomas approaching with the constable, his shoulders slumped.

"I need some help over here," I called.

Arthur and his friend ran to my side. The clouds parted and we spotted John clinging to an outcrop not far below. Arthur pulled his jacket off and rolled his sleeves up. "Give me your coat, Frank."

Frank obliged. Arthur tied the sleeves of both coats together.

"Hang on to one end," he instructed Frank Thomas. "With the added length, I think I can reach him."

They formed a human chain, with Frank braced against the wall.

"I'm headed your way, Weston," Arthur called down calmly. "Just sit tight."

The slope was steep and treacherous. I could hear bits of earth and pebbles sliding beneath Arthur's feet.

Then something caught my eye in the dark water beyond. The pale form of Dr. Gibson paddling out from shore.

"Dammit, he's getting away," I muttered.

If he was a strong enough swimmer, he could probably reach the other side. Strone Point jutted out into the loch, narrowing the distance somewhat.

I was about to summon the constable when the water began to roil, perhaps thirty yards off Gibson's starboard side. The doctor hadn't noticed yet. I considered calling out to him, but then I thought of the poor scullery boy from the Duck. Of H.N. Gryffin and the Swans. Of Finn and Ursilla Brody. Even of Duncan Montague.

I held my tongue.

The doctor's strokes were more energetic now. He, too, believed he could make it.

I watched with interest as he drew farther from shore.

A triumphant shout came from below. Arthur had reached

John's outcrop. The men clasped hands and started the laborious return journey. Frank Thomas held fast to the coat sleeve with both hands, his gaze fixed on the two men below.

I turned back to the loch. The roiling had ceased. A line of wavelets was moving rapidly toward Gibson. The doctor must have finally seen them for he'd stopped swimming and seemed to be treading water.

There was a great deal of splashing and flailing about as he turned back the way he'd come. But the wavelets were on him now. His head vanished, popped up once, then vanished again.

And that was the very last I ever saw of Dr. Martin Gibson.

Then John was clambering over the wall, scratched and bruised but whole, and we were hugging each other tight.

"It saved me, Harry," he whispered in my ear.

"What did?" My words were muffled against his chest.

"Louisa's magic amulet. T'was the cord that caught on that twig."

I pulled back and stared at him. "It wasn't!"

"On my honor."

A tear ran down my cheek. I brushed it away, embarrassed. "We'd better get the Hand of Glory before it causes any more trouble."

John glanced over my shoulder. "Don't you have it?"

"Where would I have it, John? In a pocket?"

I followed his gaze, searching the knoll. A touch of ice ran down my spine.

"Oh no," I breathed. "No, no."

The Brodys were still sitting there, telling the story—or some version of it—to Constable Robb. He'd brought a rusty set of manacles, which were around Goodnight's wrists. Miss Neiderberger had drifted over to Frank Thomas, who seemed even more smitten with her.

Mrs. Davies was accounted for, too, but she was looking around with a frown.

"Where have you gotten off to, my darling boy?" she called. "Mummy is *not* in the mood for games!"

It all came clear.

"Caesar," I hissed.

"He can't have gone far," John said. "We'll find him."

As luck would have it, my husband was right. We fanned out through the ruins. Within a minute, I heard the soft tinkle of bells.

"Caesar," I coaxed, creeping into a shattered stone enclosure. "It's me. Your friend!"

The dog might have aided us, but that was *before* it discovered its smashing new toy. A pair of cunning eyes gleamed from the darkness. He held the Hand of Glory in his sharp little teeth.

"You can't keep that," I warned, inching closer.

The dog growled and shook it like a rat.

I dove for him. He leapt through my reaching arms, but John had come up just behind.

"Help me, Harry," he sputtered as Caesar wriggled desperately to escape.

"Drop it!" I snapped.

The dog ignored this command. I was forced to prise it from his jaws.

"Oh God, it's disgusting," I exclaimed. "Cold and slimy!"

"That's the saliva," John panted. "Should be dry as a bone since it's mummified."

I'm not prone to flights of fancy, but my skin crawled as I touched it. The Hand of Glory was pure evil, through and through. I ran with it back to the box and hurled it inside, slamming the lid shut. Caesar trotted over a moment later and sniffed the box. He cast me an accusing look and returned to his mistress.

"*There* you are!" she said happily, scooping him up.

I walked over to the constable. "Did you . . . . " I swallowed. "Did you find Arran?"

He shook his head gravely. "Not yet. Master Finn needs a doctor, but I was just told Gibson tried to murder you all." He looked around. "Where'd he go, anyway?"

"Swam into the loch," I said. "I saw him drown."

The constable's white brows lifted. "Saves me the trouble of tracking him down then."

"I'll have a look," John offered, bending down to examine Finn's gunshot wound.

With the men distracted, Goodnight took a furtive step backward. Mrs. Davies raised her own revolver and aimed it at his chest. She must have found it where John had dropped it.

"Do not test me, sir," she said in a steely voice.

He shot her a sour look.

"Sit down," she ordered.

Goodnight complied, resting his forearms on his knees.

"The bullet passed through the meat of the calf," John reported after a moment. "You'll need a cane for a few weeks, but barring infection you should recover well. You're fortunate it didn't shatter the bone."

Finn nodded weakly.

"Can you get him back to the Duck?" John asked Arthur and Frank Thomas.

The two men nodded. "Of course," Arthur replied. "And I can dress the wound."

I turned to Jack Goodnight. "Do you know where the boy is? I doubt anything will save you from the gibbet now, but you've done a number of very bad deeds. One last good one might serve you when you meet your God."

He paled.

"Arran is barely older than your own daughter," I pressed. "Please, Mr. Goodnight. At least his family will have a body to bury."

He licked his lips and gave a brief nod. "Gibson said the boy was locked up in the cellar of his house."

My heart beat faster. "Alive?"

"Maybe."

I looked at John. "We'll go straight there," I said.

Ursilla jumped to her feet. "I'm comin' with ye. It's my fault the boy was caught up in this." She looked down at her son. "Will ye be all right?"

"Go," Finn said, holding her gaze. "Bring Arran back to us."

I eyed the box containing the Hand of Glory. I didn't care to let it out of my sight, but when I tried to lift the box, I realized it must be lined with lead. My arms ached within seconds. I knew I'd never make it to Gibson's house. And John still had his own wound from being grazed on the moor.

"I'm giving it to Else Neiderberger," I said.

John frowned. "Do you have that much faith in her?"

I glanced at the sturdy Swiss woman. "Yes."

"Why?"

"Don't know. I just do." I beckoned her over before John could object. "Miss Neiderberger, we're entrusting you with a singularly dangerous object, if you're willing to accept it."

She eyed the box and drew a steadying breath. "I vill."

"Just get it back to the Duck. We'll take custody of it from there."

She tilted her head, blond braids gleaming in the moonlight. "Why me, if I might ask?"

"Because I think you're content with what you have." I glanced at Mrs. Davies. "Despite everything."

Her ruddy face broke into a smile. "Zat is true, Mrs. Weston."

I gave her a little salute. "Godspeed then, Miss Neiderberger."

"

John picked up Gibson's rifle. Ursilla joined us and we hurried down the track leading back to the village.

"It's not your fault," I said to Mrs. Brody. "It's all Gibson's."

She didn't reply. I could see she was sick with worry.

"Finn's secret is safe with us," John put in. "Your son is a good man. We've seen all sorts of odd things in my wife's line of work. I just want to set your mind at ease. We needn't ever mention it again."

I felt a surge of love for my husband. He said it in just the right way, matter of fact and without a trace of pity.

Ursilla cast him a grateful look. "Thank you, Dr. Weston."

"Oh, and Gibson was eaten by the loch beast," I added. "I saw it get him. So he won't be troubling you."

John's head slowly turned my way. "Harry?"

"Sucked him under like a trout gulping a fly."

"Did it, now?" Ursilla said with a faint smile.

"I'll tell you all about it later," I said to John. "After we find Arran."

He resisted the urge to interrogate me on the spot, though I could tell it wasn't easy. We went the rest of the way in silence, the boy's fate foremost on everyone's mind.

All the windows of Dr. Gibson's house were dark. We walked up the neat path. Ursilla Brody tried the knob. The door was locked.

Her eyes looked like black wells as she turned back to John. They burned with a strange intensity and I took a half step back, suddenly unsure.

"Kick it in," Mrs. Brody said.

CHAPTER 27

John slammed his boot heel into the door. It shuddered but held. He kicked it twice more and the door flew open. Gibson's parlor was dark and silent.

"Arran?" he called. "It's John Weston!"

No answer came.

We made our way through to the kitchen. It was black as pitch, but I smelled the remains of the doctor's supper. The same meat stew that lay rank on his breath as he whispered in my ear. Then a light bloomed. John held a lit candle.

Gibson had washed up after himself and everything was spick and span. I pictured him sitting at the table, napkin on his lap, tucking in while the poor child was below his feet . . . .

I squashed this train of thought. Mr. Goodnight didn't know for certain that Arran was dead.

"Over here," Ursilla called.

She'd located the door to the cellar. It was secured with a large padlock, the metal shiny and new. After rummaging through the drawers, I found a heavy wooden mallet of the sort used to tenderize meat. John moved to take it, but Ursilla laid a hand on his arm.

"You've done enough. Let me try."

John took one look at her face and stood aside without a word. Ursilla's jaw set as she delivered a series of mighty blows to the lock. I think she vented all her frustration and rage on that door. At the seventh strike, the hasp tore loose from the wood. She used the handle of the mallet to pry it the rest of the way off.

Not a single sound had come from the cellar. No cries for help.

"Perhaps you should wait up here," I said to Ursilla.

She understood my meaning, but shook her head. "I'll go with ye."

John opened the door. A flight of stairs led into darkness. A damp, unpleasant smell wafted up.

"Me first," he insisted, raising the candle and starting down the stairs.

My heart beat in my throat as I followed him. I whispered a prayer. The talisman had left a trail of death and ruin. Couldn't God see fit to spare its last victim? Just a child! Anger pricked me. The rest was terrible, but this . . . .

"Arran?" Ursilla called softly. "Ye down here?"

"Missus?" a hoarse voice replied. It sounded distant, like it came from the far side.

My throat tightened against a rush of emotion. John turned and gave me a look over his shoulder. My husband's eyes looked damp, too.

"It's all right, Arran," he said, hastening down the stairs. "We're here now. Gibson's gone—"

"Don't!" the boy called, a desperate edge in the words. "Stay up there!"

John halted halfway down. Ursilla and I pressed against him on the riser.

"What is it?" Ursilla asked. "What's he done?"

The light danced over an earthen floor. I saw the usual stores of dry goods. A woodworking table and a few tools, all covered with cobwebs. The various odds and ends you'd expect in a cellar.

And a row of empty glass cases. The lids had been left ajar.

"There's snakes, missus," came the barely audible response. "Three of 'em."

Poor Arran's voice was a rasp. I wondered how long he'd gone without water.

"Where are you?" I called, my feet suddenly tingling.

"On top o' some boxes. They left me alone so far, missus." His voice wavered. "But I'm scairt t' climb down."

"Stay where you are," John said, sliding the bolt of the rifle with a wince. "I'm coming down."

Ursilla moved to block his way. "No, don't kill them!" she cried. "They've done no wrong. It was a man who tried to use them for evil."

John looked dubious, but he lowered the rifle. "How will we catch them?"

"Milk," she said. "Just wait!"

She cast a stern look over her shoulder and ran back up the stairs to Dr. Gibson's kitchen.

"Are you hurt?" I called to Arran.

There was a long pause.

"No, missus. But I'd rather not talk. They might hear me and come over."

We took another step down and crouched so we could see through the risers. Arran was sitting atop a stack of crates on the other side of the cellar, knees drawn tight to his chest. He held perfectly still, eyes scanning the shadows.

The sadism required to leave a child alone in darkness with venomous snakes told me everything I needed to know about Dr. Gibson—if I hadn't grasped the man's character already.

I hoped the loch monster enjoyed some sport before devouring him.

Ursilla returned a moment later with a bowl in her hands. She pushed past us and ventured to the bottom of the stairs. She looked around, then set the milk on the floor. Mrs. Brody made a rasping sound low in her throat. Like a cough but not quite.

A bright green snake slithered from a crevice between two sacks. It wiggled around her foot. Ursilla paid it no mind. She crossed the cellar in six swift strides. The boy watched her with wide eyes, still frozen in place. When she reached the stack of crates, she held her arms out.

"Come on, then," she said to Arran in a calm, no-nonsense tone.

It did the trick. He reached for her and Ursilla set him on her hip. The boy wrapped his legs around her waist, staring fearfully at the earthen floor.

By the time she returned, two more snakes were investigating the bowl of milk. One was a krait, brown with white stripes. The second was a Russell's viper, sand-colored with darker oval spots. The bright green one was an Eastern mamba. All could kill with a single bite, but they displayed no hostility as she stepped past them and carried the boy from the cellar. Arran hugged her tight, face buried in her shoulder.

"There we are," she murmured. "Let's get you home now."

The boy nodded bravely. I think he was too shocked to cry.

"What about the snakes?" John asked.

Ursilla tried to set Arran down. His legs clung tighter.

"Table, please, missus," he whispered.

She kissed his grimy cheek. "Of course. I'll be back in a titch."

Arran reluctantly let go and sat cross-legged on the table. I watched from the top of the stairs as she descended into the cellar.

"That's enough now," Ursilla said firmly, bending down to the bowl.

My breath hitched as she scooped each snake up in turn and deposited it back in a glass terrarium. She shut the lids.

"Milk's no good for them anyway," she explained, returning to the kitchen. "They like it, but it makes them sick."

Arran nodded in amazement. If he'd been grateful before, the boy worshipped her now.

"Aren't you feared of 'em, missus?"

"Well, now, of course one must be careful. But they're gentle creatures at heart. They didn't harm you, did they?" Her brows lowered. "Gibson was cruel to keep them like that. What do you say we find a zoo that takes reptiles? Give them a better home?"

For some reason, her casual attitude toward the snakes seemed to hasten his recovery. Arran nodded. Color was returning to his face.

"As long as I don't never set eyes on 'em again," he managed.

She smiled. "That's a good boy."

"The doctor said he was settin' the mice free. Gave me a farthing apiece for 'em. He made me swear not to tell, but I wondered." His face crumpled. "I'm sorry, missus!"

"You couldn't have known, Arran," Ursilla said gently. "Come on, your parents are worried to death." She turned to me and John. "The snakes'll be all right down there for now. I'll bring 'em to the inn later and decide what to do with 'em."

"The inn?" I echoed faintly.

"They're from the tropics. We can't let the poor things freeze outside, can we, Mrs. Weston?"

"I suppose not. But—"

She scooped Arran up and departed Dr. Gibson's house, leaving us to catch up with them. The boy's cottage wasn't far. Light streamed from the windows despite the late hour. John and I waited down the lane as Ursilla knocked at the door.

I wasn't eager to share our lodgings with three of the deadliest serpents on earth, but the sight of Arran's mother weeping and clutching the child to her breast lifted my spirits. His brothers and sisters crowded behind, smiles on their faces. The father, I gathered, was still out looking for him.

"Do you think he'll be all right?" I asked John.

The boy had finally dissolved into tears under the onslaught of hugs and kisses.

"By morning, he'll be telling the whole story. And the more times he tells it, the less power it will have. Loving care will set him straight. Look at them." John eyed the large family fondly. He had three brothers.

I swallowed. "We never really discussed it. . . . and I suppose this isn't the time. But . . . how many children do you expect, John?"

He looked at me in surprise. "Expect?"

"Yes."

"Well, that's for us both to decide."

I sighed. "Good. Because I'm rather a small person and the thought . . ."

He put his good arm around my shoulders. "Harry, I married you because I'm hopelessly in love with you. If you give me ten or one or none, nothing will ever change between us. Like Miss Neiderberger, I am content."

I laid my head on his shoulder, warmth filling me. "Ten?"

"That was hyperbole. Didn't you go to school? It's a rhetorical device—"

I poked him. "One sounds all right. Maybe two." I frowned. "If the first one isn't like Myrtle."

"What if the second one's like Rupert?"

Rupert was his incorrigible younger brother.

"Then we're doomed," I laughed.

The door to Arran's cottage closed. Mrs. Brody returned. She was smiling, too, but it had that melancholy edge that never seemed to go away.

"I need to see to my own boy," she said. "Well, I suppose he's a man now." Ursilla cast us a wary glance. "Ye won't tell?"

"We swear it," John replied. "But if I may ask one thing. Did he . . . inherit this from his father?"

She laughed in genuine amusement. "Nae. Nor from me, Dr. Weston. It's Finn's alone. The ability came to him not long ago when he turned eighteen." Her face closed. "But I canna tell ye any more about it. Only that my son never harmed a living soul."

"We believe you," I said.

An idea was forming in my mind, still nebulous, and I was too tired to examine it closely. We returned to the Drunken Duck and shared the happy news. Arthur was dressing Finn's leg in the kitchen. John went to assist. I took a peek through the door. Cassie was fussing over Finn, while the Cook boiled water and cut up clean linens. Adding Ursilla Brody, the kitchen was already crowded and I saw nothing that needed doing, so I returned to the common room.

Miss Neiderberger sat with the lacquered box at her feet, gazing pensively into the hearth. Frank Thomas stood behind her, one arm resting on the back of her chair.

Mrs. Davies occupied her customary place, Caesar dozing in his basket.

"I took a peek at the Hand of Glory," she admitted, as I sank into a chair across from them. "Ghoulish thing."

"You didn't touch it, I hope?"

Mrs. Davies shuddered. "Lord, no."

"She tried," Miss Neiderberger reported sternly. "I vould not allow it."

Some axis of power had shifted between the two women, for Mrs. Davies failed to utter a word of reprimand. Instead, she looked a little sheepish.

"I merely hoped to examine it," she protested. "They're so very rare."

I stared at her. "You wanted to bring Algie back, didn't you?"

Mrs. Davies flushed through her white powder. "What? The thought never crossed my—"

"Listen to me closely." I leaned forward. "Whatever walked through that door, it would not be your husband, do you understand?"

She stared at the ancient oaken door, now firmly bolted from the inside. It was a blustery night. The wind howled against the eaves and rattled the mullioned windows. Her face held both longing and fear. At last the old woman nodded, more chastened than I'd ever seen her.

"Yes, Mrs. Weston," she said quietly. "I do understand."

"Good." I gave her a warm smile, all too aware of my own hypocrisy. "Now how did Caesar find us?"

Mrs. Davies brightened. She sipped her brandy. "Well, after you left, my clever boy was fit to be tied. He stood at the door, barking and barking. I tried to soothe him, but he wasn't having it. Then one of the search parties returned. Constable Robb, Mr. Doyle, Miss Neiderberger and our dear Mr. Thomas."

She gave the Welshman a smile, which he returned with a look of pleased surprise.

"When the door opened, Caesar darted out into the night!" Mrs. Davies drew a breath, briefly closing her eyes. "Oh, how I feared for him! I knew right away that he rushed headlong toward danger. The Pekingese is a noble breed, as I told you when we met. I insisted that we all go out to find him. Happily, Miss Neiderberger had taken the precaution of sewing bells to his Christmas tunic. I have very acute hearing, don't I, Ilsa?"

Miss Neiderberger nodded.

"I directed the others toward the castle," Mrs. Davies said. "Where my dear boy had already brought that villainous doctor to heel."

I crouched down to Caesar's basket. He opened one eye.

"You were very brave," I said. "And you came in the nick of time."

I reached out to pat his head. The Pekingese growled. He hadn't quite forgiven me for stealing his prize.

"Right," I said, quickly withdrawing my hand. "Fierce warriors don't like that sort of thing."

"You may rub his belly," Miss Neiderberger advised. "Zat is usually acceptable."

I chanced a quick tickle of his nether region, which was still covered with burrs. Caesar kicked a leg and went back to sleep.

"How did the Brodys end up there?" Mrs. Davies asked, glancing at the kitchen. "Were they truly not a part of it all?"

"Both perfectly innocent," I replied. "They saw a light and went to investigate."

Mrs. Davies frowned. "But it wasn't visible until we reached the castle—"

"Where's Jack Goodnight?" I interrupted before she could pursue this line of inquiry.

"Locked up in the constable's pantry," Frank Thomas said. "They don't have a jail. But he'll be sent up to Inverness tomorrow."

"So they were partners in crime," Mrs. Davies mused, replenishing her brandy. "An odd pair, if I do say so. But I'm not surprised. I suspected them from the very start. It was the eyes. *Shifty.*" She banged her cane on the floor, causing Caesar to break wind in his sleep. "One must always watch the eyes. They reveal all, don't you think so, Mr. Thomas?"

The Welshman made a noise of agreement. He seemed to be struggling hard not to laugh.

Mrs. Davies carried on for a while, but my own thoughts turned to Louisa and Evangeline. I didn't envy the constable the task of giving them the news. Yet I did wonder.

Had Jack Goodnight's wish worked? Or were Montagues the only ones who could wield that particular power?

My companions fell into quiet conversation. I must have

dozed off in the chair for the fire had burned low when John's hand fell on my shoulder. Lines of exhaustion creased his face.

"We patched Finn up," he said. "He's sleeping now. And if I don't find my own bed soon, you'll be scraping me off the carpet."

I smiled and covered a yawn.

"What shall I do vith this?" Miss Neiderberger wondered, eyeing the lacquered box at her feet.

"Do you think you might carry it up to our room?" John asked. "I'm not sure I can manage."

She stood and hefted the lead-lined box like it was a tin of cookies. "Yes, sir."

Frank Thomas sprawled at a nearby table. He shot to his feet.

"Miss Neiderberger, I hope you don't think it too forward of me, but you are . . . ." He exhaled slowly. "A magnificent creature."

The Swiss woman's cheeks pinked.

"Oh my," Mrs. Davies chortled. "Algie used to say the same to me." She pressed her cane to the floor and struggled to rise. Frank hurried to assist her.

"Where do you live, Mr. Thomas?" she asked as he helped her walk to the stairs.

"Swansea," he replied.

"Well, you must come to London and pay us a visit."

He cocked a thick brow at Miss Neiderberger, who lowered her head to cover a grin. "I'd like that very much, Mrs. Davies."

We followed them up the stairs. The Hand of Glory was stowed inside a sturdy chest with blankets on top. I hoped it had caused enough mischief for one night and would stay put.

John and I barely managed to undress before we toppled onto our own feather mattress. I fell directly into a deep sleep.

I DREAMT OF CAER MORVAN HALL.

There was a gay party going on with men in black tails and women in sparkling jewels whirling in pairs through the ballroom. Christmas wreaths bedecked the balconies. I didn't like the sound of their loud laughter. I decided to go out to the lawn for some air, but when I opened one of the French doors to the patio and stepped through, I stood in the East Wing.

The smell of charred wood was quite fresh. The music had gone silent. I walked along the main passage and paused at the foot of the stairs, peering towards the old billiards room. It sat empty of furniture as before, but the painting of Silas Montague was no longer wrapped in a sheet.

It hung on the fire-blackened wall.

I did not want to enter that room so I started up the staircase instead. The risers creaked under my bare feet. Where I'd left my shoes, I had no clue. When I reached the top, a long corridor stretched in both directions. It seemed to go on forever, door after door. One would surely lead back to the party so I started trying the knobs, but every single one was locked tight.

It was one of those dreams that's more irritating than scary. I felt no sense of impending doom. Smoke did not fill the hallway. Yet I worried that John would be looking for me and I wanted very much to get back.

Then one of the knobs turned. I stood in the nursery.

It should have been the old one since I was in the East Wing, but it looked like Louisa's. The miniature manor with tiny people. Boxes of frilly costumes. Only the murals on the walls were different. Instead of Alice and Puss in Boots, I saw fishermen and water horses. Black hounds and pixies. A wizard dueling with a knight, wand against sword. The knight's helm was lowered, but I knew it was my husband.

"Cross my palm with silver, Mrs. Weston, and I shall reveal the shocking truths you seek."

I spun around. The photographer, Cormac Ferguson, sat at

Louisa's low table, sipping daintily from an empty teacup. Landscape pictures of the loch were spread across the table. He grinned at me.

"How do I get back to the party?" I asked, cheeks burning as I realized I was wearing a thin nightdress.

He held a hand out and waited expectantly. It had a webbing of extra skin between the thumb and forefinger like Finn Brody.

I fumbled for a coin, but I had no pockets. Ferguson looked disappointed.

"Which door goes back?" I asked again. "Please tell me."

He started rummaging through the photographs, knocking them to the floor. The pile seemed endless.

"Where is it?" he muttered. "You're late, you're late. For a very important date!"

When he looked up again, he had long white whiskers sprouting from his cheeks. I took a step back.

Cormac Ferguson thrust a book at me.

"It's all in here," he said. "But don't waste time, Alice! The hurrier you go, the behinder you get."

It was *Legends of the Sea Folk*.

I grabbed the book and ran to the door. Threw it wide and—

Sat up in bed with a gasp.

The dream didn't fade as some do. Every detail remained vivid in my mind. As motes of dust danced in the morning sunlight streaming through the window, the last bits of the mystery locked together. Mad as it seemed, they all fit.

But why had my unconscious mind cast Conrad Ferguson in the role of the White Rabbit?

"Oh!" I whispered, as John stirred to wakefulness beside me. "Could it be?"

CHAPTER 28

I told John my theory.

Together, we worked through it, filling in the blanks. Neither of us could find a flaw in the reasoning.

"We must tell her," he said at last, wonder in his voice.

"Right away," I agreed. "I hope we're right."

We hurriedly dressed and went downstairs to the empty common room. The Cook said Mrs. Davies had taken Caesar for a walk with Frank Thomas and Miss Neiderberger. Arthur was shut up writing in his room.

"Do ye want breakfast?" she asked.

The ginger cat strolled through, tail hooked in a question mark. It looked disappointed that its foe was nowhere to be found.

"Later, thank you," I said. "Where is Mrs. Brody?"

The Cook directed us to the yard, where we found Ursilla feeding the ducks next to their little watering hole. She smiled as we approached.

"Good morning," she said. "How's the arm, Dr. Weston?"

"Improving," he said, returning her smile. "And Finn?"

"In some pain, but Cassie brought him beef broth and he

seemed cheered to see her. Will ye be leaving soon?"

I glanced at John. "We'll stay for a few days more," he said. "I'd like to keep an eye on your son's wound. And we thought we might try for a proper honeymoon."

Ursilla looked glad. "You're welcome to. None of the rooms are booked at the moment."

It hadn't occurred to me before, but Drumandrochit's new reputation as the site of several murders wouldn't be very good for business.

"Mrs. Brody," I said, choosing my words carefully. "I remember Finn saying that he was looking for something else on the moor."

Her face went taut.

"Also that it was none of our business," John added quickly. "And we wouldn't bring it up except that my wife might have an idea of where it is."

Ursilla frowned. "I . . . Ye . . ." She swallowed. "Ye do?" she asked faintly.

"I think I might have seen it, though I didn't realize what it was at the time," I said. "Will you come with us?"

Mrs. Brody blinked. "Aye," she muttered. "I suppose so."

We fell into step together. Presently, the thatched roof of Kinlach Cottage came into view.

"That old place?" she said, drawing up short with a look of disappointment. "We already looked there."

"After you bought it," I said.

Ursilla nodded.

"When Duncan Montague was still alive."

She frowned. "Aye."

"But Cassie is the one who cleaned when Mr. Ferguson came two months ago. And she doesn't know, does she?"

Ursilla's wary face was answer enough.

"Gibson said Duncan Montague was about to do something rash and that's why he killed him. At the time, I thought he meant Duncan would try to destroy the Hand of Glory. But now I believe it was something else. Duncan intended to return the item he stole from you. Gibson couldn't allow that."

Her gaze unfocused. "Ye mean Duncan hid it here at some point *after* I bought the cottage?"

"It used to belong to his estate. No one was living there. What better place?"

I took her arm and steered her toward the cottage. John rapped at the door. Conrad Ferguson greeted us in shirtsleeves. "Oh, hello," he said. "I was just packing up my things. Heading back to Glasgow tomorrow."

"May we come in?" I asked.

"Of course." Ferguson stepped aside, searching our faces. "I heard what happened from Cassie. Glad you caught them." His expression hardened. "I hope they go straight to Hell."

He brought us into the kitchen and gestured to a parcel wrapped in brown paper and tied off with twine. "I suppose you're here for the photographs. I planned to bring them over to the Duck this morning."

"Er, yes," I said, having clean forgotten about the pictures we'd bought from him. "Thank you. But I was wondering, have you dismantled the darkroom yet?"

"I was just about to. Why?"

I looked down the narrow hall, which was crammed with equipment boxes.

"I'd like to show Mrs. Brody something. We won't touch any of your belongings."

"Go ahead. My negative plates are already packed." He glanced at Mrs. Brody. "It's yer cottage anyhow." Ferguson returned to his sorting.

My pulse quickened as we walked to the darkroom. It was just as I recalled, with the large sea chest and heavy coverings across the windows. All were quilts save for one of a lustrous, dark brown hue.

Ursilla's eyes fixed on it immediately. She stood stock still, then rushed forward. The innkeeper tore it loose with trembling hands and pressed it to her breast.

"My skin," she breathed. Her dark eyes turned to us, brimming with tears. "Twenty years." Her voice broke and she steadied herself with a deep breath. "Twenty years I've searched." A tremulous smile broke over her lovely face. "You cannae know . . . ."

"That was Duncan's wish, wasn't it?' I said gently. "To have a selkie bride."

Bitterness touched her eyes. "He captured me sunning myself ashore at Eynhallow. Lured me with tender words and then hid my skin so I couldnae return to my natural form."

"Did you ever love him?" John wondered.

"Once. But nae for a very long time, Dr. Weston." She stroked the sealskin in her arms. "He gave me Finn. For that I'm grateful. And in fairness, Duncan wasn't quite as cruel as the rest o' his kin. After he brought me back to Caer Morvan, he could see I was miserable. He refused to return the skin, but he let me leave the Hall. Gave me the inn."

"The children of selkies and mortals are very special," I said.

She gave a wry smile. "Finn isn't one nor the other. Just himself. He can assume many forms. All night creatures."

I thought of the tawny owl that had swooped over our heads at the Standing Stones and again at Craigmonie.

"But he chose Muckle Black Tuck to frighten Duncan," I said.

She nodded. "When Finn came of age and learned to change, I had no choice but to explain all of it. He was furious at what his father had done. He bent all his energy to getting my skin back. Shadowing Duncan wherever he went. Trying to scare him into revealing the hiding place.

"That was all not long before Duncan died. Finn swore he was nowhere near him when it happened, but when I heard about the heart attack I feared . . . ." Ursilla squared her shoulders. "But it wasn't him after all. It was Gibson killed Duncan. So ye see, I spoke the truth when I said my son's never harmed a soul."

"Do the McKenzies know?" John asked.

"Only Mr. Swan." Grief lined her face. "Such a kind soul he was. He tried to help me as best he could, but Duncan never told him where the skin was hidden." She pondered this for a moment. "I suppose he kept the Hand of Glory secret to spare Finn a terrible choice."

Ursilla rolled the skin into a ball. Despite the years locked away in the sea chest, it was fresh and glossy like a living animal.

"What will you do now?" I asked her.

"I must talk to my son. Make arrangements." She gazed at me. The melancholy was gone and her eyes shone bright and clear. "The Drunken Duck is Finn's now. I expect Cassie'll be glad to help him run it. They're sweet on each other if you haven't noticed."

"One would have to be blind not to," John said with a smile.

Ursilla chuckled. "She knows all about *him*. Just not about me. And I . . . ." Her chest rose with a deep breath. "I'll be heading home. My kin'll be mighty glad to see me again."

We returned to the kitchen, where Conrad Ferguson was busy packing boxes.

"Did ye find what ye wanted?" he asked, dusting his hands off.

"I did," Ursilla replied with a small grin.

"Care for a souvenir, Mrs. Brody? Ye treated me well. I'd be happy to make you a present."

She regarded the photographs spread across the table for a long moment. "No, thank you. In all honesty, I think I'd rather forget."

He gave a puzzled laugh. "Somethin' I did?"

"Not you." She patted his arm. "Ye were a lovely guest, Mr. Ferguson. Good luck in Glasgow."

He shrugged and waved goodbye to us. John tucked the paper-wrapped parcel under his good arm and we stepped into the sunshine.

"Ye kept my son's secret," Ursilla said as we walked back to the Duck. "So I won't ask if ye'll keep mine." She winked. "But if you're ever up in Orkneys, call my name and I might just say hello."

"LET'S GO ON A PICNIC," JOHN SUGGESTED.

It was the following afternoon. We'd been very lazy all morning, eating breakfast in bed and then lolling about in our nightclothes.

"I'd love to," I replied. "But where?"

John dragged a razor down his soap-lathered cheek. "Hmmm. The Standing Stones are out."

"So's Craigmonie."

"And Urquhart castle, obviously." He rinsed the blade in a bowl of water and examined himself critically in the mirror.

"That sums up the local tourist attractions," I said.

"Not all of them. How about the loch?"

I tugged a dress over my head. "Will we stay on dry land?"

He smiled. "I was thinking of Temple Pier."

"Sounds safe enough."

When we arrived downstairs, we were greeted with a great deal of banging and grumbling from the kitchen. I stuck my head through the door. The Cook was vigorously slapping a mound of dough. Her brows were drawn down in displeasure.

"Hello," I said. "Is everything all right?"

"All right?" She chewed the words like a tough piece of jerky. "Well, Mrs. Brody's had some family emergency and gone back to the Orkneys. She left me with them!" The Cook picked up a rolling pin and stabbed it at the pantry.

I walked over and took a look. Three glass terrariums were stacked next to a sack of sugar. The cat sat on a crate of empty milk bottles, staring fixedly at the lethargic snakes coiled within.

"She said it's the warmest place for 'em." Cook brandished the rolling pin like a scepter. "Five more days 'til the zoo people come, Master Finn says. I told him I won't go in there. If he wants something, he can get it himself."

The lids looked securely shut, but I didn't blame her.

"If yer hungry, I can make sandwiches," she said in a gentler tone.

"Sandwiches would be perfect. We were thinking of a picnic."

She nodded briskly. "I'll pack a hamper, missus."

"Snakes," I reported to John, who stood warming himself by the fire. "In the pantry."

He laughed. "Maybe we should put the Hand of Glory in there, too."

"That's not a bad idea. I don't much care for keeping it in our room, but it shouldn't be left sitting around."

I went back to our room and fetched the lead-lined box from its chest, opening it briefly to ensure the Hand of Glory still nestled inside. The mummified digits were ugly as ever, but it mainly struck me as pathetic. The Hand's power had waned. Perhaps because the last wish it had granted was a selfless one. Or perhaps because it held no temptation for me whatsoever. But somehow its power had waned and I no longer feared the talisman. I shut the lid and carried it downstairs.

"What's that?" the Cook asked as I lugged it into the kitchen. "Not another snake, I hope."

"Just . . . their carrying case," I puffed, dropping it next to the sugar.

The cat took one look at the box and arched its back. With a hiss, it streaked out of the pantry. The Cook frowned and returned to slicing bread.

I'd stuck Godfrey Montague's diary under one arm and showed it to John when I returned to the common room.

"I think we should burn this," I said.

"It's a historical artifact," he pointed out.

"Yes, but it also has instructions to make another Hand of Glory."

He nodded. "Do it then."

I drew a breath and tossed the diary into the flames. We watched the pages turn brown and curl to ash.

"They're all gone now," I said softly.

"All but Finn," John replied.

"He's not like the others."

"No, he's not."

"I wonder who Montague left his fortune to?"

"The will is sealed." John shrugged. "I suppose we'll never know."

I collected our basket of sandwiches and we strolled arm-in-arm down to the shore. John spread a blanket on the pier. I started to unpack the basket when a dark figure appeared across Urquhart Bay.

"Is that Mrs. Brody?" I murmured, shading my eyes against the sun.

"I think so," John replied. He gripped my arm. "Is she . . . ."

"Shedding her clothes? Yes." I hesitated. "We really oughtn't look, John."

"You're right," he said, still staring.

I clapped a hand over his eyes, squeezing mine shut.

"It's not the nudity, I hope you realize that," he grumbled.

"Don't be silly. You want to see her turn into a seal, but I won't allow it. She's been treated abominably by people already."

"No, you're right." He paused. "Can we watch her swim away though?"

I cracked an eye. Ursilla was gone. "I suppose so," I said, releasing him.

A breeze whipped the surface to a chop. We scanned the wavelets. I heard John's breath catch.

A small dark shape surfaced off the shore. It dove, then surfaced again, rolling playfully onto its back.

"The River Ness feeds into the Mornay Firth," John whispered, though I knew she couldn't possibly hear us.

"And from there?"

"The North Sea. I looked it up in a book of maps."

The seal frolicked gaily for a minute, wending its way along the shoreline.

"Harry!"

The fear in my husband's voice alerted me before he pointed.

Some way up the loch, the water was frothing. A line of ripples headed directly for the selkie.

"No," I croaked, the image of Dr. Gibson's last gasping breath still fresh in my mind. "No, no."

I was about to scream a warning when the seal saw the beast. She submerged.

John and I joined hands, hardly breathing. The line of wavelets subsided.

The beast had dived deeper in pursuit.

"Swim," I muttered in an agony of fear. "Swim!"

A long minute elapsed. Then a gout of water erupted, shooting high into the air. The seal broke the surface again.

She was not alone.

Galloping alongside her was a magnificent steed, sable coat gleaming in the sun. It raised its head and shook water from its mane. Then it gave a joyful whinny and sank beneath the waves.

"I think she found an escort," John said with a shaky laugh.

We sat in quiet awe as the pair raced north up the loch, the horse rising and diving to either side of the seal. When they finally disappeared into the distance, I looked over. John was brushing crumbs from his mouth.

I glanced at the picnic basket. "Where are the sandwiches?"

"Eh?" He was still staring mistily toward Inverness.

"Is that all you left me?"

A solitary sandwich remained in the basket.

"Oh!" My husband gave a guilty start. "Did I?"

I frowned. "Yes, you did."

"The excitement made me hungry. Didn't really taste it though."

I took a bite of sandwich. "We can't tell anyone what we just saw," I mumbled through a mouthful of bacon. "You do realize that."

John sighed. "I know."

"Miss Neiderberger was right. The loch beast is a kelpie."

John lay back on the blanket, lacing his hands behind his head. "They're freshwater spirits. It'll probably come back once it sees her safe to Mornay Firth."

I swallowed the last morsel and looked regretfully at the empty basket. "The final mystery solved."

"And we can't tell anyone."

"Ever," I agreed.

"Not even Arthur?"

I bit my lip. "We promised, John."

We never did tell a soul, Faithful Reader. Not even many, many years later when our children had children, and I had assumed Mr. Kaylock's place as a Vice President of the S.P.R., and John bought a motor car to drive to his surgery uptown—and a single blurry photograph would introduce the whole world to the mysterious creature that became known as Nessie.

But I get ahead of myself, as there is still a bit more to relate of this particular tale.

CHAPTER 29

The following morning, we decided to return one last time to Caer Morvan Hall.

The run of fair weather continued and it was a bright, sunny day as we approached the manor. I had no idea what our reception would be like, but we both agreed that it had to be done.

Miss McKenzie greeted us at the door with her customary reserve. I realized now that she hadn't been lying so much as protecting the memory of a man she'd known since childhood. My own opinion of Duncan Montague was not high, but I came from another world. In the McKenzies', loyalty counted for everything.

Had she suspected Jack Goodnight of wrongdoing? That, I would never know. But I did not believe her or her brother to be bad people. Just set in their ways.

The housekeeper deposited us in the drawing room and went to fetch her mistress. The Montague portraits, I noticed, were all gone.

"Are you sure about this, John?" I asked, one shoe tapping a rhythm on the carpet.

"I'm sure."

"But—"

"Hush, she's here."

"Dr. and Mrs. Weston," Mrs. Goodnight said with surprise. "I . . . I wasn't expecting you."

She looked pale and drawn. Her blonde hair was pulled into a tight chignon that emphasized her hollow cheeks. She wore a somber gown of dark gray.

We both rose to our feet. "I apologize for intruding," John said. "We just wanted to convey our sympathies for what you must be going through."

"That's very kind of you." She gave a funny laugh. "I'm not sure what to say, to be perfectly honest. My husband had some kind of breakdown. I should have seen the signs, but I was clueless."

"We have no doubts about that," I said firmly. "Did you speak with him?"

She gave a brief nod. "I had to, of course. I simply couldn't believe it when Constable Robb came to the door and told me he'd been arrested. For murder! It seemed impossible." She gave another brittle laugh. "But Jack didn't deny it."

"I heard he's been taken for trial in Inverness," John said.

"Yes. I wrote to his lawyers. I expect he'll plead insanity." Her hands knotted into fists. "Jack said he'd put everything in my and Louisa's names. The bank accounts and property . . . ." She trailed off again. "I'm sorry, but what is it you want? This is a difficult time."

"I don't know how we can help, but we wanted you to know that we bear no ill will toward you or Louisa," I replied cautiously. "How is she?"

"She has no idea, of course. I made up a story." Mrs. Goodnight noticed my gaze drift to the empty places on the wall where the Montague portraits had hung. "I burned them," she said defiantly.

"And I don't blame you," John repled. "I would have done the same."

"We should never have come here!" Her chin trembled. She sank into a chair. "When I saw Jack, he told me . . . ." She let out a long breath. "Crazy things. He begged me to try letting Louisa go outside. In the daytime."

"Did you do what he asked?" John asked.

She looked at him like he was mad. "Of course not."

The silence stretched out.

"Because . . . " John cleared his throat. "Well, there is a possibility he could be right."

"How?" Mrs. Goodnight snapped. "Nothing's changed! Jack lost his mind." She looked around with bitterness. "It was this place. I don't believe the rumors, but you had only to look at those pictures to know what sort of people lived here. He fell under the spell somehow. It's all like some bad gothic novel. I won't subject my child to the imaginings of a lunatic! He's hurt enough people already."

The speech was more or less what we'd anticipated.

"I do understand," John persisted. "But you can't be sure unless—"

"Is everything all right?"

Nurse Payne stood in the doorway. She wore a woolen skirt and sweater, her auburn hair coiled in a loose bun.

"No," Mrs. Goodnight said stonily. "They're trying to convince me Louisa's been miraculously cured!"

The nurse eyed us both. "Why would you think so?"

"It's difficult to explain," I admitted. "And we could be mistaken."

"You see!" Mrs. Goodnight threw her hands up.

"Mommy?" a voice piped up.

We all turned. Louisa pushed past the nurse. "Mommy?" she said, hope lighting her eyes. "Is it true?"

At that moment, I regretted coming there. I looked at John.

He regarded her calmly. My husband believed and his faith lent me courage.

"No, darling," Mrs. Goodnight replied. "The Westons were just leaving."

Louisa's face set stubbornly. "Tell me! Am I better now?"

Evangeline groped for words. She threw me a desperate look.

"It was your father's dearest wish," I said. "And . . . er, sometimes magic is real."

This was not the answer Mrs. Goodnight had hoped for. Her lips tightened.

"How could you?" she hissed at me.

Louisa watched us with wide eyes. To my surprise, the nurse took our side.

"Let her try, Eva," she said. "Just an instant won't do any harm."

"But—"

"If you don't, she'll find a way to test it. You *know* her."

The women exchanged a long look. I think an entire conversation unfolded without words. There was an intimacy between them and I had a revelation regarding the question of separate marital bedrooms.

Society would condemn their relationship to the shadows— or, more accurately, pretend it couldn't exist at all—but I felt glad that Evangeline had found someone to love. It would make the next months a bit easier.

"Please!" Louisa begged. "You don't believe in magic, but I do! And so does Sir Weston!"

Mrs. Goodnight cast us both a look of quiet fury. "I suppose you have to see for yourselves what happens. Better that I'm present." She turned to Louisa. "One second only, young lady."

She jumped up and down, cheeks flushed with excitement. "Thank you, Mommy! Oh, thank you!"

We walked through the gloomy foyer to the front door, our

footsteps echoing on the tile floor. Louisa ran ahead and waited impatiently. "Hurry up!" she called.

Mrs. Goodnight refused to look at us. She marched forward with a grim expression. I guessed it was less the prospect of the physical pain her daughter would experience. We had raised Louisa's hopes. And after we were gone, she was the one who would face the tears of disappointment.

Doubts crowded my mind. Jack Goodnight was not a Montague. If we were wrong, we would have done a very terrible thing.

But I remembered Evangeline calling Caer Morvan Hall a prison. It seemed to me an even worse tragedy if the wish had cured Louisa—*and she never knew.*

Either way, it was too late to stop them now.

Evangeline twisted the bolt, hand resting on the doorknob. "Put your bonnet on, darling."

Louisa accepted the huge floppy bonnet from the nurse and tied it beneath her chin.

"Ready?" Evangeline asked.

Louisa drew a deep breath. "Ready."

The heavy door swung wide. Louisa took a single step forward and flung an arm up. "It's bright!"

Evangeline moved to pull her back inside, but the child lurched away and stumbled down the steps to the lawn. She tore the bonnet off. Louisa scrunched her face against the glare, but I could see the determination in her chin. Her mother gave a shout and chased after.

Mrs. Goodnight caught the child after only a few steps. She tried to shield her with her arms. Louisa shook her off. They stood there tussling for a minute.

"Let me go," Louisa cried. "Let me go!"

Evangeline released her. A hand flew to her mouth as Louisa took another tentative step forward, tipping her bare face up to the sun.

"It's warm," she said in wonder. "But . . . it doesn't hurt."

The child sank down and ran her fingers through the grass. "How green it is," she whispered, looking around. Her gaze fixed on the distant blue-gray sliver of Loch Ness in the distance. "So much color in the world." She laughed. "I'd forgotten."

The nurse ran outside. She looked utterly shocked.

Mrs. Goodnight gave a sob, her hand still pressed to her mouth. "Are you sure . . . ? It's not . . . ?" She shook her head, tremulous laughter bubbling up.

Louisa pushed her sleeves up and held her pale arms out, regarding them solemnly. "No prickling, Mommy."

Then she lifted her skirts and ran down the drive, blonde hair flying out behind her.

"That's enough for one day," Evangeline called nervously. "Please, darling, come back!"

Louisa circled around. Her cheeks were pink as she pelted up to us.

"I want to see the village!" she declared. "And I want to go to the zoo. And . . . and . . . a million other things!"

"You can make a list," her mother said, pulling her daughter into a hug. "We'll do them all one by one, I promise."

Mrs. Goodnight glanced at me. I saw joy in her face, but also fear and bewilderment.

"I wish Daddy could see me." Louisa disentangled herself.

"He just had to go away for a while," Mrs. Goodnight said quickly. "I told you, a business trip."

"He didn't even say goodbye," she pouted.

"I know he loves you very much," I said. "He told me so."

"It was him, wasn't it?" Louisa eyed me shrewdly. "Daddy made me better."

"It was his heart's dearest wish."

She nodded, still ruddy with triumph. "And you, Sir Weston? Did the Amulet of Koth save you from the evil wizard?"

John bent a knee. "It did, Lady," he replied truthfully.

"Will you come visit us in California?"

"I hope we can."

"The hotel has a swimming pool and tennis courts and a Japanese tea garden and an ostrich farm." Louisa paused for breath. "Even a bowling alley! Everything is 'lectric."

"It sounds marvelous," John said.

She gazed up at the Hall. "I liked it here. I'll miss the pixies. But I like California better. Mommy does, too. She already put the house up for sale."

Mrs. Goodnight frowned. "How did you know that?"

"I heard you talking to the lawyer."

She shook her head in exasperation. "Eavesdropping again."

"Oh, I'd never." Louisa skipped up to the front door, the sun turning her hair to spun gold. "Can I tell Miss McKenzie I'm better? And ask her to open all the curtains!"

Evangeline hesitated, looking to Charlotte Payne.

"I . . . I don't see why not," the nurse said, studying the child. "The signs are gone. But she still shouldn't take too much sun right away. I'll want to keep a close eye."

"Go on," Mrs. Goodnight said. "I suppose this house could use some daylight."

Louisa galloped inside, shaking the reins of an imaginary horse.

"But don't mention . . . " She trailed off as the child disappeared. "Charlotte, could you?"

"Of course," the nurse replied with a quick smile, hurrying after Louisa.

"I haven't told the servants we're leaving yet," Evangeline admitted. "Perhaps the next owner will keep them, if I ever manage to sell the place." She pressed a hand to her forehead. "Listen to me, carrying on like everything's normal. But it's not, is it?"

"There's a lot to take in," John began.

"I owe you both an apology." She gazed at us squarely. "How did Jack do it? He didn't tell me everything."

I bit my lip. "Can you manage without knowing the answer to that? Just . . . accept it as a mysterious gift?"

Mrs. Goodnight searched my face. I detected that hint of fear again, quickly smothered by denial.

"Yes," she said. "I believe I can do that."

"Good." I smiled. "Have a safe journey back to America."

She regarded me gravely. "You as well, Mrs. Weston."

We departed Caer Morvan Hall and walked arm-in-arm back to the Duck.

And thus it was that the last wish ever granted by the Hand of Glory saved a young girl's life.

CHAPTER 30

W e did tell Arthur that story.

His first child had been born the previous January and his eyes went a bit damp when he heard of Miss Goodnight's recovery. In a strange coincidence, Arthur's own daughter was named Mary Louisa.

"I'd make a tale of it," he said, "but that's not the sort of thing that fits with Sherlock Holmes. His character demands a rational explanation. Makes it more enjoyable for the reader, as well. All the clues are there if they can puzzle it out."

"Do you expect to write many more?" I asked.

We sat in Arthur's room watching him pack his suitcase.

"If my new publisher treats me fairly," he grumbled. "Do you know what Ward Lock paid me for *The Scarlet Thread*? Twenty-five pounds! They kept all the rights, but I won't make that mistake again."

He shuffled a stack of papers into a pile. I caught a tantalizing glimpse of a title page. *The Hound of the—*

"What's that one?" I asked, craning my neck.

Arthur stuffed the papers into a valise and gave me a mysterious smile. "I never discuss works in progress."

"Oooh, you're horrible," I laughed.

"Call it superstitious," he replied with an answering chuckle. "But I promise to send you a copy when it's ready."

"Perhaps you'll find success as a full-time author," John said.

The remark did not seem to please him. "To be honest, I might kill Holmes off after I'm done with this next round. I really ought to focus on more serious novels."

"Kill him off?" I echoed. "You mustn't!"

"We shall see. I started writing another longish one. And a short adventure. Perhaps I can work the snakes in there . . . ." His gaze lost focus for a moment.

"Are they really traveling with you to Inverness?" I asked.

Arthur blinked. "Oh, yes. The Zoological Society expressed an interest. Some fellow will be meeting us at the train station. And I'll personally deliver the Hand of Glory to the London branch of the S.P.R., as promised."

"Is there nothing you'd wish for?" I teased.

"Only to see my dear Touie." She was Arthur's wife and I knew her health was fragile. "I've been gone too long already."

"Well, send mother and child our regards." John peered through the window. "It looks like the mail coach is here."

Finn Brody had hired two village boys to see to the baggage, which included three boxy shapes wrapped in blankets and one lacquered box. We gathered outside to bid goodbye to the quartet who was leaving the Drunken Duck. Miss Neiderberger held a squirming Caesar in her arms. She was laughing at something Frank Thomas said. The Welshman looked dapper in a suit and derby.

Mrs. Davies spotted us and stomped over with her cane.

"It's been a great pleasure making your acquaintance," she said with a beaming smile. "I told Algie all about you. He agreed that it's best we continue to commune through the Veil."

"Your husband is wise," I said.

She glanced toward the loch. "My only regret is that I never saw the leviathan, though I do applaud its choice of victims. The creature has discrimination. A certain *savoir faire*, one might say." Mrs. Davies adjusted her hat, which sported a large ostrich plume. "Well, I do hope we meet again someday."

Funny as it seemed, I hoped so, too.

"You might consider applying for membership to the Society for Psychical Research," I said, clasping her gloved hands. "They're not as stuffy as the Ghost Club. I'm sure they admit women."

Arthur, a member of the Ghost Club himself, pretended not to hear this remark, though he smiled through his mustache.

"Do they? Well, that sounds worth pursuing. Thank you, dear."

I turned to shake hands with Miss Neiderberger. Her grip was crushing.

"Goodbye, Mrs. Weston," she said. "It has been exciting."

"It has indeed." I nodded at the Welshman. "Mr. Thomas."

He grinned and tipped his hat to me.

They all clambered into the mail coach. The driver shook the reins and it sped off towards Inverness.

THE DRUNKEN DUCK WAS VERY QUIET AFTER EVERYONE LEFT.

John and I spent a few idle days walking the moors and just spending time alone together. Despite all that had happened, I'd grown fond of Drumnadrochit. It *was* a peaceful place. And the pall that had hung over the village seemed to be gone for good.

No replacement had yet arrived for Dr. Gibson so John changed the dressings on Finn's leg. The bullet wound was healing cleanly with no sign of infection, though John insisted he stay off it.

All this I heard second-hand from my husband. Cassie was the only other person who entered Finn's bedroom, but as they were newly betrothed not even the village busybodies tried to stop her.

On the morning we were set to depart, Master Brody made his way down the stairs with a cane. He'd lost weight and looked older than his twenty years, but he was still a handsome man. Luckily, he'd inherited the best traits from his father instead of the worst.

"I've been meanin' to thank ye," he said quietly. "For what ye did."

I nodded. "I'm glad your mother is back where she belongs. But I suppose you'll miss her."

He smiled. "I know where t' find her."

"And you?" John asked. "Do you and Cassie plan to stay at the Duck?"

"Aye. Though we've decided to rename the place."

"Oh?"

"I thought the Black Dog had a ring to it," he said with a straight face.

We burst into laughter. "It's perfect," I said. "I hope we can return someday."

"If we're still in business," Finn replied, the smile fading. "I don't have a single reservation at the moment."

"We'll spread the word to our friends in New York," John promised.

"Truth be told, the inn was doing poorly before all the excitement about the loch beast," he admitted. "I hope we can make a go of it."

"You took down the stuffed animal heads," John observed.

Finn made a face. "My ma hated those. She only kept 'em as reminder o' what people are capable of. I never cared for the sad auld things either. They're down in the cellar now."

He had hung some of Mr. Ferguson's landscape portraits to fill the empty spaces.

"I like those much better," I said, eying one that showed the unlucky manor house in the background. "What will happen to Caer Morvan Hall?"

"I heard someone's bought it," Finn replied. "Another foreigner."

"Already?" I echoed in surprise. "I expected it would sit empty for years."

He gazed out the window with a frown. "Did ye hire a private carriage?"

"No, we're waiting on the mail coach."

I peered through the glass. A black brougham trundled down the lane. The driver was decked out in a gleaming top hat and coat with shoulder capes. The carriage halted in the yard and a middle-aged man in a somber suit got out. He strode up to the front door of the inn. Finn went to greet him.

"Are you Mr. Brody?" the man inquired. He wore a closely trimmed silver beard and round spectacles.

"I am," Finn replied. "Are ye lookin' for lodgings?"

"No, my name is Campbell." He held a leather case. "I'm a solicitor with a firm in Edinburgh."

"Don't tell me someone's suin' us," Finn muttered.

"You misunderstand." He glanced at John and me. "May we speak privately, Mr. Brody?"

Finn looked worried, but he nodded. "Come inside."

The two men retired to a small sitting room that was rarely used and closed the door.

"What do you think the lawyer wants?" I whispered.

"Must have to do with the case against Goodnight." John frowned. "But Harry . . . is that who I think it is?"

We still stood by the window. I followed his gaze. "My God, I believe it is."

Another man had just hopped down from the carriage, this one younger by two decades. He was quite tall with sleek black hair parted on the left. The ducks in the yard scattered as though a hawk had just swooped into their midst. His bold nose did resemble a bird of prey, but when he spotted us through the window, his smile was that of a lazy cat.

"What on earth is the count doing here?" I exclaimed.

I had met Lord Balthazar Habsburg-Koháry in New York two years previous. He'd aided us in an unsettling case involving a loose daemon. Then he'd vanished—though I'd heard a few rumors.

"Let's go find out," John said.

We met him in the yard. He took his hat off and bowed gracefully from the waist.

"Mr. Weston. Miss Pell. What a surprise to see you here."

Judging by the amused look in his eye, he knew very well what we were doing in Drumnadrochit.

"It's Mrs. Weston now," I replied. "We just got married."

The count looked pleased. "Congratulations. Don't tell me you came here for the honeymoon?"

"We did," John replied.

He laughed. "What a coincidence! My own nuptials took place in Gretna Green two days ago." He glanced back at the coach, where a long-legged woman with a determined look about her had just descended. "That's my new wife, Lady Koháry."

She strode over with a friendly smile. Balthazar made introductions.

"You make a handsome couple," I said.

Everyone in sight had paused in their work to stare at the striking newcomers. Both were olive-skinned with raven hair and eyes. They wore very fine clothes. But it was the air of self-assurance that set Lord and Lady Kohary apart from mere mortals. They were both people who expected to get their way as a matter of course.

I imagined their fights were legendary—as well as the making up afterwards.

"She got away from me once," Balthazar said lightly. "Twice, actually. But I managed to track her down."

Lady Koháry shot her husband an amused look.

"How long do you plan to stay at the Duck?" I asked.

"Oh, we're only stopping to rest the horses." Balthazar gazed toward Caer Morvan Hall with a proprietary air.

"Don't tell me *you're* the new owner?" John said.

"I am." A corner of his mouth twitched. "Why? Is there something wrong with it?"

Clearly, the man knew everything. *How*, I couldn't say. But Lord Koháry collected dangerous talismans. If the Hall held any other dark secrets, I suspected they would meet their match in the Hungarian count.

It made me oddly reassured.

"Half the manor was damaged by fire," John said. "But I suppose you're aware of that already."

"Yes, we'll just stick to the other half for now," Balthazar replied carelessly.

I turned to his wife. "Where are you from, Lady Koháry? I can't quite place your accent."

"Call me Zarifa, please," she replied. "And my mother was from Egypt. My father was British." A shadow crossed her face, but she brightened a moment later. "Tell me, have you visited the Hall?"

"Oh, er, once or twice. If you find a dead cobra in one of the upstairs bedrooms, don't be alarmed."

John cleared his throat. "What my wife means to say is—"

"Dead cobra?" Zarifa laughed as loudly as a man, throwing her head back. I liked her. "This place is more interesting than I thought."

"So . . . the solicitor is yours?" John asked.

Balthazar shook his head. "He represents the Montague estate. Something about a blind trust. The agent we bought the

Hall from knew we were coming out. We offered Campbell a ride from Inverness."

"I hope you'll come to see us," Zarifa said. "We don't plan to stay forever, but I've always wanted to visit the Scottish Highlands."

"So you bought an entire estate?" I said, smiling.

"*He* did." Zarifa frowned in mock severity at her husband. "Balthazar's rolling in it. You wouldn't believe how many houses he owns."

"It's only prudent." His smile widened. "I have a lot of enemies, too."

The door to the inn opened. Mr. Campbell emerged with Finn. The young man looked white as milk. They shook hands just as the mail coach appeared.

"My firm will be in touch," the lawyer said, putting his hat back on. He strode off to meet the coach.

I hurried over to Finn. "Is everything all right?"

He rubbed his forehead. "He just told me I'm the sole beneficiary of Duncan's will. It took them a while to sort out because he'd left the whole bundle to Swan, but he was just a . . . . something or other."

"Trustee?" I guessed.

"That's it. Now that he's gone, it all goes to me." He spoke without emotion.

"I hope it was a fair amount."

Finn turned to me, his gaze unfocused. "Almost two million pounds, Mrs. Weston."

I blinked. "That is . . . quite a lot of money."

"Should I take it?"

"Yes," I said without hesitation. "Do some good with it. How long has the Duck stood here?"

"Almost two hundred years."

"Then make sure it stays." I spotted Cassie through the door. "Does she know yet?"

He shook his head.

"Go tell her. You can decide together."

He gave a strangled laugh. "Aye."

Finn hobbled inside. I watched Cassie's jaw slowly drop open. Then she threw her arms around him.

"Happy news, I take it?" Balthazar remarked when I returned.

"Quite." I glanced at the mail coach. "And I'm afraid we won't be able to visit the Hall. We're leaving ourselves."

"Another time, then," Zarifa said warmly, taking my hands.

The pair returned to their brougham. I watched it depart, their dark heads bent together. Zarifa gave another ringing laugh.

The count's reputation was hardly spotless. I'd heard all sorts of tales about him, each wilder than the last. But he had saved our lives once before. On balance, I believed he stood on the right side of things.

We bid goodbye to our hosts, who looked in high spirits. Our luggage was stowed, along with Mr. Ferguson's photographs. The ducks had returned to waddle around the yard—perhaps in search of another leaky barrel of ale.

Mr. Campbell was the only other occupant of the coach. He gave us a brief nod and buried his nose in a newspaper.

"Well," John said as the inn and the village of Drumnadrochit fell behind us, "that was an eventful trip."

I laughed. "Too eventful."

"But you did a good thing, Harry. You saved more than one life."

I laid a hand on his knee. "I hardly managed it alone."

John smiled modestly. "I suppose I did make a contribution."

I grinned back. "Actually, I was thinking of H.N. Gryffin."

He nudged my foot.

"You must admit, she got onto it all first," I said. "A remarkable woman."

"And a talented writer," John added. "H.N. will be sorely missed."

We were silent for a moment.

"Well, I suggest we take our next holiday closer to home," he remarked. "There's a quaint little town called Fall River. It's in Massachusetts. The autumn foliage is spectacular, I hear."

"From who?" I demanded. "Another monster hunter?"

He looked offended. "Not at all. An old client of my father's. Andrew Borden. He's a bank president. Perfectly respectable, Harry."

"That does sound nice," I said grudgingly. "Next year, perhaps."

"He has two daughters just a few years older than we are. Lizzie and Emma. I've been wanting to meet them."

The coach meandered along the road. Smoke drifted from the chimneys of tiny hamlets on either shore. It was a pleasant afternoon and the sun reflected on the loch, burnishing it to a silver mirror. Yet beneath that sparkling veneer lay fathoms and fathoms of black water that never saw a single beam of light.

Loch Ness guarded its secrets, I thought, thinking of how close we'd come to becoming one of them.

"Fall River," I mused. "Sounds peaceful."

John grinned. "Harry, my love, when have I ever steered you wrong?"

MORE GASLAMP GOTHIC

If you missed other books in the series and want to continue with John & Harry's adventures, check out *Dead Ringer, The Scarlet Thread* and *The Daemoniac*, which are on sale at all online booksellers.

The Daemoniac

It's the summer of 1888 and a bizarre killer is stalking the gaslit streets of New York. But are the murders a case of black magic —or simple blackmail? Harry and John follow a twisted trail of lies, treachery and madness that end much closer to home than they ever imagined.

Dead Ringer

Harry and John face off with golems, doppelgängers and New York's most devious criminal mastermind to solve one of the strangest cases of their career – a tale of murder, revenge and fairytale bogeymen to make the Brothers Grimm shudder.

The Scarlet Thread

When society girls start dropping like flies at the start of the Winter Ball Season, Harrison Fearing Pell lands her first juicy case since she was suspended from the Society for Psychical Research. The victims appear to have been scared to death. Is the culprit the vengeful ghost of Bloody Mary Worth—or something even worse?

ACKNOWLEDGMENTS

A huge thanks to Carol Edholm for her generous spirit and razor-sharp editing eye. Also to Laura Pilli and Leonie Henderson, my trusty first readers. To Mom and Nick—always.

ABOUT THE AUTHOR

Kat Ross worked as a journalist at the United Nations for ten years before happily falling back into what she likes best: making stuff up. She's the author of the Nightmarked series, the Lingua Magika trilogy, the Fourth Element and Fourth Talisman fantasy series, the Gaslamp Gothic mysteries, and the dystopian thriller *Some Fine Day*. She loves myths, monsters and doomsday scenarios.

www.katrossbooks.com

kat@katrossbooks.com

f facebook.com/KatRossAuthor

o instagram.com/katross2014

g goodreads.com/katross

p pinterest.com/katrosswriter

BB bookbub.com/authors/kat-ross

ALSO BY KAT ROSS

Gaslamp Gothic Collection

The Daemoniac

The Thirteenth Gate

A Bad Breed

The Necromancer's Bride

Dead Ringer

Balthazar's Bane

The Scarlet Thread

The Beast of Loch Ness

The Nightmarked Series

City of Storms

City of Wolves

City of Keys

City of Dawn

The Fourth Element Trilogy

The Midnight Sea

Blood of the Prophet

Queen of Chaos

The Fourth Talisman Series

Nocturne

Solis

Monstrum

Nemesis

Inferno

The Lingua Magika Trilogy

A Feast of Phantoms

All Down But Nine

Devil of the North

www.ingramcontent.com/pod-product-compliance
Lightning Source LLC
Chambersburg PA
CBHW050403260626
47156CB00003B/855